MY FINAL BREATH

PAIGE DEARTH
756

Dirt On The Author

Born and raised in Plymouth Meeting, a small town west of Philadelphia, Paige Dearth was a victim of child abuse and spent her early years yearning desperately for a better life. Living through the fear and isolation that marked her youth, she found a way of coping with the trauma: she developed the ability to dream up stories grounded in reality that would provide her with a creative outlet when she finally embarked on a series of novels. Paige's debut novel, Believe Like A Child, is the darkest version of the life she imagines she would have been doomed to lead had fate not intervened just in the nick of time. The beginning of Believe Like A Child is based on Paige's life while the remainder of the book is fiction. Paige writes real-life horror and refers to her work as Fiction with Mean-ing. She hopes that awareness through fiction creates prevention.

Connect With Paige

Find all of Paige's books on Amazon

Sign up for new book releases: paigedearth.com

Follow Paige At:

Facebook: facebook.com/paigedearth

Instagram: paigedearth

Goodreads

Twitter: @paigedearth

More books by Paige

Home Street Home Series (can be read in any order):
Believe Like A Child
When Smiles Fade
One Among Us
Mean Little People
Never Be Alone
My Final Breath

Rainey Paxton Series (must be read in order):
A Little Pinprick
A Little High

A Message From Paige

Dear Reader,

Munchausen syndrome by proxy is one of the more hidden forms of child abuse. Because caregivers are covert and calculating, their abuse often goes undetected by family, friends, and even medical professionals. For this and other reasons, it difficult to pinpoint the number of children who have and are now suffering at the hands of a caregiver with Munchausen syndrome by proxy.

All types of child abuse go unnoticed and have far-reaching, long-term ramifications on the victims. Some children lose their freedom, some lose their sense of self, some lose their virginity, most lose their voice and sadly, some lose their lives.

Children are commonly manipulated by their abuser making them too afraid to tell anyone. Please, if you know of a child being abused, help by telling someone who can make a difference.

~Paige

Foreword

Munchausen syndrome by proxy

noun

: a psychological disorder in which a parent and typically a mother harms her child (as by poisoning), falsifies the child's medical history, or tampers with the child's medical specimens in order to create a situation that requires or seems to require medical attention

- Meriam-Webster.com Dictionary, s.v. "Munchausen syndrome by proxy," accessed May 14, 2020 www.meriamwebster.com/dictionary/Munchausensyndromebyproxy

Prologue

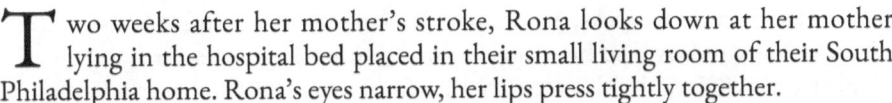

Two weeks after her mother's stroke, Rona looks down at her mother lying in the hospital bed placed in their small living room of their South Philadelphia home. Rona's eyes narrow, her lips press tightly together.

"You were always such an annoying, demanding bitch. I'll be so much happier without you in this world, I've been waiting forever for you to die," Rona says.

Her mother, Shirley, doesn't respond. Having been starved by Rona, she's even weaker than when she was initially released from the hospital. Shirley barely clings to life. She has been unconscious for three days.

Rona grabs a red throw pillow from the couch beside the bed. She looks at her mother one last time. Then she presses the pillow over her mother's face and holds it down firmly. Rona watches the rise and fall of her mother's chest as it diminishes until it stops altogether. She places a finger against her mother's neck to make sure there is no life left in her.

Rona takes a moment to enjoy the surge of power running through her.

Finally, Rona pulls the pillow away and looks into her mother's face. The face reminds Rona of a giant, gray raisin. The skin around her eyes is deeply wrinkled from dehydration and her mouth hangs open, exposing her tobacco-stained teeth. Shirley's dry tongue drapes over her peeling, cracked bottom lip. Rona's stomach churns as she jams her mother's tongue back into her mouth and walks away.

Now the funeral process could begin, and people would come to see her and pay her the attention she deserves, the attention she craves.

Rona stares at the face of the clock hanging over the kitchen sink. She is mesmerized by the long black second hand as it ticks slowly around the twelve numbers. She leans against the kitchen counter as she dials 911.

The next two hours are a flurry of activity, the kind of chaos Rona thrives on. The ambulance arrives and a short time later a funeral home director shows up. When everyone is finally gone, including Shirley's body, Rona sits on the sofa with a bottle of beer and guzzles it down.

Leaving the empty beer bottle in the living room, Rona strolls into the bathroom. She brushes her hair and flattens the front of her skirt. She looks into the bathroom mirror one last time and gives herself a warm smile, content with the person who stares back.

In the living room, Rona sits down, grabs her phone, and dials the familiar number. Filled with glorious anticipation, she holds her breath as it rings.

"Hello?"

Rona lets a sob escape her throat. "Kurtis? It's Rona. My mother died. They just came and took her away. What am I going to do now?" she cries.

"Oh, Rona. I'm so sorry. This has to be awful for you. I want you to stay calm. You're going to be okay. I'm going to take care of you. I'll be right over."

Rona puts the phone down, props her feet up, and rests her head on the back of the sofa. Yes, she thinks, I'm going to be better than okay. I'm finally going to have the life I want.

Over the next three weeks, Kurtis spends as much time with Rona as possible. He practically moves into her house to make sure he can care for her properly. While Rona is flattered by his attentiveness for the time being, she wonders where their relationship is headed. After all, she got rid of her mother so that she could spend more time with him.

One night, as they sit on her sofa together, Rona breaks down in tears. Kurtis drapes his arm over her shoulder. "I want you to remember that you're very strong. You have your whole life ahead of you."

Rona buries her face in his chest. "But now I'm all alone. My mom was the only family I had."

Kurtis strokes her hair. "You'll never be alone. We'll make our own family, I swear."

Rona looks into his eyes. "What are you saying?"

Kurtis kisses her forehead. "I'm saying that I have seven months until I graduate from college and then we can get married . . . if you want."

Rona stares at him blankly. She had expected him to move in permanently, not a marriage proposal. "Are you serious?"

Kurtis runs his fingers from her shoulder to her wrist. "I'm very serious."

Rona puts both hands over her mouth. Tears burn her eyes. Then she throws her arms around his waist. "Yes, of course I want to marry you."

***

Rona has hated her raging alcoholic mother for as long as she can remember.

By age sixteen, Rona was made up of two parts: one void of empathy and the other filled with rage. Inevitably, these two parts were bound to bond. As time marched on, she developed a deep-seated loathing for her mother, which fed her rage. With rage taking center stage in her teenage mind, Rona's ability to feel empathy remained undeveloped.

By the time Rona graduated from high school, she had become obsessed with being sick so she could get the attention from others that her mother didn't provide. She learned how to fake illnesses and often complained of mysterious symptoms. As a result, she was shown sympathy from the school nurse and eventually from medical professionals.

Following high school, Rona trained to be a nurse. She had an insatiable appetite to learn about how the body defied itself. She was fixated on illnesses and how to treat them.

Rona met Kurtis one weekend at a bar in Philadelphia a few blocks from her home. She was a full-time student at Temple University, working on her bachelor's degree in nursing, and he was a student at the Wharton School of the University of Pennsylvania. Rona's long, curly hair and honey-colored eyes immediately caught his attention. Her full lips and her smile were difficult for any man to ignore. Kurtis, who was equally good-looking, was enamored by her looks and tenacity, and so began a sizzling romance.

The days that followed Rona's mother's death was the most satisfying time she could remember. That initial attention Rona received from Kurtis and the others was equivalent to a junkie inhaling their initial hit of crack. She quickly became a hard-core addict for attention and sympathy from people.

Sympathy for hardship, Rona learned, was plentiful.

Chapter One—Twelve Years Later

My name is Molly Roslin and this is my story.

The first eight years of my life were excellent, the best a girl can imagine. My parents gave me all of their attention, and we always did fun things together on the weekends, like going to the movies or bowling, or staying at home and watching videos. I never gave a single thought to my happiness ever ending.

Then I got sick, and my life has been terrible ever since.

About a month ago, Mama took me to what seemed like my millionth doctor visit. I knew Dr. Becker, since I'd been seeing him for a while. He had a Newton's cradle on his desk, that thing with balls at the end of strings. While we waited for him in his office, Mama lifted the silver ball on one end and let it hit the next ball. For twenty minutes, I had to endure the tap, tap, tap, tap, tap of those stupid balls clanking together. Mama told me that people found it therapeutic and soothing, but I was so weak from prolonged illness that the taps hit my ears like a thousand volts of electricity with every strike.

Dr. Becker finally joined us. "Molly," he said, taking my hand, "it's good to see you. How are you feeling today?"

I had trusted Dr. Becker for a long time. "I'm not too good. I've never been this tired before and my body hurts all over."

Dr. Becker knelt in front of me. "I know you aren't feeling very well. I asked you and your mom for this meeting so we could discuss the next steps. I think it's important that you're comfortable. There's no reason for you to suffer in pain."

My eyes filled with tears. "Am I going to die?"

Dr. Becker turned to look at Mama before turning back to me. "I won't lie to you, Molly. You're very sick. I don't think you're going to die right now or tomorrow or even next week, but I have no way of knowing how much time you have left."

"Oh, no!" Mama shrieked, placing her hand over her heart. Her outcry made my pulse quicken.

Dr. Becker turned toward her. "Rona, I know this is difficult. Right now, it's important that we focus all of our energy on Molly."

Mama nodded. "Of course, Dr. Becker."

On the ride home from our meeting, I had two conflicting thoughts. On the one hand I was scared of dying because I didn't want to leave my family. But on the other hand I was relieved about the possibility of my suffering coming to an end. I welcomed the idea of not having to exist in my current state.

That was eleven days ago and now I can see that Dr. Becker was right: I have gotten no better. He had made it clear that I would only get worse, so I can't say I'm surprised. Time passes very, very slowly when you don't feel well.

For the past four years, I've fought with everything I had in me to stay alive. I believed that one day I would be well again and my life would return to what it was before I became a medical mystery that no one could solve. But now, the only thing I can focus on is the night-light plugged into the wall under my window. There are so many "lasts" that I blindly missed; I only wish I'd known they were my "lasts," but facing that black cloud steamrolling toward me seemed too much.

As I lie in bed now, unable to move on my own, I think about the things I did several months ago. If only I'd known that I had taken my final walk outside or turned my face up to sky so the sun can warm it or laughed with my baby sister, Ava, until my belly hurt, I would've been more grateful for my freedom. Little things mean so much now that I can't experience them anymore.

I try to sleep, but my breath comes in sharp gasps. I suppose this is how people feel when they drown. I can't get the air I need. It's terrifying and uncomfortable. Peace is nowhere to be found.

I think about all of my "lasts" to take my mind off of the present. Like the last time I watched my favorite cartoon. The last time I cuddled with my little sister, Ava. The last time I snuggled the teddy bear that Daddy gave me. The last time I wore my most comfy pajamas. The last time Daddy kissed me good night. The last time Mama brushed my hair and held my hand while she told me a funny story. And the last time I walked through the front door of my house.

The hard part about "lasts" is that I didn't know they were my lasts until it was too late. Now I wish I had paid closer attention to everything I did. I would've held onto those moments and burned them into my memory. Now that I'm lying here, struggling to fill my lungs with air, I know how important those simple moments were.

It is the little things in my life—the things I took for granted and never gave much thought to—that I think I'll miss the most . . . like breathing.

The night-light fades into a small white spot surrounded by blackness. I allow my eyes to ease shut, and my body relaxes.

I think, I'm twelve years old. I'm only a kid. And while in my heart I know death is reaching for me, I'm still trying to hold onto life. I'm not ready to die . . . it's too soon.

Until this very moment, death was something that lurked around on the outside of my thoughts. A dark, depressing idea I had refused to acknowledge . . . but now I can't deny it any longer. My eyes slip closed and everything stops.

Am I dead? Oh, God. I think I'm dead.

Chapter Two

S oon after I close my eyes, I wake up in a place filled with light. The first thing I notice is that I feel no pain. My breathing is pure and simple. I place my hands in front of me and turn them palms up and down, loving that my skin is soft and pink again. My body is supported by something white and very soft, the way I imagine a cloud would be.

When I was alive, I lived with my parents, Rona and Kurtis, and my baby sister, Ava. They were my whole world. Everything I knew and loved. We lived in a beautiful house in Villanova, Pennsylvania. It was a two-story home with stone siding, and large maple trees running the length of the driveway. Our downstairs was homey but huge, with hardwood flooring and oversized furniture. The foyer was enormous. There was a library that was mainly used by Daddy and we had a wide-open living room with comfy sofas and chairs where we watched television together.

Oh, and the kitchen. Mama had the best kitchen money could buy—that's what she told me all the time. Upstairs we had four bedrooms, but we used only two of them. One for Mama and Daddy; the other I shared with Ava. Mama thought it would be better for us to stay in the same bedroom until we were older. Our backyard was fenced in and had lots of trees. It wasn't just a house; it was my home and I loved every inch of it.

A movement in the distance rattles me from my memories. I look up and see a figure walking toward me. The silhouette is muddled, but from the curves at the waist and slender arms, I can see it's a girl. She comes closer and extends her hand. I hesitate for a moment, but then I'm compelled to place my hand in hers. She gives me a smile.

"Hi, Molly," the girl says. "My name is Gwen. I'm your guardian. I'm here to help you transition from your old life into your new one."

I wonder for a split second if I'm dreaming. I look around to see if we are alone. I see no one here but the two of us, so I turn back to her. Slowly I move closer to Gwen and touch her arm. I need to be sure she's real. "Where am I?"

"You're in Limbo."

My insides feel tingly, and I give Gwen a silly grin. "Am I dreaming?"

Gwen smiles politely. "No. This is where you go after you die."

My giddiness vanishes.

"I'm really dead?" My smile fades. I dig my fingernails into my palms to make sure I'm not sleeping. "I don't want to be dead."

Gwen looks down. "I'm sorry, Molly."

I back away from Gwen. I know what dead means . . . I've thought about being dead for some time before now. Gwen's confirmation this is eternal strikes me with force, and I can't wrap my mind around it . . . dead. I collapse to my knees in disbelief. "Noooo!" I mutter in a long, monotone breath. "I want to be alive. I'm not ready to be gone. Please."

I hold my head with my hands. I have so many questions. If I'm dead, then that means I'm not Molly anymore. If I'm not Molly, then who am I? A ghost? What happens now? Does my family know I'm gone?

The realness and permanence of my situation rush over me. I don't know how to be dead. I want to rewind the time and go back to my room, to the home I love. I need my mom. I don't want to be here by myself. With the massive weight of sorrow resting on my shoulders, I break into sobs.

After several minutes I breathe deeply and steadily, to collect myself. The whole time Gwen stands over me with her hand resting gently on my shoulder. It's a small gesture, but it reassures me that I'm not completely alone.

"I'm dead, and in a place called Limbo?" I ask in a subdued voice.

"Yes, you are."

"Limbo is so . . . so big. There's a lot of open space here. Where will I go?"

"That's up to you, Molly. You get to create your life here. If you think about something you want it'll appear for you. Why don't you try it? Think about something little that you'd like to have."

I close my eyes and think about my favorite jeans, and when I look down I'm wearing them. "That's crazy. The coolest thing I've ever seen," I say, even though my eyes are still swollen.

Gwen gives me a knowing smile. "Yeah, there's a lot of cool stuff here."

"Can I think about going back to my home? If I do that will it just appear and I won't be dead anymore?" I ask expectantly.

"No, Molly. You can think into existence things to appear, but you won't be able to change circumstances that are true about your life. Like that you're dead."

In an instant, my surge of hope drains from my heart, down the middle of my body, rushes through my legs, and escapes from the tips of my toes. "Oh."

"Do you remember what happened before you died?" Gwen asks.

I rub my forehead. "I was looking at my night-light and closed my eyes." I pause. "Does my family know I'm gone?"

Gwen shakes her head. "Not yet. You died about four hours ago."

"Four hours? How will they find me? Who will find me? What if nobody comes to check on me for a long time?"

"I don't have all the answers to your questions. But you do and can watch it . . . see what happens, if you'd like. But only if it'll make you feel better," Gwen says.

I look down at my hands. I would do anything right now to get a glimpse of my family again. "Yes, I'd like to see. Is that weird? I mean, that I want to watch?"

Gwen turns and I follow her. She says, "No, it's not weird. Most people want to watch. They need to know they'll be missed to confirm they were loved even though they have no doubt that they were."

Gwen and I stand before a wall made of frosted glass. She faces it, and I do the same. Suddenly I see everything from my past.

I'm lying on my bed at home. My chest is still; it no longer rises and falls. My mouth has gone slack along with the skin on my face. I look like I'm asleep. Then my bedroom door opens and Daddy walks in as he does every night when he gets home from work.

He walks to my bed and sits next to me. He talks to me. I have the urge to run. I thought I could watch, but I can't.

"I can't do this, Gwen. I made a mistake. I don't want to see my dad find me this way. He'll be really upset. I'll miss him. I don't . . . I don't want to watch anymore. Is that okay?"

Gwen turns her back to the glass wall and I do the same.

"Of course it's okay. This time belongs to you, Molly."

Thinking about losing my family makes me burn with anger, an acidy fire deep in the center of my gut. I was cheated out of my life. My fury makes me want to break something. I want to let my family know I'm all right and I want to be alive and back with them.

I wish I could cry, I do. Crying would help me right now, but my tears are stuck somewhere between shock and resentment. All of my heated emotions overshadowing the sadness of losing my life.

I close my eyes and picture my family. I'm afraid to let them go, to be here on my own. I feel lonely and long to be back with the people who mean everything to me . . . my family.

Chapter Three

My mom was the heart of our family, the person who held us all together and took care of us, especially me. She didn't work outside of the house, but she didn't need to. I don't know how much a lot of money is, but Mama told me she and Daddy made lots of it. She also told me you could never have too much money.

Mama cooked and cleaned and made sure we did well in school. She bought Ava and me the prettiest clothes. People always complimented me on my clothes. And Mama was the best hair braider ever. I could sit for a long time while she braided my hair and told me stories about when she was a little girl. Mama's childhood wasn't like mine. Her mother didn't love her very much. I can't even imagine someone not loving Mama.

Of all the people I'm forced to leave behind, I'll miss my mom the most. Even though she was strict and overprotective and sometimes I couldn't stand it, she was my best friend. The person who stood by me. That's not to say I won't miss Daddy and Ava—you can bet I'll miss them like crazy—but Mama was my hero.

When I turned twelve four months ago, I told Mama, "I hate being so short. How come I'm not as tall as the other kids my age?"

"So what if you're shorter than the other kids? It's because your growth was stunted from being sick all the time."

"Right!" I growled. "So you're saying I am way shorter than all the other kids."

Mama leaned into me. "God made you out of sugar, spice, and everything nice." She gave me a tight smile, indicating that the conversation was over. So I walked off quietly, the way I was expected to do.

Of course, Mama hadn't made me feel any better about being so short. All I wanted most in the world was to be like other kids. But if I stayed sick I knew that would not happen. That didn't stop Mama and me from praying together every night before I went to bed.

"Come on, Molly. Time to say your prayers," she'd say.

I'd move onto the floor next to her where we kneeled on the side of my bed.

"Go on now. Say your prayers," she'd tell me.

"Dear God, please bless Mama and Daddy and Ava. Please help me heal because I don't want to be sick anymore. If you let me get better I promise to be good and have faith in you always. And please let me grow taller like everyone else. Amen."

Mama added, "And God, give Molly the strength and courage to face what you have in store for her. Give her the ability and willpower to succumb to her weaknesses and find strength in your love that you send to her through me. Please fill me with the knowledge and ability to take care of my daughters the way they are meant to be cared for. Amen."

It seems funny now, but I figured since I never actually got any better that God couldn't hear our prayers or he was ignoring me. Now that I'm dead, I can only hope he wasn't ignoring me because if that's the case then I'm in big trouble.

I've been in Limbo for four hours and twelve minutes now. I've spent that time grieving my own death while Gwen sits quietly next to me.

I tell Gwen, "Right before I died, my body felt unlike it ever had before. It was like every part of me was broken and scattered. I couldn't stop thinking about the pain. It was horrible. Not even watching television took my mind off it. That's the first time I wasn't afraid to die. I knew it was the only way to stop my suffering."

"Were you scared?"

"Yeah, of course I was. But Dr. Becker had told me the last time we met that he didn't know how long I'd live. So I suspected I was at the end of my life. I didn't tell Mama about how I was feeling right before I died; I was too scared of making her sad. I was tired of making Mama miserable."

Gwen asks, "Did your mom actually tell you that you made her miserable?"

I shake my head. "No. That's just what I thought. I was sick of ruining her life. I knew Mama would be heartbroken when I died. Mama worried about me all the time, and that weighed heavily on my decisions during my last couple of days."

"How do you feel now?" Gwen asks.

I shrug. "So far, being dead is fine. I'm really glad to be rid of the pain. Dying was . . . um . . . weird. Right after I died, I felt like I was floating in a pool of silk, and my body was perfect. I relaxed and looked around; a light surrounded me that was the slightest shade of purple. Purple is my favorite color, so I can spot it anywhere. Someone who doesn't love purple the way I do might mistake the light for white. But trust me, it's purple."

"That sounds wonderful," Gwen tells me. "I remember when I died . . . the experience was similar to yours, and just like you, all of my pain and suffering were gone instantly."

I think about my journey to Limbo. It was safe and peaceful. Now I am the strongest I've been in a long time. It's weird to be happy and then sad all of a sudden. There's a glow about me I can see when I look at myself in the mirror in the beautiful bedroom I imagined into being. Gwen helped me bring my bedroom to life almost as soon as I got here so that I'd have a place that was mine.

The bedroom is as big as a house, just like the home I lived in when I was alive. There are sheets of white tulle flowing from my bedroom ceiling around the large, pink bed. The windows are twelve feet tall on one side of the room and the remaining walls are the color of wisteria flowers. The pictures I've chosen for my walls are of me and Ava. My favorite of the pictures is of me holding Ava when she came home from the hospital after being born. I was looking into her eyes and she was looking back at me.

My newfound health in Limbo makes me want to sing and dance . . . use every part of my body to celebrate my new comfortable existence. But then I remember that I've left Mama and Daddy and Ava behind, and I feel a flood of guilt. I know they're all sad that I'm gone, and their sorrow replaces my joy. I miss them so much already. I'm worried that I'll forget them, what they look like, or how their voices sound. Or worse, that they'll forget about me. I wonder if I'll ever see them again. I don't know how I'm supposed to exist without the three of them. They're my family, my life, the only reason I still want to be alive.

But the scariest thought of all is that they'll carry on without me as though I was never there. It's hard to think about being forgotten—it makes my heart hurt.

Tears pour out of me. They're hot and salty. They run down my cheeks and into my mouth. "I want to be alive again!" I yell through my sobs.

I take in a quick breath. "I don't think it's time for me to go yet. I was lying in my bed just a little while ago, and I wanna go back. My dad is going to find out I'm dead. I need to be there so he knows I'm okay."

I grab the sleeve of Gwen's shirt. "He needs to know I'm okay so he can tell Mama. How will they know? I can't stand this. It's too soon for me to die. I'm just a kid!"

Gwen faces me and takes both of my hands in hers. "No one wants to be dead, Molly. I know how hard this is for you. I know what it's like to die young."

I look into the distance to avoid making eye contact.

"Give it a chance," Gwen says tenderly. "It's not so bad here. No one here will ever hurt you."

Gwen puts her arms around me. I surprise myself when I return her embrace because I'm not supposed to talk to strangers, let alone hug one. But everything is different now. None of the rules I obeyed on Earth mean anything. I'm already dead so nothing worse could happen. Besides, I need to be held; I'm scared to be alone.

I pull back slightly and nod. I know I have no other choice but to be in Limbo.

I try to accept my situation. I learned how to do that when I was living, so surely I can do it here too.

I guess I can admit that being in Limbo is kind of cool. It's like the sensation I get when I'm watching television and I'm no longer awake, but not quite sleeping and my mind drifts and my senses are dulled. It's blissful.

But the coolest thing about being in Limbo is that I'm perfectly healthy. It feels incredible not to be sick anymore.

To be clear, I still want to change everything. I want to go back and be among the living. But I'm here, and I at least need to find out about this afterlife thing. I mean, sad to say, but when you're dead, you're dead.

Chapter Four

I glance around uneasily. We are in a small city. The buildings are old but well kept, and the streets are made of cobblestones. I can see a glistening river running alongside the streets. It's magnificent, and for reasons that aren't clear to me, I know I belong here. But my eyes keep roving, looking for something that will connect me to the time when I was alive. Something familiar, such as my school, or grocery store or movie theater. I'm trying hard to make sense of what's happening. I look for other "dead people"—I think that's what we're called because I don't see spirits or ghosts flying around—but there's no one else here besides Gwen and me.

"How old are you?" I ask.

"I'm fourteen," Gwen answers.

I look around again. When I turn, Gwen is watching me. "You died when you were fourteen?" I say.

Gwen's arms go limp and fall to her sides. She nods. "Yes, I was too young to die too."

"How did you die?" I ask.

"I was in a concentration camp in Poland called Auschwitz. I'll tell you about it if you want to know."

I'm not sure what to say to Gwen. I read The Diary of Anne Frank . . . I know of the horrible things Hitler did to the Jewish people.

My insides are jittery. I want to listen to what Gwen has to tell me, but I'm petrified of what I will learn. I mean, seriously, it's not like every day I talk to someone who was tortured by the Nazis. That's a lot of pressure for a twelve-year-old.

"I read about those camps," I say. "You were one of the people Hitler killed?"

Gwen nods. "It was terrible. I died in 1944."

I look at Gwen like she's gone mad. "That was a really long time ago."

Gwen returns my gaze but doesn't respond. Her silence makes me nervous. I wish she would say something. I can see that the quiet between us doesn't bother her. I allow myself to feel the stillness too. It soothes me.

It's strange to look at Gwen and know she was killed by the Nazis. She looks good— healthy and happy. But then again, I look good too, now that I'm not alive.

Gwen has an alluring quality about her. She draws me in with her charm and grace. She's adorable with her long curly brown hair and pale brown eyes. Her face is round, but her body is petite. She's stunning. I catch myself wishing I was as pretty as she is.

I want to know more about her as much as I want Gwen to know more about me. I think that maybe I've found not just a guardian, but hopefully a friend. Now that I know she's been dead for a long time, I think it's safe to assume she knows everything about Limbo and dying.

I point at the enormous space filled with the purple light. It's so beautiful. I want to go there immediately. "Can you bring me there now?"

Gwen shakes her head. "Not yet, Molly. You have to wait here until you get rid of all your bad feelings from your life on Earth. Once your heart is pure then you'll go on to an even more peaceful place."

I thought I would leave Limbo right away. Apparently that's not how it works. My head drops, and the blood rushes to my face. I know Gwen says I can't leave Limbo right now, but I'm eager to get on with things. I've been ripped from my family. I didn't even get to say good-bye to anyone, and that makes me angry at myself.

"Why can't I go now? I don't have bad feelings. What am I going to do here?" I ask.

"You and I will spend time together."

"Doing what?"

Gwen takes in a long breath. "Here's how it works: you can only move on when you're free of all uncertainties from your life on Earth. While you're in Limbo, I'll help you leave behind all the troubles stuck inside your heart. That's why the place you're going is perfect and filled with love, because no one brings any bad stuff from their physical life into their eternal life," Gwen explains.

It sounds a little too pie-in-the-sky for me and I have to refrain from rolling my eyes. "Maybe it's perfect for you, but I doubt it'll be perfect for me."

Gwen chuckles. "You really won't know until you get there. I'll take care of you until then, I promise."

My mom never took no for answer and suddenly I mimic what I've witnessed her say to doctors and nurses over the years. "Are you positive I can't go now? Isn't there someone else I can talk to? Someone who is in charge?"

Gwen shakes her head. I look into her eyes, and I know she's being honest. I have to believe her because she has no reason to want to trick me. There's something mysterious about Gwen and I'm curious about her.

This thing happening to me doesn't make sense and I think she's the key to filling me in on the things I need to know. All I think is . . . this has gotta be far better than my old life, because if it isn't, I will be very unhappy.

Chapter Five

I t may seem selfish, but I don't feel so alone knowing that Gwen died when she was young too. I instinctively know it's not right, but not being the only kid in Limbo who lost her life consoles me. I know already that we died in different ways. I died because I was sick. Gwen was murdered because of a madman. That's a big distinction between the two of us. I have so many questions for her about what it was like to be in a concentration camp, but I don't want to make her uncomfortable.

Gwen disrupts my thoughts by putting her hand on my cheek. "You have beautiful eyes. They're the prettiest blue I've ever seen."

This makes me smile. I love hearing nice things about myself. I mean, really, who doesn't? "Thank you," I say.

I want so badly to know more about Gwen, I'm about to burst, so I gather up my courage. "Will you tell me how you died?"

"I was sent to a gas chamber."

I tilt my head and close my eyes, remembering all the things I'd read about the Nazis.

Gwen rests her hand on my shoulder. "I was made a prisoner just because I was Jewish. Most of my time in the camp I was starved. When the soldiers did give me food, it was usually stale or spoiled. Sometimes the bad food would make me sick, but I was so hungry all of the time that I would've eaten anything, even if it killed me."

I move closer to Gwen. My stomach spins and my heart races. I remind myself this isn't about me and I need to keep myself together. This is Gwen's story, her nightmare, not mine. And the least I can do is give her all my attention.

Gwen presses the bridge of her nose with her thumb and index finger. "The Nazis tortured us for a long time. They made us work sixteen hours a day, even the really young kids. That's not easy when you're starving and dehydrated. Then, out of nowhere, the soldiers broke our work routine. It was a rainy, cold afternoon in the middle of October when they gathered us together and led us to a building."

Gwen pauses briefly. Silence falls between us. "We had no idea what the Nazis were going to do to us. You know, they were always doing things to hurt us physically or playing games with our minds. It wouldn't have mattered even if we did know we were going to be gassed because our lives belonged to them."

I watch Gwen. My intuition is telling me I should do or say something to lighten the moment, but that's something I was never very good at. Mama was in charge of making everyone feel better. It was a skill I never needed to master.

"Are you still mad about what happened to you?" I ask.

Gwen pushes a stray curl of hair behind her ear. "Not anymore. When I first got here, it was excruciating. I mean, I was happy to be free of all the emotional and physical pain, but I didn't believe I had been murdered, kind of like you when you got here. Then I went through the process you're going through now. It helped me. I don't forgive Hitler or any of his people who killed my family and me. I was forced to face the truth about my life on Earth. I wish I had lived a long life, but I didn't. Now I have this great state of being, a spiritual state that lets me meet people like you."

"Did it hurt?"

"You mean dying?" Gwen hugs herself.

"Yeah. Did it hurt in the gas chamber?"

Gwen shudders as if she were shaking off an icy chill. Her mouth is downturned. Her hair covers her face as she slumps over.

Guilt rips through me. I should have shown some self-control and not have pushed Gwen. I wish I weren't so curious, but my need to know what happened to her won out.

Gwen puts her head back. "Yeah, it was awful. Let me show you."

She points and we both look at the small city as it transforms into a concentration camp. We stare at the side of a windowless building. We watch hundreds of bone-thin men, women, and children walk like zombies toward the cinderblock building. The ground changes from cobblestones to dirt, and there are puddles and mud everywhere. Everyone is wet and dirty.

The scene sickens and mesmerizes me. I turn my head sideways to steal a peek at Gwen. I wish I hadn't asked her about the gas chamber. I'm not sure I can handle whatever it is I'm about to witness. I grab her hand. She looks at me and back at the building, commanding me to watch with her. I hold my breath and follow Gwen's gaze.

Suddenly one of the soldiers is standing behind the crowd of human skeletons. He lifts his rifle into the air and fires a shot. The sound of the gun is sharp. The blast is deafening. It echoes off the dreary, grayish buildings in the concentration camp. Everyone goes deadly silent.

The soldier yells, "Everyone remove your clothes and put them in a pile by the door! You're going to shower and see a doctor!"

"It was humiliating," Gwen says, "standing naked in front of so many boys and men. I thought I'd die from embarrassment."

The large group of naked people all huddles together. Their skin hangs from their bones like loose fabric. The bitterly cold wind and rain bite at their dry, bluish-gray skin. Most rub their arms, attempting to generate heat.

Another soldier steps forward and yells, "Get moving! Get inside the building! You all smell and need a shower!"

The inside of the building is one large room. In the cluster of naked people, Gwen comes to the forefront. One hand is covering her private parts while the other clutches her mother's hand. The immense space is packed with bodies. There is no room to move; people . . . humans are squashed against each other, inhaling the exhaled breath of the person next to them.

Several popping sounds erupt, and the unknowing group looks up at the shower heads that hang on the walls, anticipating a long-overdue hot shower. Suddenly the lights snap off, and they all stand in total darkness, which is quickly followed by screams and panic.

Gwen grits her teeth and one hand is pressing against her heart.

Gwen and I stop watching her past.

I rub Gwen's arm in a jerky movement. I'm nervous. "What happened?" I ask.

"All of a sudden, there was a tight feeling in my chest. Then it was like all my muscles were bursting inside my body. The pain was unbearable." Gwen pauses. "Let's keep watching. I need you to see this with me."

"Why?" I ask. "Why do I need to actually see it?"

"It'll allow you to see that no matter what happens to us on Earth, we can still go on and have a better life here."

I close my eyes for several moments. I give my belly a chance to settle. Then I gather up all of my strength. "Okay. Let's do this."

We turn back to the building and watch.

The people, who are victims of the slaughter, shout and cry and beg for their lives. Gwen's mother falls to her knees and pulls her daughter into her arms. They hold onto each other for several minutes, both screaming from the agonizing pain as they rock back and forth together.

The crowd sways in different directions as the group tries to move toward the doors where they had entered. Others, closest to the walls, attempt to scratch their way out with their fingernails. Everyone is gasping and choking. As time passes, they grab and claw at each other, trying to fill their lungs. Their fight for clean air is met with poison. People fall to the dirt floor, lifeless bodies collapse on top of each other.

Gwen's death scene is the most sickening thing I have ever seen. Regular people, just like me, being put to death because of who they are and because they were born into a religion. It's ridiculous. It makes no sense. I know I have just witnessed out-and-out evil. I worry about what I'll see next.

Chapter Six

I've been through my own hardships and trauma, but I can see that Gwen's experience was so much worse than mine.

I am physically suffering the way Gwen did in her final moments. My throat feels closed, swollen. The air I breathe in is rancid. It's as though I'm suffocating exactly the way Gwen suffocated in the gas chamber.

My heart is thumping hard inside my chest. The emotions and images make my body tremble all over. I want to be supportive of Gwen, but it's a struggle. "Gwen, I don't want to watch anymore. I'm afraid."

My head is pounding, as though someone is smashing it with a hammer. My insides run cold, and I can't control my shivering. I peer at Gwen as I wait for her to say something. She's staring at the past as though she's in a trance.

"Gwen?"

Tears roll down Gwen's cheeks. "It was a very lonely way to die. Even though all of those people were around me, and my mother held me, the situation prevented any human kindness to be shared because we were all focused on our own suffering. Very slowly, the cries and screams stopped. I knew my mother was dead, even though I couldn't see her in the blackness." Gwen points as though I weren't already staring at the horrific scene. "I didn't care that she was dead. I wanted to be with her no matter what happened; look at how I cling to her lifeless body."

I have no choice. I brace myself and watch more of Gwen's demise.

Gwen lies motionless on the dirt floor. Very few people still hang onto life. The screams have turned to agonizing groans. Gwen has let go of her mother's dead body and is now holding her own head, squeezing it tightly.

Gwen says, "It felt like my brain was swimming inside my skull. Like I was drowning. Slowly, the screams got quieter and quieter until I could only hear my own. Then it was like a firecracker exploded in my chest. Shortly after that, I was here. My body and mind were whole again, as if nothing had ever happened. But oddly, I wasn't the same. The Nazis damaged me."

Even though it's only the two of us, Gwen leans in closer to whisper in my ear. "For the first two weeks I was here, I wanted to go back to Earth and kill the Nazi guards who did this to me. I wanted to rip their heads from their necks for taking my life, dignity, and spirit from me. It was really hard at first, but it eventually got better."

I roll my shoulders forward so Gwen can't see my tears. Not because I'm embarrassed to cry, but I want to be strong for her. "You and all those other people died a horrible death. It makes me sick to my stomach to watch. I don't think there's anything I can say right now to make it better. Your death is overwhelming. It's scary and you were helpless. I'm sorry that happened to you."

"Yeah, every time I see what happens it makes me very emotional all over again. I know it's stupid to relive it, but it's the only way to show the difference between what I was on Earth and how I am now. I'd like to say it's all okay and that it was a long time ago. But that would be a lie. I've learned to accept my fate, but I'll never be okay with evil people killing innocent people."

I shake my head in disbelief. "I'd be exactly like you. I'd never be able to let go of someone killing me. Not ever." I lift my eyes and meet Gwen's.

Gwen gives me a strange look but quickly smiles.

"Tell me all about where I'm going when I leave Limbo," I say. "Will I like it there?"

"You'll love where you're going. Everyone does. It's everything we always want when we're on Earth. Love, happiness, trust, fulfillment, peace. It's a place of rest," Gwen explains. "But before you can go, we have work to do," she continues. "We have to sort through your life. Don't worry; I'll help you. In the end, you'll feel so much better. So let's start at the beginning."

My hands are clammy, and my breath bursts in and out rapidly. "I don't have much to say. Having to talk about when I was alive scares me. I don't want to relive being sick."

Gwen stares into my eyes. "It was the same for me. It will always be torturous, but you'll be able to see things you didn't see when you were alive. You'll understand what happened to you. I'm one hundred percent certain everything will make sense. You have to trust me."

Gwen's certainty fills me with hope that things will be better soon. Limbo is a nice place, and I don't want to think about the pain of my past. But, I'll do it for Gwen. I don't know why, but I already trust her.

Chapter Seven

I desperately need a break. I want to get out of the small city in Limbo for a while. So I imagine Gwen and me in the middle of a field of wildflowers. The sun is shining overhead and a soft breeze caresses our skin. I inhale the sweet fragrance of the flowers as it wafts past my nose.

I'm lying on my back, remembering how much I loved the ocean. I picture the waves crashing and the white foam rolling up the wet sand while birds sing overhead. I recall the smell of the bay from behind us and the hot sand under my feet.

I have the overwhelming urge to share this wonderful memory with Gwen, who's putting together a small bouquet of flowers as I talk. "I remember when I was five. Over the summer, Mama and Daddy took me to the beach in Cape May, New Jersey. Daddy played with me in the water, and Mama brought big picnic lunches. I got to eat all the potato chips and cookies I wanted."

Gwen sits down next to me and we both look at her bouquet. The flowers hold a lot of beauty for things so small and delicate. The colors of the bouquet blend, and suddenly we are watching me when I was a little girl. I'm digging in the sand with a plastic shovel. Daddy and Mama are sitting behind me on a blanket.

"Ice cream! Get your iiiice cream here!" a man yells.

I look up. I abandon my shovel and run to my father. "Ice cream man, ice cream man!" I squeal.

Daddy stands and plucks his wallet from the beach bag. I'm bouncing up and down on my toes.

"Let's go get some ice cream, Molly." He turns to Mama. "You want something?"

Mama shakes her head. She watches me with pure adoration.

I've bounced too much. I lose my balance and stumble headfirst into the sand. Mama quickly picks me up and brushes me off. "Are you okay?" she asks.

I nod, even though my bottom lip is trembling. I grab Daddy's hand and skip down the beach next to my father. Daddy stands behind me as I look at the pictures on the side of the ice cream box. I look up at my father.

"You can pick whatever you want," he tells me. My heart soars with ice cream love.

The ice cream man looks down at me and smiles. "What can I get for you?" he asks.

"That one," I say, pointing.

The ice cream man winks at my father. "Oh, the ice cream sandwich. That's a very good choice. You have excellent taste, young lady."

A smile stretches across my face.

The man opens the cooler lid. Gusts of smoke roll out from the dry ice.

"That's magic," I say to Daddy.

"Yep. That's magic, honey. Just like a magician pulling a rabbit from his hat."

I giggle and clap my hands together. Daddy and the ice cream man share a chuckle.

I take the ice cream sandwich from the man and run to Mama while Daddy pays him. I fling myself on her lap, and she pulls the paper off for me.

"I love these," I tell my mother.

"Yes, they're very yummy."

She hands me the sandwich, and I take a bite of the frozen treat. I hold it toward my mother.

"You wanna bite?"

Mama kisses my cheek. "Yes, I'd love a bite."

Gwen and I stop watching. I close my eyes and cherish the memory.

"I loved the ice cream man," I tell Gwen. "Going to the beach was my favorite thing to do. I missed going there so much when I got sick. Being on vacation in Cape May with my mom and dad are my best memories."

Gwen's face lights up. "I used to go to Gdynia Beach in Poland with my family before the Nazis forced us out of our home. We had so much fun there. We went every year. Did you go to Cape May every year?"

I look away and shrug. "Not every year; we went the next year. That's when Mama told me she was pregnant, and I was going to have a baby brother or sister. At first I was so jealous. I was the center of my parents' life, and I didn't want to share them. But when Ava was born, and I held her in my arms, I was excited to be a big sister. Do you know that picture of me and Ava looking at each other that I hung in my room here? Well, that was right after she was born. That's when I fell in love with her."

"Did your parents still give you attention after Ava was born?"

"At first my mom was busy with Ava, but after she got a little older, Mama spent more time with me because I was sick. Ava got cheated out of Mama's time because of me."

Gwen's forehead wrinkles and she tilts her head. "It wasn't your fault that you were sick."

I rest my chin on my chest and slump over. "Yeah, I know. People don't get sick on purpose; it just happens."

I look up at Gwen, a little worried about what she's thinking. On Earth, I was a silent worrier. Mama had taught me it was essential to leave a good impression. That was a lot of pressure for a kid, especially a sick one.

I say, "I still think that Ava got ripped off because of me."

"That doesn't make much sense," Gwen says sharply.

My skin prickles at the tone of her voice. Why would she tell me I don't make sense? It makes perfectly good sense to me. Right?

I fall quiet and think about Gwen's statement more. Deep down, I know she is right. I know I have no reason to blame myself for what happened. Why do I think this way?

Chapter Eight

I want to explain myself to Gwen. Silence won't fix this for me. "The reason I think Ava got ripped off is that it was impossible to be a good big sister when I took all my parents' attention away from her. Even though I couldn't help being sick, Ava must have been lonely when I was at the hospital with Mama and Daddy was working. Sometimes, when Ava and I would lay in our beds at night, she would tell me that she wished I would get better so we could all be together more."

"I'm sure Ava gets plenty of attention now that you're gone."

Gwen's comment slams into my gut like a fist of steel. I don't need a reminder that I'm no longer with my family, as in permanently separated from the people I love most.

I change the subject on purpose. "Tell me again what you know about my life."

Gwen nudges me, and I drum my fingers on my leg. I can't tell what she's thinking. That grates at me. "The only thing I know about your life is how you died. I know you were very sick, and I know that your mother wasn't always nice to you, but I don't know specifically what bad things she did to you. I see it unfold as we watch your life together," Gwen explains.

My mouth drops open. Did I hear her right? Did Gwen just say Mama wasn't nice? That she did bad things to me? Is Gwen nuts?

"I don't understand what you mean. Someone gave you bad information. My mom was nice to me," I say as calmly as I can.

Gwen leans into me. "We don't know the whole truth yet. And, when we watch, you and I see different things. I can see more than you do."

"What are you talking about? What things?"

Gwen hesitates. I can see she doesn't want to say more, but I glare at her.

"Bad things," she says.

Gwen's eyes lock on mine. She doesn't blink. My heart thumps, and I feel like I'm trapped. Maybe I went to hell instead of heaven. I'm crawling out of my skin with apprehension. I stand up and walk away from her.

I point my finger at her. "Don't ever say that again."

"Molly, I have to tell you the truth. How else will you know how you died?"

"Gwen, you're not telling me anything. You keep making accusations about Mama. It's ridiculous."

Gwen gets up and moves toward me. "Look, all I know is that your mother isn't everything she appears to be. She's a complicated woman. That's what I've been told."

I immediately wonder who in Limbo told her these things, but quickly realize it doesn't matter. I don't like it. Defiance inches its way up from the pit of my belly.

I tilt my chin up, look down my nose, and make eye contact with her. I keep my voice even and purposeful. "So someone told you all about my mom? No one knows Mama better than me."

Gwen shakes her head. "No, I swear, I don't know everything. All I know is that you were sick. A lot. Too much." She places her right hand over her heart and raises her left in the air. "I don't know all the things that happened in your life, I only know what killed you. I don't want to upset you." She takes hold of my hand. "My job is to help you fill in the gaps. As we go through your life, I'll be with you every step of the way. You're not alone."

I'm not sure what to say. I don't know what Gwen means when she says she'll fill in the gaps. What gaps? I was born. I got sick. I was a human pincushion, and I died. There are no gaps. I cross my arms tightly over my chest.

"I'm uncomfortable going through my life," I tell her. "Out of nowhere, you blurt out bad things about my mom. My mom took good care of me. You don't know anything about us. You should know that Mama is my favorite person in the world. She was everything to me. I probably would've died a long time ago if it wasn't for her."

Gwen frowns. "I guess we'll have to wait and see. But here's the thing: I have to be honest. You don't want me to lie to you, right?"

I shake my head. "No. That would be dumb."

"Exactly," Gwen says. "You and I are going to learn a lot about each other. Molly, the best thing about being in Limbo is that you learn the truth. It's very powerful."

I cringe, thinking she means I'll learn more about her life in the concentration camp. I've seen enough to scare me forever. Uneasy, I bite on my bottom lip. It's unclear what choice I have, since Gwen's the only person I've met in Limbo.

Not knowing what to do next, I shake out my hands. "I don't think you know what you're talking about. You're going to see how good my mom was to me. Then you'll know the truth."

I turn my back to Gwen. Maybe I can scare her off with a dark warning. "My life was really terrible, and I had to go through long operations and a lot of disgusting medical stuff. You might wanna rethink going through everything with me."

Gwen leans her back against mine. "I can handle whatever comes at me. I died in a concentration camp, remember?"

I nod. "Of course I remember. It was the most horrific thing I've ever seen. There's nothing that can be worse than what happened to you."

Gwen looks away. "That's not true, Molly. Many people die in cruel ways."

I let Gwen's words hang in the air like the smell of rotten trash.

Chapter Nine

G wen pulls her hair into a high ponytail and secures it against her scalp. She lifts her face toward the sky, and the sun catches the honey color flecks in her brown eyes, like stars in a dark, cloudless sky. There's a fire in Gwen I admire; she is a warrior. If I wasn't so annoyed at her remarks about Mama, I might've told her that even though she hurt me, her presence is still important to me.

Gwen touches my arm. "Will you tell me all about your mom? What was she like?"

A lump forms in my throat. I worry that everything I say about Mama will be judged harshly. Gwen's already made it clear that she thinks Mama is a bad person. But I won't let my mom down. She earned my loyalty.

I force a smile. "Mama is great. Everywhere she goes, people know her."

Gwen leans her head to the side. "Okay. But what was she like?"

I think for a few moments. "Well, people like her. They want to be around her. She's smart and funny. She makes people laugh. But she can be tough, too."

I look down at the grass and imagine a thick yellow and white quilt. Gwen and I both sit. We're silent for a long time before she speaks again. "I know your mom changed when you were seven, right before the first time you got sick. Did something happen to her?"

I shake my head. "Not really."

"Come on, Molly. You can tell me. I swear I won't make any comments or ask any questions until you finish what you have to say." Gwen draws an X over her heart with her right hand and smiles. "I swear."

I tell her, "Fine. So, after my seventh birthday, Mama stopped being happy. She said she was lonely. It started after Daddy got promoted at his company. Mama had gone to a lunch celebration at his office and she told me all about how everyone fussed over him. I was really proud of him, but Mama was upset. She acted like she was jealous of him. I felt sorry for her. Before he got a new job, I had never heard them yell at each other. But after she went to his celebration lunch, they started fighting a lot. It confused me."

Gwen and I see Mama and Daddy standing in the kitchen several weeks after his promotion.

"Kurtis, your new job is killing me. It's ruining our family. You're not the only one who works hard around here."

Daddy looks at Mama with his mouth hanging open.

"You're spending too much time at work. We were happy before you took on all of that extra responsibility. And you used to pay attention to me. Now you're barely home. You come in, eat, sleep, and do it all over again the next day."

I see myself standing just outside the kitchen as my parents argue. I'm gently rocking in place.

I tell Gwen, "I remember how scared I was. My family was the center of my entire world, and seeing my parents fight was so scary. I had no idea what would happen. The uncertainty really freaked me out. I just wanted them to get along so we could all be happy again. I had been terrified that our family would be broken up. I was drowning in fear and loss. I loved both of them so much."

I see myself later that night. As Mama tucks me into bed, I stare at her. I look worried, like a hurt puppy.

Mama kisses my cheek. "Is something troubling you? You know you can tell me anything."

I fight back tears until I can't anymore. I ask through sobs, "Are you and Daddy getting divorced?"

Mama holds me close to her chest. "No, sweetheart. Never. Sometimes we fight. That doesn't mean we don't love each other."

I don't make eye contact with Mama, and my frown pulls the corners of my lips farther down.

The next morning, I'm standing at my window, mindlessly staring out at the long driveway in the front of our house, when my mom enters the room.

"Hi, Mama," I say.

"Good morning, sweetheart. Listen, I know you were upset last night after hearing Daddy and me fighting, but I want you to know everything is fine. Like I said, sometimes people get into arguments, so it's no big deal. I decided that since Daddy has to spend so much of his time at work, I'm going to focus all of my attention on my kids, starting with you."

I skip from the window over to my mom and throw my arms around her waist. Mama kisses the top of my head and I push my body against hers.

Gwen is watching me intently. "You look really happy to get your mom's attention," she says.

I look down at my hands. "Yeah, of course. What kid doesn't want to get attention from their mom and dad? And Mama is special, she's smart and beautiful, and even though she's strict, she made me laugh."

I peer at Gwen. She waits for me to continue. My feet hurt, and I notice that my toes are curled up in my sneakers. I tell myself to relax.

"It was great having Mama so interested in me and everything I did. Before I got sick, she would cheer me on when I played basketball in the park. I was pretty good for seven and could beat most of the boys. Daddy had played basketball in high school and he started teaching me when I was only five. Being a good player made Mama proud of me."

Thinking about how happy I was then; I can't help but smile. "Right after I turned eight, I got too sick to do anything. Mama told me I had the flu, and I needed to stay in bed for a couple of days. I did everything she told me to do. But I kept getting sicker instead of better. I never thought that those 'couple of days' would never end."

Chapter Ten

My nervousness settles. I no longer worry about finding out "bad things" about Mama because I know there aren't any. To prove it, I want to tell Gwen everything all at once. There are no distractions here in Limbo, which makes it easy to talk, to feel, and to connect with her.

I roll onto my belly. "I was in the hospital a lot. When I had to stay there I was so scared, and Mama knew that, so she rarely left me. I hated being in there. I was defenseless because I never knew what the doctors were going to do to me—I always had tests and procedures."

"What kinds of tests and procedures?" Gwen asks.

"The kind that hurt. There were lots of needles and surgeries. I think the surgeries were the worst because when they were over and I woke up I had a lot of pain. They would give me pain medicine and I was so groggy and out of it I could hardly remember anything.

"Anyway, Mama stayed at the hospital to make sure I was taken care of. She said it was her duty to watch over what the doctors and nurses did for me. She needed to make sure they did everything right. She is good like that."

Gwen taps her chin with her index finger. "How did your mom know what was right? Was she a doctor?"

Gwen tilts her body toward me as she waits for me to answer.

"Mama's job was to raise Ava and me. After she graduated from high school Mama went to college to become a nurse. She dropped out six months before graduation because she was pregnant with me and had some complications. Mama never went back and finished, but she knew all about medical stuff. She asked lots of questions and always made the doctors do the right tests so that they could figure out what was wrong with me. Mama read a lot of medical books, too, so she'd be prepared. I knew I was lucky to have a mom as smart as she was. I could count on her to take care of everything."

"Did your mom take care of everything the way you needed her to?" Gwen asks.

"Yeah, she did everything for me." I shrug.

Gwen picks at the cuticles around her fingernails. "You told me you got the flu when you were eight. How long did it last?"

"Ugh. It seemed like it lasted forever. I never got better. I kept getting sick. I think the flu was what started everything that was wrong with me. Mama told me if I'd taken better care of myself, I wouldn't have caught that dumb flu in the first place. She said it was because I didn't wash my hands enough. So guess what? I washed my hands like crazy from then on."

I look over at Gwen. She sits by me and gives me a wink. "Are you ready to go back and look at your life again? We'll start from when you were a baby if that's okay with you."

"I guess so. I mean, you told me I don't have a choice if I want to move on. Right?"

Gwen nods and stands. "Come on," she says as she walks away.

Curious, I get up and follow her. We are walking together, but we are moving so fast, it's more like flying. The sensation of moving so swiftly gives me butterflies in my belly. The good kind. It's a super fun way to get around.

We stop and sit on a bench in a park, the exact bench and park near my house where I played basketball when I was young. Mama used to sit and cheer me on from this very spot. The smell of hot asphalt after a short rain shower collects in my nose and reminds me of hot summer days with ice cream or water ice. I experience that wonderful sensation of when my life was still . . . still my own.

Gwen points at something in the distance. It's me at eight months old, being held by Mama in a doctor's office. I am tiny and grossly thin.

When the pediatrician enters the room, Mama stands and steps toward her. "Oh, Dr. Morgan. I just know something's wrong with Molly. I've done some research, and I think she's failing to thrive."

After Dr. Morgan checks me over, she shares my mother's concern. The two spend time putting together a plan to help me to get stronger. Mama suggests running a couple of medical tests, but Dr. Morgan doesn't agree. She tells Mama testing is premature.

My stomach twists into a knot watching myself as a baby. I watch another scene as Mama tries to bottle-feed me, but I don't eat much. I cry a lot, so she pulls the bottle away from me. Daddy tells Mama he worries about her, being a new mother and having to cope with my situation.

"Mama told me I had a hard time eating in the beginning. She said something seemed to be bothering me, but she couldn't figure it out," I explain to Gwen.

Gwen doesn't comment. We go back to watching.

We see Mama take me to the doctor several times after my first birthday because I am not gaining weight like I am supposed to. I have a chronic diaper rash. Mama insists the rashes are caused by acid reflux, which would also explain why I cry so often.

A few months later, Mama takes me to a pediatric gastroenterologist, bypassing my regular doctor, who isn't giving her any answers. I am seen for my inability to eat enough, to hold down solid foods, and Mama's concern about acid reflux.

The doctor sits back on his stool after he examines me. "Well, Mrs. Roslin, I don't see an obvious reason why Molly can't eat normally. I could do an endoscopy, but I'd like you to give it a little more time. I have a list of foods I'd like you to try . . . things that will be easy on her belly."

"Why wait?" Mama asks. "I think we should go ahead and do the procedure. That way, if she has an issue it can be treated."

"That's true, but I'd like to give it a little more time. I never rush into procedures with children this young. I'd rather not put Molly under anesthesia unless we try some alternatives first."

Mama's eyes narrow and her chin lifts sharply. "Okay, fine. We'll try it your way, but please understand, I can't stand watching my child suffer much longer."

The doctor stands and gently pats Mama's shoulder. "Understood. I want you to bring her back in two weeks and we'll see how Molly's doing. Okay?"

Mama nods, but her stiff smile matches her rigid posture.

"Wow. Mama is very unhappy. When she stands like that . . . look out," I tell Gwen. "It's weird. I didn't know I was sick when I was a baby. Other than not eating much, I thought I was healthy."

A heaviness fills my belly, and my muscles are taut. I try to undo the tension by stretching, but it doesn't work. "Mama gave up so much for me practically from the time I was born. She never complained or told me anything about what happened back then. It's no wonder my mom worried about me all the time. I thought she was overprotective. Sometimes I would get angry at her for smothering me. Now I feel like a total jerk, and I wish I could let Mama know that I appreciate everything she did for me."

Gwen chuckled. "You're not a jerk, Molly. Besides, we don't even know the whole story yet with your mom. I think we need to wait and see what we learn."

There Gwen goes again, dropping statements about Mama. It's rude, and my face is fiery as blood rushes to it. "I'm not sure what it is you're waiting to see my mom do, but I think you're gonna be disappointed when you learn about all the things she did to help me."

"I don't mean to make you angry," Gwen says reassuringly. "But I do want you to be open-minded. There are things you need to understand about your death."

"What does that mean?" I snap, a bit harsher than I intend. It's as though Gwen is ripping my legs out from under me.

Gwen clears her throat. "It means that things aren't always what they seem. You don't see things clearly. None of us does when we're alive."

Gwen's comment rattles me. "Fine! So tell me this big secret that only you know so we can get this over with, already."

"I could, Molly, but I don't think you'd believe me. I wouldn't believe me if I were you. Being told doesn't do any good. You have to see it for yourself. It's the only way."

"You're right," I say in a monotone voice. "I would never believe anyone who said my mom was not the best in the world. So let me watch it for myself. I want to know what is so horrible about my mom. I guarantee that what you think is horrible and what I think is horrible are two different things. I know there were times when she was pushy with me because I didn't want to take my medicine . . . is that the stuff you're talking about?"

"Let's keep watching and you can make up your own mind," Gwen says.

In the space between Gwen and me, there's thick, raw tension. She turns to peer into the distance. I do the same. It's probably best we don't talk now anyway.

Chapter Eleven

G wen and I watch Mama spend a lot of time bringing me to different doctors. It's the only activity we ever do. It's an odd feeling watching myself as a baby, sick. I'm pale and thin. I don't giggle, as Ava did when she was little. I'm sort of like a lump . . . just there.

The one thing that warms my heart is seeing that Mama is surrounded by people who care for her. She is, after all, as they all tell her, a new mother burdened with a sick child. Mama's much happier, at peace, when people are there, lifting her up. Who can blame her?

Gwen says, "Nothing significant happens until you turn eight. I think we should take a break and then we can watch it. Would that be okay?"

I have to admit, I'm a little relieved. I thought something awful had happened to me. I remember most of what happened once I turned eight so I'm eager to move on, and that's where I'm sure Mama did nothing wrong. "No, let's keep going. I want you to see that Mama took good care of me."

I stare into the abyss, and I see my younger self asleep in my bed.

I am eight years old. The clock on my nightstand reads 10:00 p.m. From Limbo, I can see everything happening in different parts of the house. I watch my mother get out of bed quietly and go down to the kitchen. She opens the refrigerator and then the drawer next to it. She fills a glass with water and drinks it before going back into her bedroom and slipping into bed next to my father.

Instantly, the night turns into day, and it is almost eight in the morning. My mother calls from the kitchen. "Molly, time to get up. You'd better hurry or you'll miss the bus. Come and eat your breakfast first, then you can get dressed."

We watch Mama place a bowl of instant oatmeal in the microwave.

"Molly, get down here!" she hollers. "Your oatmeal is getting cold!"

I rush into the kitchen, run up to Mama, and throw my arms around her waist. She kisses the top of my head.

"Morning, sunshine," Mama says in a cheery voice. "Go eat your breakfast."

I smile into her shirt and take a big whiff of her perfume. I remember her smell. If smells were a visible thing it would be like she was surrounded by rainbows, butterflies, and lilacs. I imagine fairy dust trailing behind her as she moves about.

I take my seat at the kitchen table and Mama places the bowl of oatmeal in front of me. I lift my spoon and take a mouthful.

"This is cold," I say, making a funny face.

"It's cold because you took too long, sleepyhead. Just eat. There's no time to reheat it. If you don't eat now, you'll be starving by lunchtime."

Mama comes over to the table and adds a spoonful of sugar and sprinkles cinnamon on top. "That'll make it taste so good you'll barely notice it's cold. That's all we have time for right now."

Mama was right; sugar and cinnamon made it taste a little better, even cold.

Hours later, I sit at my desk in school. Beads of sweat cling to my upper lip. I'm unbalanced and swaying slightly in my seat.

The clock on the wall reads one o'clock. My teacher, Miss Patrone, is talking about American history. She looks over at me just as I vomit on the girl sitting in front of me. I remember the girl was new, so I didn't know her well.

Miss Patrone whisks me from the room and takes me to the nurse as I continue to heave. The school nurse springs into action. I am quickly put on a small bed and given a bucket. My eyes are red, and tears stream down my face as I retch.

I remember my throat burning from the bile. My stomach was hard as stone. I was terrified to be in the nurse's office without Mama . . . she was the only person who had ever taken care of me.

"I want my mom!" I bellow.

"Oh, honey, don't be upset. I already called your mom, and she'll be here in a few more minutes."

The nurse sits in the chair next to the bed and strokes my hair. By the time my mother arrives, I am covered with a blanket, sleeping.

"What happened to her?" Mama asks as she walks in.

"I think it's the flu, Mrs. Roslin. Molly has all the classic symptoms. She's running a high fever right now. She's not able to keep anything down. It's best to take her home and get fluids in her slowly—little sips of water or juice should work. You'll need to make sure she doesn't dehydrate."

Mama gives the school nurse a warm smile. "You're very kind for taking care of my baby. Don't worry; I know what to do. Molly was a very sickly child so, unfortunately, I have a lot of experience with caring for a sick kid. I'll get her feeling well again and send her back to school in no time."

"Oh, I didn't know she had previous health issues. It must have been very hard on you as a new mom." The nurse gives Mama a small smile. "You probably know this already, but if she starts to complain of an earache or a sore throat you should take her to visit the doctor because she may need an antibiotic."

Mama places her hand on the nurse's shoulder. "Yes, I'm aware, but thank you for offering that advice. I'll let this run its course. I'll only get her an antibiotic as a last resort."

The nurse nods. "You have my number here if you need to call me."

Mama gives her a polite smile. "I'll be sure to keep my eyes and ears open for any issues that she might develop."

The nurse walks over to me. "Molly, wake up. Your mom is here to take you home." The nurse helps me sit up. She wraps a blanket around my shoulders and guides me off of the bed. "I hope you feel better."

I look weak and ashen as the nurse hands me over to Mama. My mother puts an arm around me, and the nurse gives me a warm smile. "You don't need to worry, Molly. Your mom is going to take good care of you."

I manage a nod.

I shuffle out of the school with Mama and lie on the backseat of the car. Once we're home, she helps me get into bed.

In the next two days, I have horrible diarrhea and a high fever. Mama forces me to drink so I stay hydrated, but I can't hold anything in.

By the next morning I can barely pee, and when I stand from my bed I sway and stumble, holding onto the furniture and the walls to get to the bathroom. Three days after that, with no signs of improvement, Mama takes me to the emergency room.

That first car ride to the emergency room was where my long nightmare began.

Chapter Twelve

G wen is nibbling on her bottom lip. She leans into me.

"What?" I ask.

"Holy cow, you look like a rag doll. I wish I could reach in and take care of you myself."

"Yeah," I agree. "I remember how sick I was that first time. Every part of my body ached. I swear, even my hair hurt. It was the worst flu I'd ever had."

Gwen is so right and it's very hard to watch myself be that sick. The dread of knowing all the things they put me through at the hospital fills me with anxiety. I grab Gwen's hand as we continue to watch.

I'm in the car with Mama. She is driving me to the hospital. She turns on the radio. Van Morrison's "Brown-Eyed Girl" is playing. Mama sings along. Loudly.

"Mama, my head hurts. Can you turn the radio off?"

"Oh, sweetie, this will cheer you up. It's good to sing. It helps relieve stress."

"I have a headache. Please turn it off."

"Don't be silly. We'll be at the hospital soon."

I remember wanting to scream and flail my fists to show Mama I was serious. Instead, I put my hands over my ears and told myself she was just trying to get my mind off of going to the hospital.

Inside the emergency room, Mama is hunched over my gurney. I'm crying, and because I have no idea why people go to the hospital, other than for being really sick, I'm afraid something is terribly wrong with me. The people in the emergency waiting room look and behave solemnly. I hear sick people moaning, and I wonder if maybe they're here to die.

Mama looks down at me and holds my hand. "I love you so much, Molly. Don't worry; you're going to be just fine. I promise."

Mama glances at the intake nurse, then back at me. "Molly, I want you to stay here for a minute so I can call your dad and let him know I had to bring you in."

Tears fill my eyes and I shake my head. "No. I don't wanna stay here by myself."

Mama is stern. "Just do as I say. I will be back in less than two minutes."

Mama is on the phone with Daddy.

"Oh, no, Rona. Is she okay? Do you want me to come to the ER?" Daddy asks.

"No, no. There's no need for you to leave work. She'll be fine. They haven't taken us back yet, but I think she probably needs an antibiotic. If it's something serious and I need you to come, then I'll call you back. I suspect we'll be here for a while, though."

"Okay," Daddy says. "But call me and let me know how she's doing."

Mama returns a few minutes later, and a nurse calls my name.

Inside a bay, Mama gives the nurse information about me as the nurse runs an IV. I try to pull my arm away as the sharp stick of the needle breaks my skin, but Mama pins my arm against the bed.

I continuously beg my mother to take me home. I am propped up on one elbow, on the arm that is needleless. I am trying to get the metal bars down so I can leave.

"Molly, you need to stay calm; otherwise they will have to put straps on your wrists and ankles so you can't move. Do you want them to do that to you?"

Immediately my body goes slack and my head presses against the pillow.

Finally, a man walks in and introduces himself as Dr. Sunberg. After checking me over, he sends in a nurse. She gives me a smile and holds up a needle for me to see. I cringe.

The nurse frowns at my reaction. "This is going to make your tummy all better."

The nurse puts the tip of the syringe into the IV line and empties the mystical fluid. Within moments I'm asleep.

Dr. Sunberg returns a while later while I am still sleeping. "Mrs. Roslin, it looks like Molly has the flu. As you suspected, she's dehydrated. We're going to keep her overnight on the IV fluids. I think you'll be able to take her home tomorrow. We want to make sure we get her hydrated before she leaves."

"Oh, thank you, Dr. Sunberg. I think that's the right thing to do."

"As a precaution, we could give her an antibiotic."

Mama glares at the doctor. "Why on earth would you do that? Antibiotics aren't used to treat the flu."

"You're right, but as I said, maybe as a precaution in case she's developing an infection."

Mama runs her hand up to her forehead. Her tone is bitter. "Okay, well, it concerns me that you would even suggest giving Molly something she may not need. Unless you know she has an infection, I don't want you to give her antibiotics. You know as well as I do that giving her antibiotics can cause her to develop antibiotic resistance, and if she ever truly needs them they'll be less effective."

Dr. Sunberg shoves his hands into the pockets of his white coat. "I understand, and that's perfectly reasonable. I'm only suggesting we give them to Molly just in case, but if you don't agree, we'll refrain."

Mama's lips press together. "You're correct. I don't agree."

I watch Mama grab at the collar of her dress and turn away to dismiss him. If it were possible for steam to roll out of her ears, it wouldn't surprise me.

Gwen clears her throat and turns to me. "You were very sick. Don't you think it's strange that your mom wouldn't let the doctor give you antibiotics? You know, just in case."

I turn my head away from Gwen and shrug. "You don't know Mama. She's powerful, and no one tells her what to do . . . not even Daddy. She never let those doctors say what was gonna happen to me. Not like some of the other kids that were in the hospital that had to do whatever the doctor said. Mama is special, and people listen to her."

"That's the problem," Gwen says.

"Why is it a problem that people listen to my mom? I don't understand why you'd say that," I say.

I keep my eyes on Gwen, waiting for an answer. She squirms a little under my gaze.

"Is everything okay? Is there something else you want to say?" I ask.

Gwen glances in my direction. "Let's keep watching. You'll see for yourself."

Chapter Thirteen

B y the time I wake up, I am lying in bed in a room in the children's ward. I lean over and tap Mama's hand. "When can I go home? I don't want them to give me any more needles."

Mama gives me a sweet smile. "I know you don't, sweetheart. Don't worry, you're not getting any more needles today. You're going to lie in bed, and the nurses will keep replacing these bags," she explains.

Mama points to the bag of clear liquid attached to the tube in my arm. "That's going to hydrate you, and once you feel better, then I can take you home."

I clamp down on Mama's hand. In a trembling voice I say, "But why can't I go home now? I don't like being in the hospital. There are too many people and I hate all the smells, and there are weird machines. Can't we just leave?"

Mama pries my hand from hers. "No, Molly, you can't leave right now. Stop complaining and relax. As I said, once you're hydrated I'll take you home. There's nothing more to discuss. Understand?"

My bottom lip quivers. I pull my covers up and turn my head away from my mom so she doesn't see me cry.

As it turns out, Mama is right. I don't have to endure any more needles. That afternoon, just before dinnertime, she takes me home. I get into my bed, and she turns on the television so I can watch cartoons. I snuggle under the thick comforter.

Gwen and I watch Mama as she stands next to my bed. "I'm going to bring you a glass of water," she tells me. "You need to drink so you don't have to go back to the hospital. I can't believe that the doctor was going to give you an antibiotic. Thank goodness that I know what needs to be done. Otherwise he could've made you sicker than you already are."

I smile at Mama. "Thank you."

Mama brushes the hair gently from my face. "You're welcome. I'll always take good care of you. You're my sweet child."

After seven days of bed rest, I emerge from my room and walk down to the kitchen. I sit at the table, limp, like an overcooked noodle.

Mama rushes over to me and puts her cheek against my forehead because that's how she checks for fever. "How are you feeling?"

I put my arms on the table and rest my head on top. "I feel a little better. But I'm tired, and the room spins when I stand up."

"Well, you'll eat a piece of toast, and we'll get you back to bed," Mama sings.

"Do you think I'll be better tomorrow, Mama?"

She kisses my forehead. "You'll be better soon, Molly. I think in the next day or two you're going to be well again.

"There are many things in life that are rushed, Molly. You'll learn that illness is not something that can ever be hurried along; an illness takes its good old time to leave. You remember that and you'll be much better off."

Chapter Fourteen

I close my eyes to stop watching my younger self. "I hated being sick. Mama would tell me I needed to be patient. That there was something God wanted me to learn from being ill."

Gwen scoots closer. "I need to tell you something. It's going to be hard for you to hear, but it's important that you know."

"Okay, what?"

"Remember when your mom went downstairs the night before you first got sick in school?"

"Yeah. So what?" I ask.

"Well, you saw her open the refrigerator and one of the kitchen drawers. Right?"

I nod. I already don't like where this is going.

"When your mom did those things, she took out a carton of eggs from the refrigerator and placed two of them in the drawer she opened."

My stomach flip-flops. "I don't understand."

"The eggs had gone bad overnight. Your mom put them into your oatmeal the next morning."

I move away from Gwen. "I didn't see her do that."

"Because you don't want to see it."

I stand and look down at Gwen. "That's a lie!"

"No, it's not. And your mother knew that antibiotics would have helped you get better quickly; that's why she didn't want Dr. Sunberg to give them to you."

My thoughts are whirling. Gwen would have no reason to lie. But this information defies everything I know about Mama. She spent all her time taking care of me; there's no way she'd do anything to make me sick. It can't be true.

"My mom got up to get a drink of water; if she took the eggs out she must have been sleepwalking. There's no way she'd do that on purpose. She would never hurt me."

"Okay, let's say she was sleepwalking. Then how do you explain that she took the rancid eggs out of the drawer the next morning and mixed them in your oatmeal?" Gwen asks gently.

"I don't know how, Gwen. I just know that Mama would never hurt me. Period."

"I think you see what's happening but don't want to admit it."

I fidget with the hem on my dress. "Why would I do that?"

Gwen turns to face me. I look away from her. My knee bounces like it has a mind of its own.

"Because it's hard, almost impossible, to face that your mom harmed you. But you need to learn the truth," she says.

"I need to learn that my family was trying to hurt me? Is that what you're saying?"

"I didn't say your family. Just your mother."

I put my hands over my ears. "Let's stop talking about this. Please. Just. Stop."

The pressure builds in my chest. Gwen is saying unimaginable things about my mom. Things that can't be true.

I calm myself by looking into the clear, blue sky and focusing on its beauty. When my breathing is level again, I look at my hands to avoid Gwen's eyes. We don't speak for a while. I know in my heart that Gwen is trying to help me somehow and that she's been sent here to get me to where I'm going. I want her to know that I appreciate her staying with me, but her words are too painful.

Finally, I ask a question to break the silence. "Are you sorry you got picked to help me through Limbo?"

"Nope. I'll never be sorry about getting to know you. We're just getting started."

I glance at her sideways. "Does that mean we're friends?"

Gwen puts her arm over my shoulder. I move closer to her. The warmth of her skin is soothing against my own.

Gwen and I sit on the bench together, enjoying the sound of the birds chirping. I have to admit that I'm a little conflicted about our friendship. She gives me comfort, and yet, when she talks about Mama, I am vulnerable.

"I want you to be open with me," Gwen says, seeming to read my mind. "I know it's much easier to get angry with me when I tell you stuff you don't want to hear. There are a lot of things that you don't know about yet."

"I wish I could react differently, but I can't. And, I can't let anyone take away the special bond I had with my mom . . . with my whole family," I say.

Gwen slides her arm away from me and twirls a curl of her hair around her index finger. "I know how hard it can be to face the unthinkable things that have happened. It's just that sometimes we are so close and tied up in our own situation we can't see what's going on even though it's right in front of our eyes. Like the way I saw your mom put the eggs in the drawer and you didn't. Please know that I don't enjoy telling you what I see, but I have to."

I stare at Gwen. "I know what happened to me. There's not much to it other than I was a really sick kid my whole life. I'm not saying my mom is perfect, but I still don't believe she'd do anything to hurt me. Maybe you're seeing things that aren't there and I'm the one who really sees things that are real."

Gwen rubs her palms on her thighs. "It'll take time for you to see the whole picture. We only get what we can endure. Just like in life, the more time that passes, the more you'll be able to handle."

I look out over the grass. "You mean, like how I was scared to death to go to the hospital the first time, but then I became, like, a pro at it?"

Gwen pulls a small leaf out of my hair for me. "Yeah, like that. On Earth, when bad things happen, sometimes we convince ourselves that we've imagined them or there's some other explanation because we won't allow ourselves to face the truth. But here, once you've made peace with your life, you can clearly see the lives of those that were around you. I'm here to make sure you see things the way they were. Someday soon you'll have that clarity too."

"So are there lots of things I don't know?"

"Probably," Gwen answers with a small laugh. "But hey, you're in good company—we all live our lives not knowing things. In a weird way, sometimes it's actually for the best."

I squirm on the bench next to Gwen. A minute ago I was telling her to stop insulting my mom, and now I have to know what she's talking about so I can decide for myself. Not knowing what's real creates confusion for me. I can't help but wonder what "things" I don't know about myself. My insides run cold, and I'm shivering.

"I think I need to be alone," I tell Gwen.

Chapter Fifteen

I am alone, and the images of my life are gone for now. I take a deep breath, dragging in the fresh air. Even though I'm dead, the simple act of filling my lungs with air makes me feel alive.

Thinking about all the information Gwen has shared with me makes my blood course rapidly through my veins. I've spent my last three years with Mama and almost no one else. It's good because I was so close to my mom, but it's also bad because I didn't take part in my own life. My only goal was to do as I was told by my mom so I would get well again.

When I was alive, I worked hard to convince myself I would be okay someday. The way I coped was by pretending I would get better. Accepting my fate would have made me hopeless and bitter. I did my best to block out the truth. But self-deception has made death that much harder on me. Denial is brutal when truth slams you in the face.

I think back to my first illness. I never completed a full school year after. During my school absences, Mama picked up my work from my teachers. She would meet with them every week, then she'd come home and sit with me to teach me what I needed to know. Mama was so happy after her school visits, yammering on about how impressed my teachers were with her dedication to my education and that she was such a good mother.

"Your teachers feel sorry for me," Mama would say. "But I keep telling them this is my job. To take care of my children, and no matter how bad it gets, I'll always do what's best for my two girls."

When Mama would relay these stories, my chest would puff up with pride. Mama always put me first. That was the one thing I could count on, and that was a big deal. After all, every kid wants to be their parents' top priority. Plus, it was nice to see Mama happy. She spent so much time in the hospital with me; she barely had a life.

Mama talked about my being sick to anyone she knew or met. I didn't like being the topic of her conversations and wished she'd stop. I guess it was her way of getting through her own hard time. After a while, Mama's need for attention became background noise. Sort of like when you read the same sentence fifteen times and the words don't stick or make any sense.

Honestly, it was okay because I knew that all the attention Mama got from other people would help me get better. She told me the reason she talked about me all the time, especially to doctors and nurses, was so they'd work harder to make me well. I used to wish that every sick kid had a mom like mine. Mama loved us, Ava and me, and she showed us that all the time.

Feeling a little better after remembering Mama's devotion to me, I look around for Gwen, but I don't see her. "Gwen? Come back, please."

"I'm here," she says, as she sits next to me.

"Where did you go?" I ask her.

"Limbo is a big place. I envisioned myself in the Yiddish movie theater from my small town before I was taken to Auschwitz. I went to watch a film so you could be alone for a while. Whenever you need to be alone, I'll disappear until you call me back."

"Oh. But don't your feelings get hurt when I tell you I want to be alone?"

"No," Gwen replies and shakes her head. "It's all part of the process. I know how much it hurts to see yourself in a way that isn't pleasant. To find out the truth about people . . . about ourselves. We all have to face it, and well . . . when you're alone, it gives you time to make peace with what you've learned."

Gwen left out "scary." Reliving bad things from the past is scary.

"Gwen, I need to tell you something I've been thinking about. Something that bothers me."

She rests her chin on her hand. "What is it?"

"My life doesn't make any sense. I lived so that I could be sick, and then I died. I don't see a reason for me to have ever been born. Do you?"

Gwen shrugs her shoulders. "It's hard to say."

I had hoped that Gwen could clear up my confusion, but I suppose it's dumb of me to expect she'd know my purpose in life. I look away before turning back to her. "Will I ever make sense of what happened?"

"I don't know if anyone makes sense of why they had to suffer," Gwen says.

My frustration with not having answers to my questions makes me want to scream at the top of my lungs. But also, like when I was alive, I swallow my words and feelings, bury them deep inside my belly, and change the subject.

"Hey, is there anything I'm not allowed to do in this place?"

Gwen giggles. My muscles relax at the sound of her laughter. It's light, and it softens the mood.

"Nope. You can do anything you want here. You can stomp your feet, throw things at the wall, or laugh until your insides ache. That's the point of being here."

"That's the kind of freedom I wanted when I was alive. I've been a prisoner of my own body for a long time."

I run my fingers through my hair. I notice it feels like satin. "I hope my life makes sense before I leave here."

"It's a journey, Molly. In the end, you'll have peace; it's worth it. Trust me."

Trust me. Those two words tumble around in my head. I trusted that my body would heal itself. I trusted that my doctors and nurses would make me better. All that got me was dead. I realize I have to give trust one more try . . . but only because it is Gwen.

I hope I don't regret placing my trust in her.

Chapter Sixteen

I watch Mama from Limbo with longing. "She is making me her life-restoring food," I tell Gwen.

Gwen squints as she takes a closer look.

I turn to Gwen. "I remember that's what she called it. Mama came up with all kinds of things to make me better, faster. She did a lot of research and would always put powerful herbs and vitamins into my food. After I had the flu, she tried all kinds of remedies until she came up with a special medicine she made from scratch. I wanted the medicine to work so badly, but it didn't. Mama went through a lot of trouble to make it for me. But my body didn't respond. It was a huge disappointment."

Gwen and I watch another scene. I wake one morning and struggle to a sitting position so I can look out my bedroom window. The rainy weather casts a depressing mood over me.

Mama, carrying a glass of ginger ale, enters my room.

"Mama, I thought I'd be better by now," I bawl.

Mama sits on the bed and scoops me onto her lap. "You listen here. You're a strong girl, and you have to keep fighting. Life is full of ups and downs. It's how you react when things aren't going your way that counts the most."

"Yeah, but I've had lots of downs already. I want some ups."

Mama strokes my hair. "I know you do. And trust me, your time is coming. I can feel it in my bones."

I remember that her words didn't make me feel any better about what was happening. I was frustrated and resentful that my life was confined to a bed.

My flu-like symptoms persist for a few more days, so Mama takes me to the emergency room as I cower in the backseat of the car on our way to the hospital.

By the fourth ER run, I am laboring to breathe.

When the doctor comes in to see me on that last visit, Mama is almost hysterical. "I'm afraid of what is going to happen to my daughter. My husband and I decided we won't continue this way. Molly has barely eaten in more than three weeks. Every time she eats, she gets sick."

I turn to Gwen. "It was true. I had hardly been able to eat anything in all that time, and when I did, I'd have to hurry to the bathroom. But when Mama got that upset I knew how serious my illness was. It was the first time I worried I might never get better. That freaked me out so much."

I wipe the sweat from my forehead. It is unnerving to see and remember how I experienced all the bad things. "This isn't easy to watch," I tell Gwen.

"I know. But let's go back to when you started being sick again. I want you to concentrate on every single thing that happens. You need to look really hard."

"Okay, what is it I'm supposed to see?"

Gwen moves a little too close. "Open yourself up to see what's in front of you. Focus on what's real. Are you ready?"

I try to inch away from Gwen, but she fills the space between us and puts her arm over my shoulder.

We watch Mama in the kitchen again, right before I get sick a second time. It's early in the morning. She takes ground beef out of the freezer. She walks to the back door and places the meat on the patio, in the sun.

"What is she doing?" I ask.

Gwen gives me a nod and put her index finger over her lips.

Much later that day, the meat is brown. Mama carries it into the kitchen and breaks the plastic wrapper. Her head jerks backward, and she makes a face when the rotted smell hits her sinuses.

Mama's cooking. There is one pan of food for her, Ava, and Daddy, and another one just for me. She uses rotten meat in my pan. No one notices. Ava is too young and Daddy usually comes home after the dinner dishes are clean.

I wrap my arms around my knees. Gwen tightens her grip around my shoulder. We watch.

For the weeks that follow, Mama feeds me more contaminated food. By that fourth ER run, Mama is sitting next to my gurney. She cries and one of the ER nurses embraces her for a long time.

I can remember my heart aching for Mama, and at the same time I was petrified by her breakdown. I'm tense and nervous about what I'll see next. I let out the breath I've been holding in.

"Are you okay?" Gwen asks.

I nod. I don't speak. If I do, I'll only cry.

Mama talks to the ER doctor. "This has been going on for years. She eats, and then she can't eat. I can't send her to school this way. Look at her," Mama says.

She turns to me lying on the gurney in the emergency room. "She's so thin. Molly can't afford to lose any more weight. You have to do something about this right now. This can't go on any longer. I won't let it. I know this isn't a preferred option, but I think we have to consider a feeding tube, at least for now. Then we can assess things as she gets proper nutrition and progresses."

The doctor hesitates, but Mama scowls at him and lifts my bone-thin hand in hers. "I don't know what I'd do if anything happened to my child. You have to do something. Right, Molly?"

Mama and the doctor look at me, and I unwittingly nod in agreement.

As I watch my pathetic past, it plays like dark memories that I'd rather forget. The truth is, I would've done anything not to be sick anymore, and Mama knew it too.

The doctor turns to Mama. "That's a serious step. I wouldn't consider a feeding tube until I make sure we aren't masking another issue. I want to admit Molly and do an endoscopy, and perhaps a colonoscopy. We can talk about the next steps after we do some tests."

"Oh, thank you, Dr. Martin. I swear it's a stroke of pure luck that you're working the emergency room tonight. I'm so grateful that Molly is under your care."

Dr. Martin gives Mama a sad smile, then says to me, "We're going to keep you here for a while so we can get you better."

Behind the oxygen mask, a bright expression blossoms across my face.

One week later, after undergoing three tests and one procedure, all with normal results, I am released from the hospital with a feeding tube.

I remember being so hopeful that the doctors would find something treatable, but they didn't. The feeding tube was degrading. I didn't like having plastic sticking out of my stomach; it was as though my insides were exposed to the world, and as though when I left the hospital there was something significant I had left behind.

I steal a peek at Gwen and shake my head. My eyes lock on her profile. She lowers her head as if she is about to pray. I want to erase the images I've just seen. My mind is whirling. Maybe Gwen made those images appear.

"I can't even think straight right now. I don't know what to say. We just watched Mama poison me, right?"

Gwen keeps her head bowed. She's saying so much without uttering a single word.

I say, "I'm going to sleep now, and I hope I never wake up."

Chapter Seventeen

W hen I do wake up, I tell myself that it is all a dream. Mama never fed me
spoiled food, and it was all an illusion.

I look around. Nothing has changed. It isn't a dream. It's real. I'm still dead.

Gwen is sitting up, watching me. I stretch my arms and legs. It's liberating to
be limber again.

I think about what I've learned so far. I'm deeply disturbed, and yet denial
comes to the forefront of my mind. I want to stay in the moment, but not
believing is much easier and far more pleasant.

I try to stand but my knees give out. "My heart is like a lump of clay in my chest;
it's heavy, and I think it may be broken. Nothing is real. I keep telling myself that
I'm dreaming. If I'm still alive, then this is all a nightmare, and I'll wake up soon.
That's what I want to believe."

Gwen gives me a blank stare.

"Was I ever really sick?"

"You'll have to see for yourself. It's the only way you'll be able to believe it."

Gwen takes off her shoes and socks and wiggles her toes. She's so casual about
some of this stuff it makes me crazy.

I slump over, my head hanging and shoulders rounded.

Gwen grabs my hand. "Look, I'm here with you. You're not alone. I won't leave
you by yourself. I promise."

I lift my head but look away from Gwen. "But I loved my family, and I wasn't
ready to leave them. This is all nuts. How didn't I know what Mama was doing?
I must be an idiot."

I lay on the grass and curl into a fetal position. There's nothing left to do but
cry. I'm racked with endless sobs. I try to stop crying, but my emotions are like a
tornado, destroying everything in their path.

"I didn't want to die," I tell Gwen. "I've missed out on my whole life. It's not
fair."

Gwen moves closer. She is my rock. When my tears have all been shed, I collect
myself and roll over to face her.

69

She gives me the sweetest smile, and for a passing moment I don't hate being dead.

"This is hard, and you didn't deserve what happened to you. No kid deserves to be treated poorly." Gwen's smile turns playful. "You're a fighter and the nicest person my age I've ever met here," Gwen says.

I press my forehead to Gwen's. She's simply fantastic.

I return a sly smile. "You're the kindest girl I've ever met . . . even when we don't agree," I confess.

"Hey, you know what?" Gwen says with renewed enthusiasm. "I bet if we met when we were alive, we would have been best friends."

I sigh. "Except you're way stronger than I am. I envy you."

Gwen blushes. "I wasn't like this when I first got here. I was even more upset than you are. That's why I push you."

"I don't know how that's possible, but if you say so, then I believe you. The truth is, I'm young and dead, and that makes me mad."

Gwen rolls onto her belly and props her chin in her hands.

"I'm just curious. That thing with the meat that your mom did, you saw that, right?" Gwen asks.

"Yeah, I saw, and it enrages me. I'm disappointed in her, but the worst is this deep sense of betrayal. I have so many thoughts in my head, and it's hard to make sense of them. I want to go back to Earth and ask Mama why she did that to me. I don't see the point of her wanting to have a sick child or me having a feeding tube when she could've kept giving me bad food to eat. I want to cry for every day that I lost in my bed, in hospitals, and in emergency rooms. I want to know how Mama could've done this to someone she supposedly loved."

Gwen sits up. "What's most important is that you understand you couldn't have changed the outcome. Your mother was the only person who could've done something differently, or maybe your dad could have paid closer attention, but there's nothing you can do about that now or then. It's that simple, Molly."

"How do I accept that? There's nothing simple about a mother hurting her own child."

"You must believe there's something better for you. You need to stop blaming yourself for not knowing. You clearly carry a lot of guilt about being sick. Sometimes things are outside of our control and we can't do anything about it. Unfortunately, this is one of those times."

I sit up quickly. "I don't think I can do that."

"Forgiving yourself is hard," Gwen explains. "You can't beat yourself up for not knowing what wasn't shown to you. And I get that you might think you didn't stand up for yourself enough. But you couldn't have fought a war that you didn't know about. When you forgive yourself, you show yourself love. Carrying the anger will eat at you day and night. When we're finished here, you'll go to a place that's pure and blissful. All the things that bothered you in life will be a distant memory. You'll find true happiness."

"I'm not so sure. Maybe I don't belong in that pure place. I don't think I can be a forgiving person. I have a lot to figure out and I don't even know everything that's happened in my life yet."

Gwen stands, and I follow her to my bedroom I've created in Limbo. I flop down on a green sofa and sink into its mind-blowing coziness. Gwen lies on the opposite end. Our legs entangle, our feet press against each other's, and I look up and can see into the clear sky, right through my ceiling. It's awesome.

I tell Gwen, "I'm ready to go back and see more of my life."

I'm lying in my bed with the feeding tube sticking out of my stomach. I remember my life became much worse after it was inserted. Mama no longer let me eat solid food because I'd developed so many food allergies; she administered my liquid nutrition on a strict schedule.

But on this afternoon, I look like I'm finally feeling better. Ava is rolling around on our bedroom floor, pretending to wrestle her doll, and I am laughing.

I hear Mama in the kitchen, and I see myself take Ava's hand in my own. We walk down the stairs for lunch. Mama smiles when she sees us. "What are you doing down here, Molly?"

"I'm feeling better. I wanted to come down and sit with you while you eat lunch."

Mama places a grilled cheese sandwich on the table in front of Ava, who picks up half. The cheese oozes out from between the crispy, buttery bread. I remember my mouth watering as I stared at the sandwich in her small hand. Ava takes a bite and smiles as she chews.

"It's good, huh?" I ask my little sister.

Ava drops the sandwich back on her plate and nods briskly. "Yeah."

"I can't wait to be able to eat one of those again."

Ava picks up the sandwich and takes another bite. I look at it wistfully.

"Mama . . ." I start.

"What is it, Molly?"

"I need to ask you something."

"You seem so serious. What is it now?"

"When can I go back to school?"

Mama swallows her food. "I don't know. You're on a strict feeding schedule, and I wouldn't want the other kids to think you're different. Kids are cruel, and they might say things to hurt your feelings. It's my job, as your mother, to protect you. You have enough to deal with."

"I don't care if somebody hurts my feelings," I snap at her.

Mama raises her eyebrows and gives me a slight smile. "You say that now, but if someone gets you upset, you'll care. Kids are mean, Molly."

I sit forward on the kitchen chair. "But if I go back to school maybe I can find a friend, someone who wants to play with me. Then they could come here, or I could go to their house."

Mama's brow tightens, and she turns to look out the kitchen window into our backyard.

When she turns back, her expression has changed. "It may be good for you to have a friend. That may be an excellent thing."

I sit up straighter in my chair. "So I can go back to school?"

"Yes, Molly, you can go back. But first I need to talk with your father to make sure he agrees."

A huge smile spreads across my face.

"We should clean up lunch and play a card game . . . hello?" Mama sings.

I look up at her, then blink a few times. "Sorry, Mama. Did you ask me something?"

"I said, we should clean up lunch and play a card game. Go Fish?"

Ava bounces on her chair and giggles. I look at her and laugh.

"Yeah, that sounds like fun," I say.

I turn my attention to Gwen. "I was nervous about going back to school. I knew the kids might tease me. It already sucked because I didn't have any friends in my grade. I knew some of the kids, but I never got close to any of them. I prayed the others would be nice to me. Do you know what I mean?"

Gwen looks away and shakes her head.

"Oh, you were one of the popular kids," I say.

"Yeah, I had friends. My life was amazing until we were forced into the concentration camp. I'm sorry it wasn't the same for you."

Gwen stretches out like a cat waking from a nap.

I stretch too. "I was super nervous about going back to school. But I knew if I told Mama I was nervous, she'd keep me home."

Gwen leans over and pats my leg. "So you know that your mom overreacts to things?"

"I guess. I didn't think of it as overreacting. More like protecting me, but I didn't want to give Mama any reason to make a decision that I wouldn't like. I didn't tell her everything all of the time."

Gwen stares at me but says nothing.

"What?" I ask.

"I think it's good that you had your own opinions even if you never let them be known."

"That's a weird thing to say. What good is an opinion if I didn't say it out loud?"

Gwen shifts toward me. "It's good because it means you have a mind of your own. And if you could think for yourself when you were alive, you can definitely think for yourself here."

It's empowering to hear Gwen say positive things about me. It's not something I am used to. I love that Gwen believes I can think for myself. Her belief in me gives me the hope I need. Maybe I'll get through Limbo and find that peace she told me about.

Chapter Eighteen

I've been trying to sort out my feelings since I saw my mom feed me rancid meat. On the one hand, I am enraged and heartbroken. She was supposed to protect me. On the other hand, I also still love her. I know that sounds crazy; I should probably hate her. But it's difficult for me to turn my love on and off like a faucet. In any case, she must have had a good reason for doing what she did to me. Right?

It's hard to know that Mama invented a story for the doctor so I'd get a feeding tube. I agonize for hours, searching for some logical explanation. Short of understanding her motives, I don't think I'll ever have a pure mind and heart, which will leave me stuck in Limbo forever, reliving my life. There is so much I don't understand about Mama it makes my heart hurt.

In life, I was taught to look to the future, live for the moment, and forget anything rotten about my past. In Limbo, everything is wonderful and I'm filled with hope, but I have to watch everything disturbing that happened in my past. I love and hate Limbo now.

Plain tired and in need of a change, I conjure up a tire swing and climb inside. Letting my arms hang over the top, I sway back and forth along the edge of a pond I've also imagined. The soft movement lulls me. It helps to clear my mind. My body is strong. I am healthy, the way I was meant to be.

I look into the sky and soak in this moment of bliss, not worrying about the past and what happened. Those were gloomy times, and I look forward to putting my memories to bed. I wish this process didn't take so long.

Suddenly Gwen appears next to me. She's watching as I swing back and forth. "Are you ready to keep going?" she asks.

My eyelids are heavy. I nod.

A week after my conversation with Mama, she allowed me to return to school. I wasn't allowed to ride the bus because Mama was afraid the kids would tease me or mess up my tube, so she drove me.

Once we arrive, our first stop is the nurse's office. I sit on a chair with my shirt up above my belly button. Mama and the school nurse are going over my feeding tube.

The nurse turns to Mama when she finishes explaining. "Your instructions are perfect."

Mama beams. "Thank you."

The school nurse nods. "I think we have it all covered. Why don't you go home, and I'll take it from here. You don't have to worry; I'll take excellent care of Molly."

Mama presses her lips to my forehead. "Oh, one other thing. If anything goes wrong or if Molly doesn't feel well, you must call me immediately." Mama points at me. "That includes if any of the other kids tease you. Understand?"

"Yes, Mama. If anything happens, I'll tell my teacher just like you told me to do."

"That's my girl," Mama says and brushes her hand over the top of my head.

My book bag is flung over my hunched shoulder, my arms are crossed, and my head hangs as I walk toward my first class.

"You look like you're marching to your death," Gwen says. "I thought you would've been happy."

"I was scared the other kids would tease me," I tell Gwen. "My mother had talked so much about the possibility of my classmates being mean, it stuck in my head. What if they think I'm a freak? What if everyone hates me and I don't make any friends? If no one likes me, will Mama make me stay home?

"I also hated being the center of attention. I was always sick and I didn't have any friends. Most of them didn't even know or remember me."

When I enter the classroom, the other kids are silent, and all eyes are on me. Miss Petrone, my teacher, brightens and rushes toward me.

Miss Petrone's arms extend out and I'm not sure if I should run into them for a hug. Her smile is so big it almost swallows the rest of her face. I stand still with my hands clasped together and smile back.

"Molly, it's so nice to have you back. We've missed you while you were away."

My face turns bright red. "Thanks, Miss Petrone, I'm happy to be back," I say.

Miss Petrone turns and faces the students. "Let's all make Molly feel welcome. Can you all say hello?"

The class grumbles a hello in unison.

"I was so embarrassed I wanted to shrink down to the size of a gummy bear," I tell Gwen. "See the girl glaring at me? She's the one I barfed all over. What was her name? Judy? Julie? Jenny? I can't remember; it was one of those J names."

Miss Petrone puts her hands up and loudly clears her throat. I look up at her.

"We saved your seat," she says, pointing to the girl with the J name.

I weave my way through the desks and give J girl a smile. She responds by rolling her eyes. I slide into my seat, and Miss Petrone goes back to the lesson.

I lean forward in my chair so my mouth is close to J girl's ear. "I'm really sorry I puked on you."

J girl jumps.

"I didn't mean to scare you."

She turns and scowls at me.

"Right," I say under my breath.

"Molly?"

I look at Miss Petrone. "Yes?"

"I asked if you were able to keep up with your reading."

I cough quickly to clear my throat, not wanting to gurgle out the first full sentence I'm about to speak. "I finished Charlie and the Chocolate Factory last week."

"That's wonderful. We all finished it last week as well. It doesn't surprise me a bit, though. Your mom assured me that you'd stay up on your studies. You're lucky to have someone like her who was able to help you while you were sick."

I nod with tightly clamped lips and big, round eyes.

Luckily, the girl in front of me raises her hand.

"Yes, Jessica?" says Miss Petrone.

"That's it! Her name was Jessica," I say to Gwen.

"I'm nervous Molly's gonna puke on me again."

The classroom breaks into laughter. My neck disappears as my shoulders rise to meet my head.

"Children, it's very rude to laugh at other people," Miss Petrone says. "Molly has been through enough and certainly doesn't need any of you being mean to her."

I turn to Gwen, "I wanted the teacher to stop talking and I kept staring at her hoping she would read my mind and just be quiet."

Gwen nods and we watch again.

A girl's voice comes from the back of the classroom.

Miss Petrone looks over. "I'm sorry, did you say something, Veronica?"

Veronica stands. She has long brown hair down to her waist, and her bangs are cut stylishly, straight across her forehead.

Veronica places her hands on her hips. "I said I'll switch seats with Jessica. I'm not worried about Molly puking on me."

I let out a loud sigh of relief and Jessica snaps her head around and glares at me.

"Well now," Miss Petrone begins, "Veronica is showing us all how to be a good, respectful person. We can all learn a lesson from her selflessness."

Veronica doesn't smile; her expression remains serious. "Is that a yes?" she asks impatiently.

"Yes, Veronica. Thank you very much. Jessica, gather your things and move to Veronica's seat."

Jessica sits up tall in her seat, turns, and looks down her nose at me. "But that's all the way in the back of the room. I like sitting up front. Can't Molly switch with Veronica?"

Miss Petrone glares at Jessica. "I think it would be better if you moved your seat, Jessica. Come on, get moving. We've wasted enough class time on seating arrangements."

A few minutes later, Veronica sits down and turns to smile at me and I smile back.

Just as Miss Petrone finishes giving us our new reading assignment, it is lunchtime. The class stands next to their desks at the teacher's command.

Veronica leans into me. "You can sit with me at lunch."

My mouth drops open, but no words come out. Veronica watches me closely and I look away. "I have to go to the nurse's office. I can't eat regular food."

Veronica's smile dips. Then her eyes widen. "Maybe I can come with you and eat my lunch there? That way, we can talk. Let's ask Miss Petrone."

Veronica hangs back, and I wait with her. We are the last two left in the classroom.

"Molly, Mrs. Falcone is waiting for you in her office."

"Can I eat lunch with Molly in the nurse's office?" Veronica asks eagerly.

Miss Petrone studies us for a moment. "I think Mrs. Falcone would be fine with that. It's nice that you two get along. And Veronica, I'm especially proud of you for stepping up."

Veronica pinches her lips together. "Miss Petrone, being nice to someone isn't stepping up; it's being a good person."

Chapter Nineteen

Veronica is intrigued by my feeding tube. She looks at it from every angle. My face is neutral, even though I remember her curiosity was a source of angst. Instead, I sit there as though it's perfectly normal for me to eat my food through a tube.

Mrs. Falcone talks through the entire feeding process, and Veronica hangs onto every word. Once my bag of food is set up, I lean back in the hard plastic chair.

Veronica opens her lunch bag and pulls out her lunch. I stare achingly at her peanut butter and jelly sandwich. She reaches back into her sack and pulls out a bag of potato chips.

"That was agonizing," I tell Gwen. "When I saw those potato chips I swear I wanted to jump up on the table and dive face-first into the bag and chomp them down like a dog."

"Yeah, I get that. Potato chips are about the greatest food ever invented."

Veronica and I chat for a little while and then she looks at my bag of liquid food. "You almost ate half of it."

I smile politely. "'Ate' is a strong word."

We both laugh.

I place my restless hands on the table between us. "So how come I don't remember you from before?" I ask.

"I moved here two months ago. The kids aren't that nice here. There's this girl I sit with at lunch, but she doesn't talk much."

"Maybe you can come over to my house and play," I suggest.

Veronica smiles at me. "That would be fun."

"Good. I'll ask my mom when she picks me up from school today."

Veronica shoves chips into her mouth (crunch, crunch, crunch, swallow). I remember wanting to ask if I could lick the salt from her fingertips, but I knew that would be really creepy, and probably the end of our friendship.

"How are you two girls doing?" Mrs. Falcone asks.

I look over at the school nurse. She's a kind lady, and I give her a thumbs up.

"Your bag is finishing up. As soon as it's done, I'll get you out of here."

"Thanks, Mrs. Falcone."

Ten minutes later, Veronica and I walk back to class as she chats away.

"So, my neighbor is a real jerk. He's fourteen and thinks he's cooler than everyone on our block," Veronica gushes.

I give her a sideways glance. "I don't play outside too much."

"Why?"

"Because I could get sick. My mom says no good ever comes from being outside except to catch other diseases."

Veronica puts distance between us. "You have a disease?"

"No, not really. I just get sick a lot. The doctors can't figure out what's wrong with me."

"Oh," Veronica says, closing the gap between us. "Well, maybe there isn't anything wrong with you then."

Gwen touches my elbow and we stop watching. "Veronica made a good point," she says.

A surge of uncertainty courses through me, and I gently move my elbow away from Gwen's hand. "But I died of kidney failure, which has nothing to do with eating bad food. So something was definitely wrong with me."

We go back to watching.

At the end of the school day, Mama is waiting at the curb and I climb into the quiet of our family car as the other kids run to their buses, laughing and shouting back and forth.

"How was it? I want to hear everything," Mama says.

"It was excellent. I met a girl named Veronica. She said she would love to come over to our house and play. Can she?"

Mama grins, and her light pink lipstick frames her straight, white teeth perfectly. "We'll see. Did Miss Petrone say anything about me?"

My smile vaporizes, and my voice goes flat. "Yeah, she told the class that you're great."

"Really?" Mama says as she looks at herself in the rearview mirror. She shoots herself a quick smile before looking at the road again. "Tell me exactly what she said. I think Miss Petrone is such a good teacher. She's very perceptive."

When I hesitate, Mama slaps her palm on the leather seat. "Come on. Tell me. I'm dying to know."

"Miss Petrone says you're very capable and that I'm lucky that you're my mom."

Mama grabs the collar of her blouse. "Oh, she's so sweet. I knew your teacher liked me. Every week when I went in to pick up your schoolwork, she raved about what a model mom I was. I want you to remember this because someday when you're a mom, I want you to treat your kids the same. You have to love your kids unconditionally. That's what a good mom does."

"Sure," I grumble into the window.

My head is cocked to the left, and I stared out the front window. My eyes glaze over.

"Did the school nurse say anything about me?"

I make a loud noise as I fill my lungs with air. "Only that your instructions for the tube were perfect."

Mama smiles like the Grinch after he stole Christmas from Whoville.

I rest my head against the window, and out of the corner of my eye I see her glance over at me.

"Are you all right? Do you feel sick, Molly?"

My head springs up. "No, I'm fine. I was thinking, that's all."

"Are you sure? I want you to tell me when you don't feel good."

"I will, Mama. I promise. I feel great. Better than I have in a long time."

I can see Mama's eyes grow dark. Her mouth turns downward, and her hands grip the steering wheel so tightly her knuckles turn white.

Sitting next to Gwen, I squeeze my eyes shut and try to wrap my mind around what I've just seen.

"Molly?" Gwen says.

I open my eyes. My breath is shallow and raspy.

"Why do you think your mom got upset when you told her you felt great?"

I flinch. "I don't know. Maybe it's because she thought I was lying about feeling good. You know, like I was exaggerating so that she didn't think I was sick."

"But you weren't exaggerating. You did feel great, right?"

"Yeah, sure I did." I'm trying to think of something clever to snuff out Gwen's line of questioning. I'm not at the point where I want to talk about it.

I stand up and take a few steps away from her. "I know you have questions, but I need to think through what we've seen. There's a lot to wrap my head around; it's like I'm watching someone else's life."

"You're right," Gwen says. "I think it's good that you take time to think about things. Your emotions must be all over the place. I totally get that."

"Thanks. You know, there is one thing. I want to hate Mama, but it's not that simple for me."

I sit down and pick at the blades of grass. I think about the rancid meat that Mama fed me. I wish I could see her objectively, like Gwen. But because I've always loved her, betrayal is a difficult thing to accept. It's hard to know my feelings weren't reciprocated.

If I see any more, I fear that I'll lose everything about myself and my mom that was good. And yet I know that in Limbo, that's inevitable.

Chapter Twenty

Gwen and I watch scenes from my past again. I see Mama in the kitchen the morning of Veronica's visit.

"Molly, I'm making my famous homemade brownies for your new friend," she tells me excitedly.

I spin around and glower at her. "Do you have to make them?"

Mama glares at me. "Why would you ask that?"

My bottom lip quivers. "Because I love your brownies and I won't be able to have any. It's not fair."

Mama purses her lips together and looks away. "Well, life isn't fair. I think not being able to eat a brownie is a small price to pay so that you can stay healthy. It's selfish that you want to deprive your new friend of something just because you can't have it."

My chin drops to my chest and my shoulders slump forward.

Mama turns back to watch my reaction. I avoid making eye contact.

"I'm sorry, Mama," I finally say. "It's just that I love your brownies."

Mama's face slowly softens. She shuffles over to me and gives me a quick hug and smiles. "It's understandable. I do make the best brownies. I mean, every time I make them for the bake sale at church they're the first things to go."

I flop down in a chair and push the hair from my face. "I know. You don't have to keep talking about how good they are; it's just making me want to eat them more."

Mama kneels in front of me. "Someday I'll pass my brownie recipe on to you and Ava. You'll make them for your kids, and by that time you'll be able to eat them again too."

"How did that make you feel?" Gwen asks.

I wince. "I was totally panicked. It was as though Mama had thrown a bucket of ice water in my face. I didn't want to wait until I had kids to eat a brownie again. And she seemed to be warning me that I'd need a feeding tube until I was old. I felt terrified and powerless."

In the kitchen, I cross my arms. "What do you mean? I'm not going to have this stupid feeding tube that long, right?" I ask.

Mama ignores me and moves to the sink. My face is bright red as I watch her.

"Mama. Say something. Did the doctor say I had to keep the tube in until I grow up?"

"Molly, please. Don't be so dramatic. No, the doctor did not say you have to keep the tube until you grow up. But there's no telling how long you'll need it. I'm just trying to make you feel better by saying you'll make these brownies for your own children someday. Okay?"

From Limbo, I can see the shock on my young face . . . I wish there had been someone, other than Mama, who would've listened to my concerns and answered my questions.

When Veronica finally arrives that afternoon, Mama gives her a tour of the house.

"Wow. You have the prettiest room," Veronica says as we all walk in.

My cheeks flush. "Thanks," I say. "My mom did it all."

My room is the palest shade of pink. Ava and I have sleigh beds covered with thick purple and white comforters.

Mama comes up from behind us. "That's very sweet of you to notice. I worked extra hard to make this room perfect for Molly and Ava."

Mama wrings her hands together. "This is where Molly spent most of her time when she wasn't in school . . . when she was sick. You know, before she had the feeding tube put in."

My chin pops up and my teeth are bared, but neither Mama nor Veronica notices me.

Veronica walks over to my wall-to-wall bookshelf. "Did you read all these books?" she asks.

I glance at my mom, then back at Veronica.

"Well, I've read some of them. And Mama has read me a lot of the others."

Mama pulls To Kill a Mockingbird from the bookshelf. "That's right. Reading is the key to everything good in life. Now, this book here"—she holds it up so Veronica can read the title— "this book won a Pulitzer Prize."

As Mama talks about various books, Veronica looks bored. When Mama finally goes downstairs, Veronica and I stay up in my room, talking and playing card games. Then we play dress-up. Two hours later, we are bouncing around my room, having a great time when Mama calls us and we go downstairs.

When I reach the door to the kitchen, I screech to a halt. There's a pizza box on the table. I look at Mama, and she scurries over and gives me a quick squeeze.

Gwen leans into me. "Why do you look so mad?"

"Because I loved pizza and seeing it on my kitchen table was torture. Mama told me I was allergic to dairy. So even before I had the feeding tube, we hardly ever ordered pizza. And, even when we did get it, Mama took all of the cheese off of mine. So, as if the brownies weren't enough, she had to go and order pizza. I thought I was going to die. Brownies and pizza . . . it was horrible for me."

Gwen scratches her forehead. "What happened when you ate dairy?"

I flip my long hair over to the right side. "I have no idea. I don't remember getting sick from pizza, or ice cream, or milk . . . I don't know . . . plenty of nurses snuck me ice cream or pudding during my hospital stays."

Gwen shakes her head. "It sounds awful. Something doesn't add up, though."

I nod because Gwen's statement is right, but I remain silent.

Gwen and I turn back to the scene.

Mama waves Veronica over. "Come on, sit down and eat."

Veronica rushes to the table, and I follow with short, hesitant steps. Mama opens the box, and the glorious smell hits my nose. As Mama serves Veronica the first slice, the cheese stretches out like a long piece of yarn as she places it on Veronica's plate. I sit at the table quietly and focus on Ava, who also has a few pieces of pizza that Mama cut up for her.

I turn to Gwen. "I've been thinking. When I was released from the hospital with my feeding tube, the doctor said I could try to eat food, but when I asked Mama, she insisted that eating solids would make me sick again. So I was always too scared to even try."

"It must've been awful for you. I know what it was like being starved in the concentration camp, but to have food around and not be able to eat any of it would've been a whole other level of torture," Gwen says.

As I sit at my kitchen table sipping my cranberry juice, Mama asks Veronica a ton of questions about her life, especially her mother.

Finally, after Veronica finishes her pizza and shoves the last bite of brownie into her mouth, my mother dismisses us.

"You two can go play. I'll clean up here." She looks at Veronica. "Your mom will be here soon to pick you up, and I want to make a pot of coffee so we can sit and chat a bit."

Back in my room, Veronica rubs her belly.

"I can't believe I ate two slices," she says. "They were big, but it was so good. And your mom makes the best brownies I've ever had."

"Yeah, I remember," I say, rolling my eyes.

Gwen and I are lying on our bellies. My chin rests in my hands. "That was the first time my mom really irritated me. She was usually great, but whenever Veronica was around she kind of changed. She was nicer than normal. She wanted to impress her, and I used to think if she just acted like herself, Veronica would love her. Mama told me when she was young, my grandmother would tell her she was a nasty, rotten person and that no one would ever love her. Mama said all she ever wanted was to be loved by her mom, and she never understood why her mother hated her. I guess that's why she acted a little weird around strangers, and always wanted to impress them. Mama wanted everyone to like her."

Gwen spins the ring on her finger. "Your grandmother sounds mean. Maybe that's why your mom is odd."

I sit up quickly. "My mom isn't odd."

Gwen sits up next to me. "Look, I'm not trying to hurt your feelings. It's just that, well, your mom isn't anything like my mom."

"So what?! That doesn't make her odd. Maybe there was something wrong with your mom."

Gwen slowly shakes her head. "I don't understand. You've seen with your own eyes that your mom intentionally hurt you and you still stick up for her. So when I say she's odd, I mean she's sick in the head."

"Yes, I've seen. You know I saw everything. I'd just rather you didn't call her things like odd."

I lower my head. Of course I know my mother is sick. And obviously, I am very angry at her. I'd say I don't like Mama very much right now. "Let's watch some more," I mumble.

The doorbell rings. Mama opens the door and sings hello in a high-pitched voice. I despise when she uses that voice. It is, well . . . fake.

"Oh, welcome. Please come in," Mama says. "I'm so happy we're able to spend a little time together."

Veronica and I are in my bedroom. I push the playing cards into a pile. "I think your mom is here. Let's go down. I want to meet her."

"You're gonna love my mom. She's really cool."

I brush my hair away from my face. "Cool how?"

"I don't know. She wears cool clothes, and she doesn't . . . worry all the time."

I whip around and glare at Veronica. My nostrils flare. "My mom worries because she loves me!"

Veronica steps back. She looks at the floor. Her shoulders slump forward. "I wasn't trying to be mean. It's just that when she told us to be careful not to swallow any of the buttons from your dress-up clothes, I was like, what? We aren't babies. It's not like we're gonna chew a button off a dress."

I look at Veronica with wide eyes. The color drains from her face.

"Let's go," I say with a softer voice. "I want to meet your mom."

Downstairs, our moms are sitting in the living room, and Ava is relaxing on Mama's lap. Veronica's mom smiles and stands as we enter the room. Veronica runs to her mother, and they hug. I stand awkwardly in the doorway.

"Well, you must be Molly. You can call me Lola."

"Nice to meet you, Lola."

"Molly will call you Mrs. Fisk," Mama says quickly. "I don't think it's appropriate for her to call you by your first name."

Lola shoos Mama off with a flick of her hand. "Actually, I love my first name much more than my last. Really, Rona, I prefer that everyone calls me Lola. Mrs. Fisk makes me feel old."

Mama's eyes narrow for a split second. "Okay, then Veronica can call me Rona so I can feel young too."

"That's the spirit," Lola says, sitting down again. "So, Rona, I appreciate how much you've shared with me about Molly. I think you're an amazing woman. Now that Molly's feeling better, you'll have more time to yourself. How would you like to join our book club? We're always looking for new members. We read one book a month." She leans up on the edge of the chair. "But the best part is when we get together for wine and dinner to discuss the books. We all take a turn hosting at our homes. What do you say?"

Mama looks ecstatic. "Oh, that would be wonderful. As long as Molly doesn't get sick, you can count me in."

Mama looks at me and raises her eyebrows.

Ava wiggles off of her lap and comes over and takes my hand. Then she yanks on it. "I want juice," Ava tells me.

I stand and raise my hands over my head. I can feel Gwen watching me. I know she has something on her mind.

"Go ahead; what do you want to say?"

"Even Veronica noticed your mom's strange behavior. Doesn't that make you wonder if what I'm saying is true?"

"Of course, it makes me wonder about everything," I say. "There's so much I didn't know, and honestly, it's too much to handle."

I go back to my bedroom in Limbo, lay on the bed, and pull the covers over my head. I think about Mama. I couldn't have known the extent of her betrayal. But I know I'll soon find out.

Chapter Twenty-One

W hen I wake, I find Gwen and we go back to watching my life.

At my next doctor's appointment, I am doing so well that the doctor tries to talk Mama into introducing food back into my diet. He assures her it would be good for me. He even tells her that once I'm able to eat all of my meals, the feeding tube can come out.

I look so happy. I sit on the examination table, my feet swing back and forth, and I glance over at Mama. She isn't happy. She crosses her arms over her chest.

"While I agree we might try to introduce some foods back, there's no way we should be talking about removing Molly's feeding tube. In fact, saying such things in front of her gives her false hope. It's not fair to her. And it's entirely too soon to have this discussion."

The lines on the doctor's forehead deepen. "I don't agree with you, Rona. How about if we wait a while longer and see how it goes? We can check back in a month and talk about it some more. How's that sound?"

"Fine," Mama says sharply.

Gwen and I watch that same night as Mama tells my father about my appointment.

"I'll tell you, Kurtis. That doctor didn't make one bit of sense. I'm bringing Molly to a new doctor. I swear these doctors say things without doing any research."

Daddy leans in and kisses Mama on the cheek. "Well, this family doesn't have anything to worry about. It'll be a cold day in hell before my beautiful wife lets someone tell her what's best for her children."

Mama chuckles. "Stop. I'm not saying that I know everything, but all the research that I've done indicates Molly would need to go a year or longer without getting sick before we could consider removing the tube. This doctor is jumping the gun, and I think that's irresponsible."

Gwen shakes my shoulder, and I look at her. "Your mother made that up. You didn't need to keep a feeding tube in for a year."

I think I believe Gwen, but to take her word means my mom is lying again. I'm probably being silly. But it's hard to accept that someone I love and trust is actually a monster. In our family, Mama was always right, always the best, and always smarter than everyone else, even the doctors.

Feeling overwhelmed, I give Gwen a slight wave. "I'm pretty agitated and disappointed with Mama. I'd rather keep watching because I don't want to prolong this agony."

Daddy pulls my mother into his arms. He kisses her so hard that I have to look away until I hear their kissing sounds stop.

Once they part, Daddy looks into her eyes. "You're magnificent. If you need me to come to the doctor with you and Molly, I'll take a few hours off of work. I don't mind."

My mom nuzzles her face into the crook of his neck. "That's a nice offer, but you don't need to worry; I won't be introducing food until Molly goes a year without getting sick. I'll decide what's going to happen. As they say, we are all in charge of our own health care."

Gwen rakes her hand through her hair. "Did you ever see that doctor again?"

"Nope. I developed other issues, and getting the tube taken out didn't come up again."

Gwen rolls her eyes. "Your mom is a piece of work. She fooled so many people. It's not right what she's gotten away with."

"I get what it looks like. But Gwen, there has to be some explanation. Something, right?" I ask calmly.

"If there is something that's missing, I hope we see it soon," Gwen says.

In the summer between third and fourth grades, my health was reasonably stable and, thankfully, I had Veronica to play with. For a while, having a friend helped me forget about being sick. A few days before school started, I spiked a fever of over one hundred and two, accompanied by nausea.

Gwen and I watch my mom walk into the bathroom to check on me.

"Oh, Molly, you're going to be fine. No need to cry."

I slump on the edge of the tub; my movements are slow and clumsy. "School starts in two days."

"Yes, I'm aware. But here's the thing: if you go back to school and you're sick it's more likely you'll catch other things because your resistance is low. Let's wait and see how you feel tomorrow. We don't need to decide about school right now."

I wasn't doing well. My new illness put me back in bed, back into my prison of pillows and comforters. I may as well have been lying on shards of glass.

"I remember being really sick. Whatever was in my belly kept sloshing around and making me puke," I say to Gwen.

Gwen and I watch my mom enter my bedroom on the first day of school. I'm already awake.

"How are you doing?"

I roll onto my side and face her. The sudden movement is just enough to make me hurl the contents of my stomach.

Mama springs forward. She pulls me from my bed and whisks me into the bathroom. When I finish puking, I curl up on the small rug in front of the bathtub.

Once Mama changes my bedsheets, she tucks me back under the covers.

I look up at Mama. "I don't want any liquid meals put into my feeding tube today. I'm scared I'll get sick again."

Mama places a hand on her hip. "That's ridiculous. Since you've been vomiting it's even more of a reason that we need to get nutrition into you."

I turn over so I'm not facing her. After several seconds, she stomps out of my room.

That night, Daddy comes into my room and sits on my bed.

"Mama told me you weren't able to go to school today."

Tears roll down my cheeks. "Yeah, I'm sick again. I don't wanna be sick anymore."

Daddy pulls me into his arms. "I know, Molly. But your mom is going to keep an eye on you and help you get better."

I pull away from him. "Why did I have to be born like this?"

Daddy pulls me back to him. "I think this is something you'll grow out of. Sometimes people, even kids, get sick, and there's no good reason why. There are kids, younger than you, who have horrible diseases. Now, I know that doesn't make your situation any better, but it should give you hope that someday soon you're going to be well."

I gently pull away from his embrace, lie down, and turn my back to him. Daddy kisses the back of my head. "I love you very much. All I want is for you to be happy. I know I spend a lot of my time at work, but I think of you all the time. You and Ava."

Daddy leans in closer. "But you're my favorite person in the whole world."

I look over my shoulder at him and give him a quick smile.

"Hey, I almost forgot. I brought you a present."

I lay flat on my back. An expectant smile stretches across my face. Daddy holds up a book and my smile disappears.

Daddy shakes his head. "This isn't just a book you read. This one you write in. It's a journal. You can write everything you're thinking. Put all your dreams and wishes down on paper."

My eyes brighten as I take the journal in my hand and sit up to kiss my father's cheek.

"Thank you."

After my father leaves my room, I watch myself doze off and wake up to loud screaming. Mama and Daddy are arguing. It's a much different conversation this time.

"Rona, what are we going to do? We can't sit around and hope Molly gets better. It's been several days, and she's still not well. There could be something seriously wrong with her."

"Are you saying I don't know what I'm doing? Or are you telling me I'm not taking good care of her? While you're at the office all goddamn day and night, I'm here taking care of our children. You try to remember that the next time you accuse me of not being a good mother."

There is an extended silence until Daddy finally breaks it. "I'm not accusing you of being a bad mother. I know that you take good care of the girls. And I know that Molly may have gotten worse if you weren't so attentive to her every need. But this is a new year, and I was hopeful she would finally get better."

Mama paces the floor before she responds. "Kurtis, I want Molly to get better too. I'll see how she does over the next couple of days, and if she improves, I'll send her to school. Which in itself unnerves me. She could get sicker, and that scares the shit out of me."

"Well, you told me you liked the school nurse, and that you thought she was competent. I'm sure she can keep an eye on Molly and call you if anything happens."

Daddy's voice gets deeper. "Look, Rona. I love you so much for taking care of our girls."

There's an extended silence. "Really?"

"Of course. You're the perfect wife and mother."

"Are you just saying that to make me feel better?"

"Do I ever say things just to make you feel better?"

Mama lets out a schoolgirl giggle. "No. You can be a selfish jerk with your compliments. It's not easy being a stay-at-home mom. It's lonely. And there are very few rewards, and it would be appreciated if you could be a little more generous with your words. I do my best to give Molly and Ava everything they need."

Daddy grabs her hand. "I'll try harder, I promise. The girls and I depend on you. I don't say it enough, but I am grateful for the life you've created for all of us. I spend too many hours at the office, and I should be here more, but these are my growing years. Doing well in my career now means I'll be able to take care of all of us financially for a long time to come."

Mama lets out a loud sigh. "I know. You're right."

Up in my bedroom, I pick up my new journal. On the first page I write:

I'm Molly. Daddy gave me this journal so I can write down everything I'm thinking. I will call you Alice. I promise to write to you as much as I can.

I turn the page and add my first entry.

Dear Alice,

I want to do something nice for Mama to let her know she's special. Tomorrow I will make her a bracelet with my jewelry kit. Good night.

I seem puzzled about why I got sick again. When I ask Mama whether the food she put into my bag was spoiled, she tells me she had the same thought, but then she checked the expiration date on the formula, and it was still good.

Gwen clears her throat. "It's kind of weird that you and your mom both questioned if the food in your bag was spoiled."

I shrug. "Yeah, I guess so. I didn't think about it too much. When it came to food, I considered myself akin to a plant. I was watered three times a day and given a little sun."

Over the next few days, Gwen and I watch my health improve, and Mama decides I can return to school.

On my first day back, Veronica sits with me in the nurse's office while I "eat."

"I was so worried you weren't coming back today," Veronica says as she takes a bite of her cookie.

"Yeah, me, too. But all of a sudden, I got better. Now all I have to do is not get sick."

***

Back in Limbo, I imagine the perfect sundress and change into it. It's yellow with white flowers and flows around me. I love it. It's like wearing a piece of summer.

I peer at Gwen. "So I thought maybe we were going to see something bad that Mama did to me to make me sick again. I'm happy that we didn't see anything. You know?"

Gwen snickers. "You know, you've come a long way so far. You've taken the first step by admitting to yourself that things weren't all that they seemed. We just saw you were sick at the beginning of fourth grade without any reason or explanation. But Molly, it was because of your mom. She made you sick. Months later, she was still making you sick, and she became sicker herself."

Gwen tapped her finger against her skull. "I already told you, but I'll say it again, your mom is sick in her head. I wish I had better news for you."

Gwen's words make me want to lash out, fight someone, be angrier than I've ever been in my life. I want to scream and pound my fists on something. I just want to get this whole thing over with and move on. This slow drip of information is agonizing. If I could die from Limbo and go to heaven I swear I'd do it right now.

Given what Gwen tells me about my mom makes it certain that I will see Mama do something that will crush the pieces of my broken heart. I need to know what it is. I need to know what Mama has done.

Chapter Twenty-Two

Returning to school was a needed break from my life. Many kids hate going to school, but those kids have never been held in their bed like a prisoner. I liked learning because it kept my mind off of what might happen to me.

Over the next several months, Daddy came home earlier than usual. Gwen and I watch one of his interactions with Mama.

"Hi, Rona. How was your day?"

Mama gives him a quick smile. "It was fine. I worried about Molly all day long, but she got through it without any problems."

Daddy moves closer and pulls out a bouquet of flowers from behind his back.

"Oh, Kurtis," she breathes. "They're beautiful. It makes me so happy that you were thinking of me today."

Gwen weaves her fingers together and cracks her knuckles. "Your mom was happy whenever your dad paid attention to her, huh?"

"Yeah, you have no idea. Mama was so sweet when Daddy was home. He'd always tell her what a good mom she was to me and Ava. She ate that up."

"How did things go once you were back in school?"

"I'll tell you, after that first day back at school I was careful about everything I said and did. I didn't ask for food, not even at Christmas. I was too scared something terrible would happen. I would've rather never put another morsel of food in my mouth than be held captive, poked, and prodded by the doctors."

Gwen and I watch another scene.

It's February and the ground is covered in several feet of snow.

Mama is in the kitchen when she answers the telephone.

Daddy says, "Hey, sweetheart, it's me. I got caught in a meeting, and I didn't realize the snowstorm was this bad. It's just too dangerous for me to drive."

Mama's body stiffens and she places a hand firmly on her hip. "And? What are you trying to tell me, Kurtis?"

"I'm telling you that I need to get a hotel room close to the office tonight and I won't be able to make it home," he explains.

Mama clenches her teeth. "Right, so I'm stuck here to take care of the girls by myself tonight. Trapped in this damn house during this ridiculous snowstorm."

"Come on, Rona. It's not like I did this on purpose. I thought you'd rather I be safe than driving on the highway. I'm sorry I won't make it home, but it can't be helped."

In the early morning hours, the temperature outside drops to below ten degrees. The next day, after the snow stops, the frigid temperatures ice over our winter wonderland. The tree limbs hang low; some freeze into the snow on the ground, as though they are part of the earth. Bushes flatten with heavy ice. In a deep freeze, the beauty of the storm quickly becomes ugly, with odd shapes and hard edges.

The next night, because of the ice, Daddy tells Mama he won't make it home again and will have to stay at the hotel another night.

"That was a horrible storm," I tell Gwen. "We were stuck in the house for almost a week. I got sick. My muscles were like stone. Then I could hardly walk."

Gwen doesn't comment. My stomach is tied up in knots. "I can remember that I was very sick, and Mama seemed disturbed. Daddy being away unexpectedly for two nights upset Mama."

"You need to watch this," Gwen says. "It's important."

My mother kneels next to me in the bathroom. "I don't want you to worry. I'm going to give you a vitamin to help you get better. I read about it at the library."

"Really? Do you think it will work? Can you give it to me now?" I practically beg.

Mama snickers. "Okay. Slow down. First let's get you back to bed. Then I'll get your bag ready, and I'll put the vitamin in with your food."

I cock my head to the side. I look for the right words. "Why can't I just swallow it?"

"Good question, Molly. Well, because it's not a pill, it's powder. I'll dilute it into the liquid, and it'll work much faster. That means you'll feel better quicker."

When Mama hooks up my bag, I focus on the healing liquid going into my body. But Mama is wrong. The vitamin doesn't make me feel any better.

"The vitamin isn't working!" I yell at my mom during my third trip to the bathroom.

"You need to be a little more patient. These things take time."

I sit with my back against the bathroom wall. "But you said it would work quicker and it's not working at all."

Mama's eyes narrow. Then her face snarls into a scowl. "Hey! Do you have any idea how much time it took me to research this vitamin?"

I stare at her blankly. I have no words left.

My look of bewilderment seems to settle my mom down. Her stern voice turns into a lull. "Sweetheart, I know it's frustrating to be sick. You have to trust that I know what's best for you. Can you do that?"

I nod.

Gwen moves closer. I am quiet. I stare at my hands, taking in the lines around my knuckles. There was a big tree in our yard with a large limb removed. The skin pattern of my knuckles reminds me of that spot on the tree.

"I'm not going to like what I see next, am I?" I ask Gwen.

Gwen places her palm squarely in the center of my back for support. "You can handle anything from here."

I stand to put distance between Gwen and me. Sometimes, when I'm really upset, I don't like to be touched. "Fine. Let's see it."

Chapter Twenty-Three

A va and I are in our bedroom, and Mama is in the kitchen, getting my bag ready. She reaches into a cabinet above the refrigerator and pulls out a large container, from which she spoons out two heaping tablespoons of powder, which she mixes with my formula.

Gwen nudges me. "What did your mom just put into your bag?"

"Probably the vitamin."

Gwen shakes her head.

"What?"

"Read the label on the jar," Gwen says.

I look closely at the print. "Potassium chloride. What is it?"

Gwen pulls on my shoulder gently, so I'm facing her. "It's used for people who have low potassium levels. It's not good for people to take it if you don't need it. It can be harmful."

"Maybe I needed it?" I suggest.

"Why would you have needed it? None of the doctors we've seen said you did."

"That's true." I put my hands over my mouth for a moment. "Oh, Gwen, what have I let Mama do to me?"

"You didn't let your mom do anything to you. She did it all on her own without anyone knowing," Gwen says.

"Let's see what happens," I say hesitantly.

Hours after my bag has finished, my eyelids are drooping as I attempt to walk downstairs, but my legs won't work. The best I can do is call out for Mama.

"What is it, baby?" Mama says, dropping to her knees next to me on the floor.

"I . . . I . . . my legs won't work."

Mama's eyes jut out. "What do you mean? Do you have pain?"

Mama's voice has a hint of panic.

"I'm thirsty, Mama!" I cry.

"I'll get you some water."

Mama rushes into the bathroom and grabs a paper cup. She fills it with water. Before leaving the bathroom, she looks in the mirror and smiles at herself.

I gasp, and Gwen grabs my hand. My mouth hangs open. The blood drains from my head and I fear I'll faint. I take several hard swallows to stabilize myself.

"Did my mom just smile at herself?"

Gwen rubs my arm. "She did."

I sit for several moments. My thoughts are scattered and random. I can't think clearly.

"Gwen, I was so scared. I thought I was never going to walk again. I don't know what to say right now."

"There's nothing you have to say. You need to see the rest of this. To understand how this all happened to you."

Even though my body trembles, I watch again.

My symptoms persist throughout the night, and by morning I am slightly better, but still not strong enough to get out of bed.

When Mama comes in to check on me, I am sobbing.

"Molly, what is it?" she asks.

"I peed my bed. I couldn't go to the bathroom by myself."

"Oh, that's nothing. I'll get everything cleaned up, and we'll get you back to bed."

When Mama finishes, both me and my bed are clean. She sits next to me and takes my hand in hers.

"I'm going downstairs to get your bag ready."

I shake my head. "I don't want anything right now."

"Molly, you have to keep up your strength. Plus I have to get the vitamin into you. It's the only way you're going to get better."

Gwen and I watch Mama put more of the potassium chloride into my morning and afternoon bags. By early evening, I am delirious.

That night, when Mama comes into my bedroom, I try to speak, but can only babble nonsense. Then I become hysterical.

"Molly, why are you so upset?"

"Because I can't feel my hands and feet. I think there's something wrong with my heart, too. I think there's a bird stuck inside my chest, flapping around, trying to get out."

She sits down next to me, then lays her ear against my chest. After a few seconds, she bolts upright.

"I'm scared. What's wrong with me? Am I dying?" I cry.

Mama looks at me. Her eyes are wide. She doesn't attempt to ease my worries. "We need to get you to the hospital."

I cry. Not a chest-heaving, uncontrollable cry, but a softer, tears dripping from the side of my eyes kind of cry.

Mama picks up the phone and calls our neighbor, who rushes over to stay with Ava. Then she gets me into the backseat of the car, and we drive at a snail's pace on the icy roads to the closest emergency room.

Gwen strums her fingers on her thigh. "Your mom made you sick with the potassium chloride in your food. And she didn't let up. She kept making you more and more sick."

"Yeah, I know. I saw what she did to my bags. Weird thing is, I want to see it and I don't want to see it. Does that make any sense? I'm afraid. If what I've seen is real, that means my entire life was a lie. It means Mama didn't love me."

With that realization, I get up and move away from Gwen. I sit next to a wooded area where the sun is warm and a breeze flows through my hair. I need to think. I need to process. I need time to accept that Mama thought my life was worthless. How will I ever move forward from here?

Chapter Twenty-Four

I think about Mama putting the white powder into my food. It makes me livid. I'm a ball of anxiety. I return to Gwen and sit next to her.

"I'm sorry, Gwen. I hope you don't think I'm mad at you because I left suddenly. I'm hurt and confused right now. My mother was the cause of my suffering."

"I get it. It must be the worst thing in the world to watch your mom do things that harmed you. I know you can handle it, though, if that helps."

It doesn't help. All I want is to be done with Limbo and move on.

"Let's watch," I say to Gwen.

We're watching my mom pace my small room in the ER. She pulls at the hem on the bottom of her shirt, her long, thin fingers nervously looking for something to occupy them. I am lying flat on my back on a gurney. My mouth is wide open as I breathe in deeply, but my chest barely raises with each inhalation. I let out several faint moans. My mother continues to pace, without looking at me.

When the doctor arrives, he shakes Mama's hand. She sits in the chair beside my gurney.

"I'm Dr. Malik. We think this little lady," he says, looking directly at me, "has something going on with her heart. We're going to do an EKG. That will provide us with more information."

Mama nods with enthusiasm. "Yes, of course. I would do the same."

Dr. Malik tilts his head slightly. "Are you a physician?"

Mama lets out a nervous snort. I wait for her to tell the story I heard so often when I was alive, and she doesn't let me down. And now, to my knowing ears, her story sounds senseless because I know she wanted to learn about medicine to use it against me.

Mama tells her same old story and ends with, "I try to stay up to date on my medical knowledge so that when my two girls are grown and off to college, I might be able to finish my education and start working."

Dr. Malik steps closer to me. "That's very admirable. If you have questions as we go through everything, please be sure to ask. I'll have a nurse run an EKG and then we can see what we're dealing with."

I am on the gurney. Suddenly my eyes pop open, and my hand flies to my neck. I look like I can't breathe. The doctor is still standing over me and yells for the nurse, who rushes into the room.

Dr. Malik slides a device inside my mouth to hold it open, then inserts a flexible plastic tube. I can hear the air flowing through the tube, giving my lungs life again as my chest begins to rise and fall.

Mama appears to cry, but from Limbo, I can see she's working hard to manufacture her tears. Watching this is like jabbing a spear through my heart. I don't point out to Gwen what Mama is doing. By now I know that Gwen sees it for herself.

When the doctor turns to Mama, she covers her face with her hands and bobs her shoulders up and down.

Dr. Malik moves near Mama and puts his hand on her shoulder. "It'll be all right. Molly's stabilized. We have her hooked up to a ventilator to help her breathe. We'll keep her on that until I feel it's safe to take her off. In the meantime, I'll run tests to figure out what is going on with her."

Dr. Malik turns to leave, but before he does, my spine arches, my eyes roll to the back of my head, and my body vibrates and jerks simultaneously. It looks like I've been hit with a thousand volts of electricity. The doctor and nurse quickly hold my limbs down as I have a full-blown seizure. By the time it's over, I am in a coma.

Mama later told me I took a long nap. I'm slowly and painfully learning that Mama told me lots of things that aren't true. That my mom is a big, fat liar. She is the queen of lies and deception. A complete and utter disappointment.

As the days pass, and I lay in a hospital bed, Mama keeps putting potassium chloride into my bag. There seems to be no end to her vile acts.

Gwen and I listen to my mom as she talks to my doctor. "Dr. Malik, I'm worried that Molly hasn't woken up yet."

"I think she'll be okay. I really do," Dr. Malik assures her. "The tests we've performed have come back with fairly good results. She definitely has something going on with her heart, but I don't think it's anything we can't fix."

Mama puts her right hand over her heart. "Thank God you feel that way. That gives me comfort. What do you think we can do for her heart once she wakes up?"

Dr. Malik clears his throat. "I've recommended we perform a catheter ablation. I've consulted with pediatric cardiology. They're going to come and see Molly. They would perform the procedure. Given the list of heart medications she's tried without success, the catheter would be the logical next step."

Mama looks like a bobble-head doll the entire time Dr. Malik speaks.

I grab Gwen's shirt. "My mom lied to the doctor. I was never on heart medicine. I never had a heart problem."

Gwen says, "That's true. Your mom lies a lot."

We watch.

Dr. Malik reaches for Mama's hand. "It's going to be okay. The procedure will take two to three hours. The doctor will insert a catheter into Molly's heart and use radio-frequency energy, like the heat from a microwave, to destroy a small portion of heart tissue that's causing her heart to beat too rapidly."

When Dr. Malik finishes, he looks into Mama's eyes. "Is there anything I can do for you? Any questions you need me to answer?"

Mama shakes her head and plops down in the chair near my bed.

I am lying flat on my back, a machine is breathing for me, and I am in a state of deep unconsciousness.

After the doctor leaves, Mama whispers in my ear, "These doctors don't know how smart your mama is. Of course I know about the procedure; it was my idea in the first place. Ha! The big, bad doctor thinks he's talking to someone who is stupid."

I spring to my feet in Limbo. Gwen watches my every movement. My voice is soft, almost unintelligible. "Did Mama say the procedure was all her idea?"

"Yes, she did. Your mom is extremely calculating. She knew exactly what she was doing to you."

All that's left to do now is break things. Mama has literally broken my heart, and that fact is intolerable.

I imagine I'm in my bedroom in Limbo. I lift my desk chair over my head and throw it into the twelve-foot window. It smashes into a million shards of glass that shatter into the air.

I turn quickly and rip the sheets and comforter from my bed. I stomp on them before I pull the mattress off, drag it over to the window, and chuck it into the dark pit I imagine is below. I walk with purpose to the small table beside my bed, and lift the only picture of Mama and me I've put in my room here. It's my favorite one of the two of us, standing on the beach in Cape May before she ruined my life. I smash the frame on the corner of the table, pull out the picture, and tear it to pieces.

The broken glass cuts my fingertips, but I don't care. I drop to the floor and catch my breath. Gwen is beside me. She says nothing to try to make me feel better. We both allow the anger and rage to recede on their own. I try to understand and think of what I'm supposed to do next, but nothing comes. I am a blank slate.

"I don't know what to do now," I confess.

"You'll keep going. You've been through the worst of it now. Acceptance is the hardest thing any of us ever has to learn," she says.

"It's more than that. I have to come to terms with the fact that I never knew who Mama was. I don't recognize her. She's like a monster from a scary movie," I say.

Gwen tucks her hair behind her ears. "I'm so proud of how strong you've been through this process. Every day you come closer to your end goal. Soon this will all be over."

My bottom lip trembles. I refuse to shed a tear over Mama right now. "Gwen, it's hard to believe that the person I knew is the same person we just watched. It doesn't make any sense."

"You know, there are times in life when things or people don't make sense. Some things can't be explained. Your mom's words and actions are so unbelievable it's not surprising that you're confused. I'm confused, too. But I can tell you that when I get jaded about the past, I tell myself it's not my job to figure it out. In the end, it doesn't matter why someone did things to hurt me; all that matters is the knowledge that it was about them and had nothing to do with anything I did or didn't do."

Gwen's eyes lock on mine. "Look, your mom may have convinced them to kill off a piece of your heart, but your heart is so big it would've been impossible for her to change who you were."

I shake my head. "You're just trying to make me feel better."

Gwen nudges my shoulder. "That's true, I am trying to make you feel better. How am I doing?"

I unclench my fists. "I guess you're doing fine."

A coldness settles over me. My joints ache. I see a thick blanket, grab it, and wrap it around myself. My fingers are restless. "If the truth is anything like what we've just seen, I don't think I can handle any more. Mama pretended to have painstaking devotion and love for me; boy, was I fooled. I can't figure out what drove her to keep me sick."

I look around me. Limbo is a place where I can have peace and joy if I allow myself those pleasures. But for reasons I've yet to understand, I can't. I want to be happy, I really do. But my life was snuffed out when I was young. And now I've just learned that my mother may have caused my death.

"This is harder than anything I ever had to do when I was alive," I say to Gwen.

Gwen puts her forehead against mine. "Right now you're being called upon to be brave, to find courage, and to keep moving forward even though I know how much you'd rather quit. This is your time. We aren't done here yet." She turns and walks away.

"What does that mean? We aren't done here yet? What else could there possibly be?"

Gwen looks over her shoulder at me, and I know there's more I need to see.

Chapter Twenty-Five

I wake from the coma after two weeks. When I first open my eyes, I blink repeatedly. I look confused. I try to move my body, but find myself trapped under the tubes and blankets.

I turn my head to the left. A girl is resting in the bed next to mine. I struggle to speak. The plastic in my mouth prevents me from forming words.

I grunt loudly, trying to signal to the girl next to me. I need her help.

She turns toward the sounds I'm making and looks at me.

"You're awake! I'll get a nurse," the girl says.

A few minutes later, a heavyset, gray-haired woman comes in and walks over to the girl in the bed next to me. "Everything okay?"

My roommate points to me. "She's awake. She was trying to say something."

The nurse hurries over to me. "Molly?"

My eyes are open and I grunt.

The nurse's eyes meet mine. "Oh, how wonderful. You are awake. I want you to stay still, and I'll get one of the doctors."

My eyes grow wide. Tears are running down the sides of my face. I force noises out of me.

The nurse takes hold of my hand. "There's no need to worry. The doctor put a tube down into your lungs to help you breathe. I'm going to get him in here right away. We'll see if we can get that tube taken out."

I give her a slow-motion nod. It's the best I can do. I'm thinking, Yes! Please get the tube out of my throat!

An hour later, the tube is removed, and I am breathing on my own. After the doctor leaves the room, I turn to the girl. "Thanks for getting the nurse," I croak.

"Sure. I've been waiting for you to wake up."

"You have?" I mutter.

The girl nods.

"What's your name?" I manage to ask through my dry, burning throat.

"Rainey."

"Your name is Rainey?"

My roommate says, "Yeah. Rainey Paxton."

"Just so you know . . . your mom hasn't been here for two days because she got sick and the doctors told her she had to stay away. She didn't like that too much. I heard one of the doctors and your mom fighting outside our room. Your mom kept saying she was fine, but when she was here she kept running to the bathroom and throwing up. Turned out she had a fever and everything. The doctor was really pissed she came in here, and they sent up a person to clean our entire room and bathroom."

Watching the scene play out, I almost feel sorry for Mama.

Unlike when I was alive, in Limbo I do these odd mind gymnastics. One minute I'm angry with Mama, and the next I am mad at myself for being a fool. My heart is conflicted.

Gwen looks at me. "Molly, I hate to state the obvious here. But you know why you got better, right?"

"Yeah, I see it. My mother is malicious," I say.

Gwen offers, "Let's watch something a little lighter. Rainey seemed like a nice person."

I nod. "I liked her."

"Good. Let's watch you and Rainey for a while."

Gwen and I turn and look into the distance.

Rainey's lying on her side, talking to me with a big smile on her face. "Anyway, the doctor said you should drink the water on your table. He said it'll make your throat feel better. Weren't you listening to him?"

"Not really. I was too busy worrying about how much it would hurt to have the tube pulled out."

It's a struggle, but I grab the Styrofoam cup and take a few sips of water from the straw.

The silence that follows between Rainey and me is awkward. I search for something to say.

"Did your mom and dad come while I was sleeping?"

Rainey sits up in the bed and wraps her arms around her knees. "Yeah, my mom stopped in for a few minutes. She came to ask me where I hid my money. My parents suck." Rainey stops talking to fluff her bed pillow. "I didn't tell her where I stashed it, though. I mean, it's only twelve dollars. I use it to buy food for me and my little sister. Anyway, I lied and said I buried it in the backyard."

"Why do they want your money?"

"So they can buy drugs and booze."

I draw in a sharp breath. "Are you serious?"

Rainey lifts her chin. "Dead serious. I wish I was lying."

I tug my covers up higher. "Do your mom and dad visit you every day?" I ask.

Rainey thumps her head back on the pillow. "Nah, they'll forget about me while I'm in here, but it's okay. I'm used to being by myself."

"Wait! What? How will they forget about you? Aren't you scared?"

Rainey smirks at me. "No, I like being here without them."

Rainey looks around the room. "This place is like being in a hotel. The police found me on the sidewalk down the street from our dump of a house three days ago. I was drunk, so they brought me here, and because I was dehydrated and dizzy the doctor admitted me. The only problem is that my little sister is home and I'm not there to watch her. One of the women who stay at the house came to visit me and she promised to keep an eye on her until I get home."

My eyes practically pop out of my skull. "Hold on! You were drunk?"

Rainey grimaces.

I pull the sheet up under my chin, and my eyes are cast down at my lap. I shake my head slowly. "I'm sorry. I didn't mean to be rude."

Rainey slumps down farther into her bed. "Well, the thing is that I didn't get drunk on purpose. The people my parents hang out with are crazy and ridiculous and out of control. But that's a whole different story for another time."

I look over at her. "Our lives are so different. It's hard to imagine how bad your home must be for you."

"Hey, look. Just forget it. There's nothing to get worked up about. It's my life."

I can't help myself from prying further. "Will you tell me more? I want to know everything. I've never met another kid who had parents that take drugs."

"Sure, but I hope you can handle it," Rainey warns.

Chapter Twenty-Six

Rainey rolls onto her back and puts the arm without an IV behind her head. "Let's see. Where should I start? Okay, because my parents are high all the time, they forget about me, so I have more freedom than most kids I know except I pretty much have a kid—my baby sister—to watch."

I put the back of my bed up higher. "Having freedom doesn't sound horrible."

"But my house is a piece of shit. My parents' friends and people they hardly know are there all the time, and they're weird. Whenever I'm at home, I have to avoid the bodies passed out on the floor because my parents let everyone stay there as long as they pay money to spend the night."

"Really?"

"Yep. And the worst thing is word gets around that my two idiot parents let people stay overnight if they pay, and random people show up. Plus, every morning, when I turn on the lights, there are bugs or mice in our kitchen. There's hardly ever any food in the house. My parents and everyone who hangs out at our house eat takeout and junk food all the time, so that's all I ever eat. Most times I don't have toothpaste or shampoo or soap. So basically I don't have any of the things that I need to live normally."

"That sounds scary."

Rainey flings her feet over the side of the bed. "It is scary and it sucks. But it's all I've known since I was little, I guess. Now you know why I don't mind being in the hospital. I have clean sheets and clothes, three meals a day, and people who care if I'm dead or alive. It's weird—when I'm in here I know I'm not alone."

I relax against my pillows and breathe in. Rainey and I are silent for several minutes, and I close my tired eyes.

Rainey says, "The thing that scares me most are the men that come around. They creep me out. My mom and dad don't see the way some of them look at me, but I do. Sometimes, I get freaked out that one of them will take me and kill me someday."

"Isn't there someone you can tell? Like the police?"

Rainey shakes her head. "No. I keep my eyes and ears open. That's all I have right now. The police will only take me away and put me in some other horrible place, like foster care. My mom told me all about how bad foster care is."

"How does she know it's bad?"

Rainey shrugs. "Good question. But I don't want to have to find out that she's right. Anyway, I've been wanting to tell you that your dad is really nice."

I stretch my legs out straight. "Did you talk to him?"

"Yeah. He's been here every night while you were in the coma. He talks to you."

I smile. "He does?"

"Yeah. He was really bummed out when you wouldn't wake up."

I stop watching and grab Gwen's hand. "I want to go back and watch my father. I need to know the things he said to me."

Gwen's eyes meet mine. It's like looking into a calm, clear sea. She nods.

My father sits next to my hospital bed. The room is dark except for the glare from Rainey's television. He slumps over the bed, holding my limp hand and stroking my hair. He takes a jagged breath.

"My little Molly. Please wake up. I miss you so much. It's been too long, and I need you to wake up. I want to see your smile. Every day when I'm at work, all I can think about is coming here to sit with you. Mama doesn't feel well, but she'll be back soon. You know, when I found out your mama was pregnant with you, I was so happy. I imagined the kind of child you'd be. We didn't know if we were having a boy or girl, but it didn't matter; I was going to teach you how to play basketball and throw a football no matter what. Anyway, you're perfect in every way. I'd give anything for you to be healthy and happy. I've prayed that your illnesses become mine. I want so much to make you better. I'd do anything to make you well again. Please, just wake up, sweetheart."

I look over at Gwen with tears streaming down my cheeks. "He was so sad. He would've done anything to make me better. I miss him so much."

Chapter Twenty-Seven

G wen and I are still watching.

A nurse walks into my hospital room. Rainey and I are silent.

"I'm Shelly, and I'll be your nurse today. How are you feeling, Molly?"

I give her a weak smile. "Tired. My arms and legs don't feel like they want to move."

Shelly brushes my hair back from my face. "It's normal to feel tired and weak after what you've been through. No need to worry, we're going to get you strong again."

"Do you know when my mom is coming back?"

Shelly adjusts my covers. "As soon as she's better. It's too risky for her to be here right now. She could get you sick. Do you want to try some apple juice?"

"Yeah, that would be great."

"How about some graham crackers? Just a few to get something solid in your belly?"

"What about my feeding tube?"

"It'll be fine. You're not due for another bag for two hours."

"But what if the crackers make me throw up?"

Shelly rubs my shoulders. "I don't think we have a reason to be concerned about that as long as you take it slow."

"I'm not sure. Mama doesn't let me eat food. I drink water and juice, but she's scared I'll get sick if I eat real food."

Shelly is unaffected by what I tell her.

The nurse readjusts my pillow. "Well, some parents get a bit paranoid about a feeding tube, not that I blame them. I'd be nervous, too, and I'm a nurse. Anyway, I talked to your doctor before I came in to check on you, and he suggested that if you could eat and drink a little that would help you get your strength back quicker."

I touch Gwen's sleeve. "Those crackers were so delicious. It reminded me how much I missed eating real food. But seeing things from Limbo makes me wonder why I didn't think it was weird that I could have food in the hospital but not at home. I didn't question anything Mama did. I just did whatever I was told."

Gwen says, "Yeah, but in fairness, most kids believe what their parents tell them. There's no reason to blame yourself for not knowing. You didn't do anything wrong."

Gwen's words take the pressure off of me and lighten the moment. "Me and Rainey did have some fun." I rock my shoulders up and down for effect.

"Oh, yeah, let's see it then," Gwen says, feeding into my excitement.

Rainey and I are in our room talking about what we'd rather be doing. We want to get out of the room and explore, but my legs are still too weak for me to walk.

"I know what we'll do," Rainey says. "We'll get you a wheelchair."

Before I can say anything, Rainey calls for our nurse.

Maria, our night nurse, comes bouncing into the room. "You girls rang?"

Rainey raises the back of her bed with the remote. "Yeah. Do you think we can get a wheelchair for Molly so we can go exploring?"

Maria studies me. I give her my healthiest smile.

"Exploring, huh?"

"Yeah, we won't go far," Rainey promises.

"As in you'll stay on this floor and not get into any trouble, right?"

"Right," Rainey and I sing out together.

Maria points her finger at Rainey, then me. "You two better not make me regret doing this."

"Scout's honor," Rainey says, holding up the three fingers between her thumb and pinky.

Maria put her hands on her hips. She exaggerates a frown. "When were you a Girl Scout?"

Rainey giggles. "Never."

"Exactly," Maria huffs. "You can't scout's honor me then."

"Okay, sickie honor."

I join in. "Yeah, sickie honor."

I hold up three fingers on my right hand, the same as Rainey. I let out a long giggle. It is all in good fun. Maria laughs hard as she leaves our room and comes back a short while later with a wheelchair. Maria helps me into the chair, and Rainey pushes me out of our room as we both squeal with delight.

Chapter Twenty-Eight

"Gwen, I need to tell you something. I've been thinking about a lot of things since I got here. I didn't always agree with Mama about my health. There were different things, like I had eaten several times in the hospital without getting sick while Mama was stuck at home, caring for Ava. I believed that I was finally getting better. Then, as soon as I left the hospital with Mama, everything changed, and I was sick again. That really scared me."

"It would've scared me too," Gwen says. "I'd like to see what your mom does when she comes back to the hospital. That'll tell us everything we need to know."

A day after Mama returns, she has the cardiac team come and evaluate me. The head surgeon agrees that I'm stable enough to go through with the heart procedure.

The next day they perform a catheter ablation. It takes ten hours—four in the operating room, where the doctor kills off a small section of my heart—and another six in recovery, where I am closely monitored.

I stay in the hospital another full day and night before they release me. At ten o'clock that night Mama finally leaves the hospital. After she is gone, Rainey and I cruise the hallways, watch television, and play cards.

"I'm gonna be so lonely when you leave tomorrow," Rainey says, teary-eyed.

"Me too. If I could stay here with you for another year that would be fine with me. I like being with you. I like how you don't do everything the adults tell you to do. I wish I was more like that," I admit.

Rainey let's out a sigh. "Yeah, well, I've had to grow up fast. My mom and dad never spent much time with me, so I learned to be resourceful when I was little."

I push myself up on my elbows and gaze over at Rainey. "I'll miss seeing people. At home I only see my family, mostly Mama."

"Maybe you can go back to school. You feel better."

"Yeah, I guess so," I say. "My heart doctor told me I was as good as new. Now I need to prove to Mama I'm well enough to go to school."

The next morning, on a chilly day at the end of October, I am released from the hospital. Daddy and Mama both come to bring me home. Once I settle into the backseat of our car, Mama tucks a blanket around me so I don't catch a cold.

"Mama, can I go back to school on Monday?"

Daddy looks at Mama expectantly. She looks back at him. The edges of her lips turn downward and she rolls her eyes to let him know he needs to drop it. "I think Monday is a little soon, Molly. Let's see how you do, and if all goes well, maybe you can go back in December."

December is a little more than a month away, but I don't argue with Mama. I settle back against the seat and turn to look out the window as the world passes by me.

***

Gwen removes one of the gold bracelets she's wearing and puts it on my wrist.

"Is this mine to keep?" I ask, touching the bracelet.

"Yep. I want you to have it."

"Thank you, Gwen."

Gwen says, "Your friend Rainey from the hospital was really nice. Did you ever get to see her again?"

"No. But I thought about her a lot after I got home. I always wondered what happened to her. We had become good friends, and we had so much fun together. It's weird, though. There was something about Rainey that haunted me. Most nights I could hear her crying when she thought I was asleep. I think she was lonely and hurt that she didn't have anyone who really cared about her. But more than anything, I worried that she wasn't safe in her house. I didn't know that my house wasn't any safer than hers."

Chapter Twenty-Nine

I've been in Limbo a while now. I'll admit, it's not pleasant seeing the old me. It's jarring to find out things about Mama I never knew. Things that break my heart and make me doubt all mankind. I know I'm being dramatic, but if I can't have faith in my own mother, what is left?

I'm like a jigsaw puzzle, but some of my pieces are warped and a few are missing. No matter how hard I try, those damaged and missing pieces prevent me from being whole.

An overwhelming sense of loss fills me. It's a tormenting emptiness. I realize now that I never lived. I barely existed. My life wasn't what I would consider good. Mama had taught me that if I was loved and cared for, that was living. I hung on to that belief when I was alive. Now that belief is wearing away, along with the love I once felt for my mother.

I've never been this hurt in all of my living days. It's like someone is driving nails into my heart, leaving me with a piercing, fiery burn.

When I was alive, I lived in constant fear of getting sick. I dreaded going to the hospital. I hated all the needles and tubes and machines that invaded my body. I'd take medicine so I wouldn't be sick and then more medicine to offset the side effects of the medication that was supposed to make me better.

In Limbo, I'm finally accepting that I was never wanted or loved by my mother, the person I believed loved me more than anything in the world. It's a hard pill to swallow.

Sadly, I can't remember many good times in my life. The good memories I have were short-lived and went by in a blur, but most don't seem to stand up to the suffering I endured.

Lately I've been thinking a lot about Ava. I loved my little sister and still do. She brought me joy in small ways. Her silly chatter. The way she laid next to me in bed and latched onto my fingers when I would cry. How she called me Olly because she couldn't pronounce Molly. Ava knew of my misery even though she was too young to fully understand. She may have been only six years old when I died, but Ava was wise for her age. I hope she will have a better life than I did.

Gwen puts her hand on my shoulder and gently shakes me, pulling me out of my thoughts. She leads me to a comfortable spot under a large oak tree. It is the biggest tree I have ever seen. I look up at its long, thick limbs. I need an escape . . . something to take my mind off of the tragedy that was my life.

"Let's climb up," I say.

Gwen nods and follows me. As we effortlessly climb higher into the branches, I can see farther into the fields and sky beyond the small, quaint city where we are staying. I adjust myself on a large branch and rest my back against the tree's enormous trunk. Gwen sits next to me.

"It's so cool up here," I say.

Gwen looks around. "Yeah, it's really something. When I was young, I loved to climb trees. I would imagine that I could climb right into the clouds. I wondered how it would feel to lay on a cloud." Gwen chuckles. "It's silly the things you think about when you're little. How about you? Did you ever get a chance to climb trees, or is this your first time?"

"I climbed a tree once. I didn't climb too high. It didn't turn out too well for me. I was unlucky like that. I'll show you if you want to see it."

"Sure," Gwen says.

We are watching my past again. It is May, and the weather is warm. Veronica has come over to my house, and she has the idea to build a tree fort in my backyard. We have a decent-size tree, so we grab a sheet from the linen closet and head outside.

"If Mama catches us, she's gonna be furious."

"We'll tell her it was my idea. Besides, you've been out of the hospital for a while, and you haven't been sick at all."

"Yeah, but she won't care."

Veronica rolls her eyes. "Come on, Molly, don't be such a chicken."

I put my hands on my hips and glare at her.

Veronica pulls the sheet from my hands and throws it over her shoulder. "Come on, Molly. Don't be such a baby. Are you mad at me now? Please don't be mad."

I lower my eyes and shake my head. "Just don't call me names anymore."

I follow my friend outside and up the tree. I use the same footholds she does. Once we are up about ten feet high, we stand on a limb and throw the sheet over the branch above us. In an instant the world is blocked out, and we are cocooned in our own private space. It is so cool.

I draw in a sharp breath. "Wow! I feel like I can hide from anybody up here."

Veronica adjusts herself on the limb, straddling her legs on either side. "Here, sit like me."

I look nervous as I swing my right leg over the limb to straddle it, and sure enough I lose my balance and tumble from the tree. I land on my back and am momentarily dazed. Without hesitating, I quickly get to my feet. I see Mama rushing from the house, screaming my name.

"Molly! What were you thinking?!" Mama hollers. She touches my arms and legs to make sure they aren't broken.

"I'm fine, Mama. I'm not hurt."

In Limbo, I see that my eyes are open wide. My hands are twisted together, and I'm bouncing from one foot to the other, as though I have to go to the bathroom.

Gwen sees it too. "Did you lie to your mom about getting hurt? You look like you're about to pee your pants."

I fuss with the ends of my long hair. "No, I told Mama the truth. I was worried that she was going to take me to the hospital. I got so nervous I couldn't breathe right. And my adrenaline was soaring, which threatened to make me cry. I guess I was just so freaked out, I couldn't stand still."

"That's awful," Gwen says. "You lived in fear a lot."

"You can say that again. There was nothing I was more afraid of than being sick, because it meant being isolated, and that was torture."

I look back at the vision with Gwen.

Mama towers over me. "I wouldn't be able to live with myself if anything happened to you!" she shrieks.

Unable to hold back my tears, a few slide down my cheeks.

"What is it? What hurts?" she asks, running her hands over my head and down my back, as though she is feeling for broken bones.

"Nothing hurts, I swear, Mama."

With that, Mama whisks me into the house for a full-body inspection. Veronica runs inside behind us.

Mama turns to my friend. "Call your mom and tell her to come and get you. Let her know I have an emergency because you two did something reckless."

Veronica's eyes lock onto mine. She mouths I'm sorry and goes into the kitchen to call her mother.

Mama focuses all of her attention on me. "Come on. I want to take a look and make sure you didn't sprain anything. I want to be certain your tube is still okay too. Sometimes you don't feel injuries right away, and then, after the shock wears off, it hits you hard."

Up in the bathroom, I get undressed. Mama examines me while I stand in my underpants and a T-shirt. When she's done, I slip into a tub of warm water. I lean my head back on the edge of the tub and my eyes ease closed.

"I'm going to check on Veronica, I think I heard her mother pull up," Mama says before leaving me alone in the bathroom.

I tell Gwen, "I was so happy that nothing terrible happened to me when I fell. I couldn't believe my good luck."

I've been in the tub for twenty minutes. The water turns tepid. My fingertips and toes are wrinkled and I'm shivering. Mama finally returns to the bathroom. I stand quickly, and she wraps a towel around me as she speaks. "Veronica's mom is worried about you. And so is Veronica. That was a very dumb thing the two of you did. What would make you think it was a good idea to climb a tree?"

Mama looks at me sternly, waiting for an answer.

"I don't know," I say weakly.

"Well, you need to think about what you're doing. You could've killed yourself."

"We didn't climb that high," I argue in a soft voice.

"Molly!" she screams. Her voice sounds like a loud crack of thunder before the acid rain follows.

I pout and lift my eyes to meet Mama's.

She puts her arm around my shoulder and gives me a gentle squeeze. "Come on, you can get in your warm pajamas and I'll get you all comfy in your bed so you can rest. I'll bring you something to relax your muscles so that you won't be sore. I'm still worried that you sprained something or that you could have a concussion."

As I get into bed, Mama gives me a long lecture about why I should think before I act and tells me again that it was a dumb decision to climb the tree in our yard.

I keep a serious expression and nod. "Mama, I promise I'll never do another stupid thing for the rest of my life."

Mama smiles at me. "Good. Now get some rest."

And I do get some rest, for a while. Then everything changes again.

Chapter Thirty

I'm lying in my bed for quite some time after my bath, with the TV and radio both on. My eyes drift around the room but don't focus on anything for very long.

Gwen and I watch Mama in the kitchen. She opens the cabinet and reaches for a pill bottle she keeps on the top shelf so Ava or I won't accidentally get into it. She places a thin brown bottle on the counter. I zoom in to get a better look, and I read the label: Diazepam. Brand: Valium. Ten milligrams. May cause dizziness. Avoid alcohol, which may intensify the effect. Do not eat grapefruit or drink grapefruit juice while taking this medication.

Mama shakes a small blue pill from the bottle, places the pill on a plate, and crushes it to blue dust with the back of a teaspoon. From the refrigerator, she pulls out a carton of grapefruit juice, pours it into a glass, and adds the crushed Valium. The spoon hits the sides of the glass as she stirs . . . clink, clink, clink.

Gwen's expression is grim. She looks at me. "That clinking is the sound of you being poisoned."

Her comment sends chills up my spine. I'm unable to respond. My eyes are glued to the past.

As Mama is stirring, the spoon clinks on the glass, making an ear-piercing sound. "This will relax you," she says to herself.

I'm watching so intensely that my eyes go dry. I reach for Gwen's hand.

Mama pours the mixture into my bag and fills the remainder with the formula used to feed me. Shake, shake, shake, and it's all one color. Mama pushes her hair away from her eyes and heads up to my bedroom. She talks while she cleans my tube. Mama turns the pump on, and it sends the cocktail—the forbidden contents—directly into my stomach. Mama tells me to open my hand and gives me two children's pain relievers. I wash them down with more grapefruit juice.

I let go of Gwen's hand as an ice pick stabs clear through my heart. This is all wrong. Mothers don't intentionally hurt their children. I'm stunned by what I've seen her do. The bottle specifically warned not to take the medicine with grapefruit juice. Mama's smart; and I know she did this on purpose. I lean back, and Gwen meets my eyes.

"I'm fine," I say quickly, then we both go back to watching.

Mama smiles at me while the bag empties into my stomach. It's not long before I'm babbling. I'm not making any sense.

It looks like I'm having trouble holding my head up. My eyes ease closed. Mama studies me. The sides of her mouth turn up. Is she smiling? What the hell is she doing? Bitch!

I reluctantly look at Gwen. I turn away quickly. My shame is intense. I don't know if I'll ever be able to look Gwen in the eyes again. I'm mortified at all the horrible things Mama is doing to me.

I look ridiculous in my bed. My arms and legs flap around my mattress. I mumble incoherently. I choke on my own saliva. I appear senseless.

I can't take it anymore. "What's happening to me?"

Gwen hesitates. "I can help you understand. Do you want me to explain?"

I shield my eyes with my hand. "Yeah, I guess so. I'm so embarrassed right now. I look like a clown."

"The grapefruit juice mixed with the Valium made it so you couldn't absorb the drug. That meant the medication passed through your gut directly into your bloodstream. It messed you up real bad. It confused you. You were delirious. You saw that you couldn't even speak. Basically, you were really, really high."

I'm doing the best I can to keep it together. I hug myself tightly. All I want to do is die. But I'm already dead. Gwen doesn't say another word. I'm grateful for her silence.

I lift my head and look into the distance.

My limbs are thrashing around. "Manna, I not feeeel gooood. I'msa fraid."

My mom is squinting, focusing on what I'm trying to tell her.

"I'm drizzy. I'ma throw up."

I puke on myself and it splashes down my pajama top. Mama grabs towels, strips my clothes off, and gets me clean again. Then I am lying on Ava's bed. I'm in a haze. I watch Mama put clean sheets on my bed. I am back in bed again, and I settle down.

At almost eight o'clock that evening, Daddy comes into my bedroom. My mother is clutching his arm.

My head bobs up and down like a buoy bouncing on a choppy sea. "See, I told you, Kurtis. She's completely out of it. When she fell out of that tree, she must have hit her head."

Daddy sits on the bed next to me and lifts my hand in his. He gently brushes my cheek with his other hand. "Molly? Molly? Can you hear me? Can you open your eyes?"

My eyelids flutter. I let out a long, garbled groan.

"What do you think happened? Daddy asks my mom.

"Well, the best I can tell is she hit her head when she fell out of the tree."

Daddy looks up at my mom. "She's not doing well, Rona. I'm scared. What should we do?"

Mama places her hand on Daddy's shoulder. "I think we let her rest and see how she is in the morning. I'll sleep in here with her tonight, so I can keep an eye on her. Ava can sleep with you."

Daddy's expression is grave. His brow is knotted, and his lips are pinched. He squeezes my hand and watches me like he's waiting for me to respond. I don't.

"My nerves are shattered," I tell Gwen.

I get up and weave my way to a quiet spot. I kneel down in the grass. My shoulders slump. I'm overwhelmed by confusion and embarrassment. My body shakes, and instead of trying to stop the shaking I allow myself to experience the grief that's been building inside me since shortly after I arrived in Limbo.

I look over my shoulder. Gwen watches me. I stagger to my feet and slink farther away from her. I want to be alone with my morbid thoughts.

I walk until I'm alone in the middle of a darkened forest.

Chapter Thirty-One

I know everything that Mama did to me was intentional. It's baffling and sickening at the same time.

I want to expose Mama. I want Daddy to know she hurt me and that she created my illnesses. The only thing wrong with me was that I was born to the wrong woman. Actually, not a woman, but Satan disguised in a mom suit made of human flesh.

The realization that my discovery of the truth has come too late pulls on my heart. I am stricken with the grief of my own demise. I wail wildly until my chest hurts. Then I lay on the damp pine needles, and eventually I fall asleep. When I wake, I'm more myself, a little less deflated.

I walk back to where Gwen is waiting for me. She greets me with a smile, and it feels like a warm embrace. I sit down next to her in the tall grass. "I'm so embarrassed. My mother's love meant the world to me. Now I know it was a charade. At least I know my dad and Ava loved me."

Gwen touches the charm hanging from her necklace. "Yes, they loved you very much. You know you have some serious endurance and perseverance. All that stuff you went through in the hospital, those tests and procedures, I never could've dealt with them."

I smile. It's good to hear something positive about myself. Gwen and I go back to watching.

The day after my fall, and after Daddy leaves for work, Mama enters my bedroom. I am doing better than the night before.

"Morning, baby," she croons.

"Hi Mama," I mumble sleepily. "What happened to me last night? I was really scared."

"You had quite a fall from that tree, that's what happened," she states plainly. "I think you may have a concussion. I'm glad you're feeling a little better. But if you have a concussion, everything you felt last night can come and go. We'll see how you are today."

"Can we call the doctor? I don't ever wanna be sick like that again," I plead.

Mama pats the top of my hand. "You must be feeling awful to want me to call the doctor. I'll tell you what: let's get your breakfast done, and we'll take it from there."

I nod. My eyelids are heavy even though I've been awake for thirty minutes. I struggle to keep them open.

Gwen and I watch Mama repeat the crushed pill and grapefruit in the feeding bag routine.

I turn to Gwen. She looks back at me and opens her mouth to say something, but stops when I hold up my hand.

"Yes," I say with an edge because I'm annoyed at my mother. "I saw what Mama did. More crushed pills in my food. More sickness to follow. More cruelty and injustice."

I gulp because I suspect Mama has many more demons in her closet I have yet to see.

Chapter Thirty-Two

T hirty minutes pass since Mama gave me the breakfast bag. My eyes roll to the back of my head. By the time Daddy gets home that night and comes in to visit me, I am incoherent. Mama stands next to my father as they look down on me.

"What did they say at the ER?"

Mama crosses her arms over her chest. "The doctor confirmed she has a concussion. I blame myself, really. Molly's a kid and doesn't know any better. I never should've let her play outside. These are the things that can happen."

Mama walks to my dresser and pulls a wet rag from a plastic basin. She twists the water from the cloth and lays it over my forehead. My father watches her with adoration.

I lean my shoulder into Gwen's. "How come we didn't see me in the emergency room?"

"Because she never took you there. She lied to your father. She was teaching you a lesson."

A loud grunt escapes from my mouth. "She lies about everything. And what lesson was she teaching me? Not to climb trees? Do you hear how silly that sounds?"

"The lesson is about control, Molly. Your mom has a sickness. She made you sick so she could get attention and sympathy from other people."

"Wait! Mama has a sickness?"

Gwen speaks calmly and I listen intently. "Yeah, a sickness. Like any other person who sets out to hurt other people. Your mom needed to control you, Molly. The more she convinced you to believe her lies, the more you'd let her do what she wanted without questioning her."

I wipe the sheen of sweat off of my forehead. My adrenaline is pumping through my body. I am outraged . . . again.

Gwen continues, "It wasn't just you. She controlled the information she gave to the doctors who made the wrong decisions and diagnoses about your health.

She not only lied to your father but also your teachers, the school nurse, basically every person she talked to about you."

My frustration mounts. "I've died once already. Learning these awful things about my mother is like dying all over again."

"Yeah, this is some hard stuff," Gwen affirms.

"Let's just keep watching," I say.

All my feedings for the next five days are the same. I cling to my mattress like a dead-weight while Mama has visitors over to the house. Veronica's mom, who carries the burden of my accident, comes every day. A few neighbors bring coffee and pastries in the mornings and sit with Mama at the kitchen table. My mother's expression looks troubled, her eyes stay downward, and her hair is uncombed. After they leave, she goes about her business, humming and moving swiftly through the house. On the sixth day, Mama puts only one crushed pill in two of my bags. On the seventh day, she again only does it once. And on the eighth day, she stops.

On the ninth day, I shuffle into the kitchen and sit across from my mom, who is just finishing her breakfast.

"Morning, Molly."

"Morning," I mumble back. "Mama?"

"Yes, love?"

"What was wrong with me?"

Mama gives me a sympathetic smile. "I think your concussion was fairly severe. And I know we've talked about it, but I don't ever want you climbing trees again."

I nod. "But I was fine after I fell and my head didn't hurt or nothing."

Mama's lips pinch together. "Well, you asked me why it happened. I told you. If you're going to argue with me, then don't bother to ask."

Mama abruptly leaves me standing in the kitchen, alone.

The rest of that day, I remain quiet and respectful.

Two days later, I approach my mom again.

"Can I go back to school?

She frowns and puts her hands on her hips.

"Do you have any idea how exhausted I am from worrying about you? You feel better for three days, and you ask if you can go back to school?"

"Yeah, but it's the end of the school year, and the teachers do a lot of fun stuff with us."

"I can't believe you would even be thinking about returning to school right now."

"I can't help it. I'm bored, and I wanna do something fun."

Mama glares at me. I squirm under her fiery eyes. I remember thinking, I wish the floor would open up and swallow me whole because her scowl was unbearable.

"I'm sorry," I say.

"You should be sorry. Sometimes life is boring. Do you think I have any fun when you're sick? Seriously, Molly, you have no idea how much work it is to take care of you. A little appreciation would be nice."

I look away and try to let her judgment bounce off of me. "I know you take good care of me and I'm really lucky you're my mom. But Daddy told me that when I'm sick people come here and visit you, and he thinks that's good. I don't have anybody, and I think it would be good for me to be around people too."

"I see. Now I'm nobody."

"Noooo," I whine. "I'm not saying you're nobody. I don't mean it like that."

The tension on Mama's face eases. She turns anger on and off in an instant.

Mama gives me a smile. "It's okay. I understand. However, I'm going to have to say no to you returning to school. I'm sorry I can't give you the answer that you want, but it's for your own good."

I spin away from her and stomp up the stairs to my room.

I turn to Gwen. "Sometimes Mama was so unreasonable that I couldn't stand her, but back then I still believed she had my best interests at heart. That's what she told me. Now I know she was self-serving and cruel."

Gwen tilts her head to the side. "There's more. Much, much more."

Chapter Thirty-Three

K nowing what Mama did to me means having to accept that I was unimportant to her . . . disposable, like trash.

When I was alive, I loved looking at pictures of the Great Smoky Mountains along the Tennessee–North Carolina border. I thought it was the most beautiful place on Earth. I'd never actually been there, but I always hoped that one day I would visit. I would look at those pictures often as an escape. So now, I imagine Gwen and I are at the bottom of the Smoky Mountains. It's breathtaking. We sit together in the stillness and look up to where one of the mountain peaks disappears into a white cloud.

"My mom and dad taught me to love people and that it's a sin to hate," I tell Gwen. "Do you think it's a sin to hate?"

Gwen puts her head back and stares into the deep velvety blue sky. "It's hard to say. I guess it depends on why you hate someone. We're human, or we were human. You have a right to feel whatever is going on inside of you. Stop being so hard on yourself. You've been through enough."

I think Gwen is right. I have been through plenty of horrible stuff. I've witnessed the ugliness that lives within my mom's heart.

On my wrist I touch the charm bracelet that Daddy gave me for my birthday. "You know, I died before my life began. I never had a chance to live."

Gwen shoots me a sideways glance.

"Mama used to tell me that if I had a good heart, I would always be rewarded with happiness. I grew up thinking that was true, but it wasn't."

Gwen squeezes my hand. "What would you have done differently? Like, if you could do it all over again. What would you change about your life?"

I pull my knees up to my chest. "I've been thinking about that a lot. I'm not sure there was much I could've done. I suppose I could've asked my dad to come to the doctor with me more often. He was rarely with us because Mama assured him she had everything under control. I don't know. I'm not sure there's anything I could've changed based on what I knew."

"That's exactly right. When you believe that—I mean, really believe it—you'll be liberated."

"You know, I worried about having cancer all the time," I admit.

"Why were you worried that you had cancer?" Gwen asks.

"Let me show you," I say.

I'm back in the hospital again. There is a girl, no older than I was, in the bed next to mine. Her mom and dad sit with her. The girl, named Clair, is wearing a scarf on her head and she lays flat most of the time. I'm too ill and weak to be present, but I hear and see her parents talking to Mama.

"How's Clair doing this morning?" Mama asks her mother, Cassandra, as she enters our room with two cups of coffee.

"Not too good. The cancer is destroying her brain. She's failing quickly." Cassandra is weeping. "I don't want her to have to live like this. She's in so much pain."

Mama rushes to the woman and embraces her. "We should have the nurse get the doctor. He can up her dose of pain medication."

Clair's mother looks to her husband, and he silently agrees.

"Listen, Cassandra, I understand what it's like to have a sick kid." Mama glances over at me and so does Cassandra. "Molly's been sick for a very long time, and I've often thought about what I would do in your shoes. Have you talked to the doctor yet about hospice care?"

Cassandra cries. "The doctor mentioned hospice to us the other day. But, in some ways, it feels like we're giving up hope that Clair will get well again."

Mama looks into Clair's face. Her voice is sympathetic. "Cassandra, I don't think Clair is going to get well. I've been here for the past four days and she has nothing but pain. You should listen to the doctor. It'll relieve Clair of her pain. You said that's what you want, right? I know this can't be an easy decision for you. I'm very sorry for all that you're going through."

The next thing we watch is the doctor coming into the room. Mama is by my bedside but she's hanging on every word of the conversation between the doctor and Clair's parents.

The doctor says, "You're making the right choice. We'll get her set up in hospice tomorrow. In the meantime, I'll up her dosage of pain medication to help."

Gwen and I watch the sun come up through the hospital window the next morning. Cassandra is sleeping in the chair next to Clair's bed, and Mama is in the chair next to mine.

Cassandra wakes slowly and reaches for Clair's hand. Then she stands quickly and puts her head on her daughter's chest. A sob breaks free from the woman as she pushes the bed rail down slowly and climbs into the hospital bed, taking her small, lifeless child in her arms. Cassandra cries as she strokes her dead child's hair.

We watch Mama wake a few minutes later and look over at them. She springs from her chair and presses the call button for the nurse, then slowly makes her way over to Cassandra and rests her hand on the woman's shoulder.

"I'm so sorry," Mama tells her. "I called for the nurse."

Cassandra's tears run down her cheeks and she looks up at Mama. "My baby is gone. She's dead. Oh, God, I've lost her. We've lost her."

I am crying too, but Mama's eyes are dry as she looks on. Then she gazes over at me and quickly hurries back. "Oh, sweetheart, I'm so sorry you have to see this," she whispers so Cassandra doesn't hear her.

The next moment, Clair's bed is empty. Cassandra and her husband are gone from my hospital room.

Mama is standing beside my bed and holding my hand. "That's a mother's worst nightmare. Losing a child." She watches me for a reaction. My eyes are round and I'm clutching at her hand. "This is why I'm so obsessed with you getting better and avoiding things that can hurt you, because of that," Mama says, pointing to the empty bed.

I say to Gwen, "I was so scared after Clair died. I kept imagining that I had cancer too. I was so confused by everything. Her death changed the way I saw my own life. You know, like it could be gone in a flash. I thought about dying all the time, to the point where I got irrational."

"I think it's normal that you were scared. I would've been afraid to die too," Gwen says.

"Well, the weird thing is, that by the end of my life, I wasn't afraid to die anymore."

Gwen rests her head on my shoulder. She has a way of doing small things that comfort me. "Tell me more about not being afraid to die," she says.

"After Clair died, I was so scared about death. Over time, I would watch Ava playing and giggling and rolling around on the floor. She could stay entertained for hours with a stuffed animal. She was free and happy. I secretly envied her. I mean, I loved her to pieces, but I wanted to be her. Some days I would wish it was Ava that was sick and not me. Then I would suffocate myself in guilt for wishing my problems onto my little sister. I didn't really want her to be sick. I just wanted someone to take my troubles away. Then, toward the end of my life, I was so tired of fighting that I was able to accept that being dead might actually be better than being alive."

Gwen lowers her chin to her chest and shakes her head softly. "There's something else you should know. Something I only just learned."

I stand up. "I'm sorry, Gwen. I can't watch anymore right now, but I promise that I'll be ready soon."

Then I walk away. I keep walking. I walk until I'm so tired that I can't walk anymore, so I lie down. I fall asleep dreading what Gwen needs to show me.

Chapter Thirty-Four

When I wake, Gwen is by my side. She pats the open space between us, and I inch closer.

We sit close together, shoulders and thighs touching. The contact feels right, complete, as though we are one.

"I don't mean to be pushy about wanting to show you more about your mom. I just want what's best for you," Gwen begins. "I know how much you love your mom, I really do. But I've been curious about something. Weren't the doctors and nurses concerned about how many times you were taken to the hospital with all these different problems?"

I shrug. "There are tons of hospitals in Philadelphia . . . in the city and the suburbs. We always went to a different one. Mama told me she brought me to whichever hospital specialized in my current problem. So she took me to the best place to treat my illnesses as they happened."

"Did you ever think your mom was lying to the doctors?"

I rub my temples with my index fingers to ease the pressure building inside my head. "No, I never suspected that anything was wrong. I didn't have any reason to think she was lying."

"No, I guess you didn't."

I rub the back of my neck to relieve the growing tension. "There were a couple of times when I probably should've known."

"Can you show me?" Gwen asks.

"Sure."

We look down at the grass, and the past appears. I'm sleeping in my bed at home. I must have a fever because there is a pile of covers on top of me. My eyes are open and my back is facing Mama as she paces next to my bed; she doesn't know I'm awake.

Mama says, "If I couldn't take care of Molly I don't know what I'd do with myself." She bounds back and forth across the carpet. Then says, "No one would give me the time of day if it weren't for her."

We see my eyes squeeze tightly.

"We'll just have to keep going on this journey, me and Molly," Mama says. "Someday it'll be all over, so best to enjoy this time while I can."

"She's insane," Gwen blurts.

"I know. When I heard her say those things I was really baffled. But I was so scared that I talked myself into believing she hadn't meant what she said. So I kept my mouth shut and didn't tell anyone."

"You didn't even tell your dad?"

"No. I was afraid he'd confront Mama and she'd be mad at me. I was stupid."

As I tell Gwen this, hot fluid whirls in my belly. My reaction is partly because I am so angry with Mama and partly because I was too blind to see what was happening. When I was alive, I was trapped. I had little interaction with the world that existed outside of my home or hospital room, I had no idea Mama was such a big, fat liar.

Gwen and I fall silent.

Gwen lies on her back and closes her eyes. "The sun feels great," she says, breaking the silence. "I love it here. I couldn't appreciate anything in nature for a long time before I was sent to the gas chamber. Did I tell you what the Nazis did to my hair?"

I fill with angst at the mere mention of the Nazis. Her death was vile, but I imagine Gwen thinks the same about watching all the stuff that happened to me. I focus on Gwen's life and leave mine alone for a while. There must be a reason I need to hear about her; whether it's for her sake or mine is unclear.

"No, you never told me about that."

Gwen runs her fingers over her curls. "This man took big scissors, you know, the kind people use to cut thick fabric, and he hacked off all of my hair a handful at a time. He got really close to my scalp with those blades too. He didn't care that he cut me a couple of times. When I whimpered, he slapped me hard on the side of my face and told me to shut up. Before that happened, I never thought it could hurt to have a haircut. It was awful. It made me feel like I wasn't human."

I touch Gwen's cheek where I imagine the man had slapped her. "That's horrible."

"Yeah, it was humiliating."

Gwen touches her hair. "This was the way my hair looked before I was forced into the concentration camp."

I reach over and take a curl of her silky hair between my fingers. "It's beautiful."

Gwen nods. She shifts her body away from mine. "I have my mom's hair. It looks just the same."

"Is your mom here with you?"

Gwen looks at me and smiles, but her eyes reveal an arcane sadness. "She is. She didn't want me to be a guardian because whenever I'm in Limbo, I can see what happened to me when I was alive. But I told her it's important that I be here. I've been coming to Limbo for a long time. I like helping other people. I mean, my mom doesn't have any say over me now. Up here, I have control over what I do or don't do. Because I love her, I talked to her about it before I decided to do this."

"What was your mom like when you were alive?" I ask.

"She was fun. She taught me how to paint and play the piano. We went to the movies together all the time, and when the weather was nice, we rode our bikes along the waterfront. My mom always listened to me. You know, she really listened to what I had to say. That meant everything to me."

I fill with envy, and a slight noise escapes my throat. My relationship with Mama was different, twisted. I realize now that she never took much of an interest in me beyond my physical health. Mama spent a lot of time with me, but she was never there in the way I needed her to be. "Your mom sounds great."

"Yeah, she still is."

I stand and twist at the waist to give my back a good, long stretch.

Gwen stands up next to me and looks into my eyes.

"What?" I ask and smile.

"I don't tell all the people I help in Limbo how I died. You're one of the few."

"Really? How come?"

"Well, up until now, most of the people that I've helped have died tragically from house fires, car accidents, drownings, chokings . . . things like that. But you and I are more alike than anyone I've helped so far."

"How?"

"In the way, we both died at the hands of someone else for no good reason."

I think Gwen is hesitant to tell me something, but I can't be sure.

Gwen continues, "I was drawn to you. I asked for you because I knew how you died and I thought I'd be able to help."

I put my arms around Gwen's shoulder and pull her into me. "You're a good friend. You've been so much help already. That means a lot to me."

"We both get something out of this. Besides, maybe once you're finished here and have peace for a while, you'll join me in Limbo to help others. We need more guardians."

"I'm not sure I'd be any good, but I'll think about it. I promise." Changing the subject I ask Gwen, "What was your guardian like?"

Gwen's face lights up. "Betsey." The name rolls off of her tongue like a sweet lullaby.

"I like that name," I say. "Tell me about Betsey."

Gwen sits in the grass and picks a dandelion from a small patch of flowers. She puts the flower to her nose and draws in the fragrance. "Betsey is great. She was a slave in South Carolina."

Chapter Thirty-Five

"Betsey was a slave?" The word drips from my tongue like poison in my mouth.

"Yeah. She was born in Africa. When she was only seventeen years old, her whole family was captured and brought to America. Betsey was on a ship called the J. Dillinger. She was separated from her family right from the start. She never got to say good-bye to any of them."

My eyes widen. "What happened to her?"

"Wait a minute," Gwen says.

The two of us sit in silence for a few minutes before I look over at her. Gwen's eyes are closed. Her lips are moving slightly, as though she's in prayer. I can no longer feel Gwen's presence even though I'm sitting right next to her. I watch her, mesmerized.

Gwen opens her eyes and looks at me.

"I thought something happened to you. What was that all about?"

"I was talking to Betsey."

Now, I think, this is creepy. I mean, a dead person talking to another dead person in their head.

"I can show you," Gwen says. "Betsey told me it would be okay. She thinks it'll help you understand you're not the only person who lived with pain and died without getting to say good-bye to anyone."

I have a morbid curiosity to see what happened to Betsey. "Okay."

Betsey is leaning against the entry of a wooden shack without a door. Other shacks, like this one, are lined up for three blocks. Betsey has dark brown skin. Her black hair is long, hanging below her shoulders in tight curls. Several curls cross over her right eye and hang just below her mouth. Her eyes are dark brown, almost black, and her lips are a dark shade of pink, but they're dry . . . cracking and peeling. She is wearing a long-sleeved blouse and a skirt that reaches the ground. It's hot. The film of sweat on her skin makes her appear to sparkle.

"Gwen, she's beautiful."

"I know. She's even more gorgeous on the inside," Gwen says.

We see a tall, muscular white man walk toward Betsey. Her eyes widen. She looks away from him as if she's seen a ghost.

I rub my arms. "Who is that? He gives me the heebie-jeebies."

Gwen explains, "His name is Bernie Hunton. He's lives on his family's plantation in South Carolina. He owns Betsey."

"What's he doing?" I ask.

"Watch," Gwen says.

Bernie thumps up the two wooden steps. He stands next to Betsey. He puts his nose in her hair and takes a long whiff.

"You smell good. You got cleaned up just like I told ya. I like that. I don't wanna have to tell ya anything twice. Ya hear?" Bernie says and smacks her butt.

Betsey's eyes pivot to three children staring at them. A bead of sweat slides down her temple.

"Ya hear?" Bernie barks in her ear.

"Yessa, mass'r."

Bernie smiles. "That's a good girl. Let's get on inside."

Betsey takes Bernie's hand and leads him into her shack. Inside, there is a bed and a chair. Her mattress is nothing more than a pile of scratchy hay.

"You got that fabric I gave ya?" Bernie spits out. "Get it and put it on the bed. I ain't gonna be layin' in no hay. And when you're done doin' that ya can take those clothes off too. I ain't courtin' ya. I'm only here for one reason."

I can't take my eyes off of Betsey. My heart bangs against the inside of my chest. I want to look away. I want to tell Gwen I can't watch anymore. But I need to know what happens to Betsey. To see her life through my eyes and feel her pain with my soul.

Betsey lifts her shirt over her head and unfastens her skirt, letting them both drop to the dusty wooden floor. She stands naked in front of Bernie. He smiles. He licks his lips. His hands shoot forward and roughly grope her breasts. Betsey flinches and tries to back away. Bernie backhands her, and she lands on the bed with a thud. He pounces on top of her like a starving animal.

Betsey's on her back. Her eyes bulge out. She searches all around her, as if looking for someone to rescue her, but no one else is there to help. Bernie is on top of her. He undoes his pants with one hand; the other hand is clasped around her neck. He bites into her breast at the same time he enters her.

Betsey gasps and expels a pained breath. Bernie rapes her for a long time before collapsing his sweaty body mass on top of her. Then he gets up, dresses, and leaves. As he is leaving, a white woman in a blue dress climbs the steps of Betsey's shack. She holds her chin high in the air, and exhales through her nose strongly, which makes a fluttering sound.

"Who is that?" I ask Gwen.

"That's Bernie's wife, Rebecca. I don't know who was more malicious, Rebecca or Bernie. They were hateful people."

We watch more.

Rebecca stops short and glares at her husband.

Bernie shrugs, tucks in his shirt, and brushes past his wife. "See ya up at the house for dinner."

Rebecca rushes into the small shack. Betsey is fumbling with her clothes, trying to get dressed quickly. Rebecca drives her hand into Betsey's hair and snatches a handful. She drags Betsey outside and pushes her off the wooden porch. Betsey lands face-first in the dirt at the bottom of the steps.

"You think you can sleep with my husband, you dirty prostitute? You think you can come here and live on my land and seduce my husband? Do you think I'll let you get away with it?" Rebecca screams in Betsey's face.

Betsey huddles into a fetal position. "No, mistress. I didn't do nuffin'. I swear. Mass'r made me," Betsey pleads.

Rebecca pulls a knife from the pocket of her dress. The tip of the blade has been broken off. She looks into Betsey's eyes, and with full fury plunges the knife into her.

"Liar! My husband wouldn't have anything to do with you. This is all your doing, not his. You were trying to gain favor, maybe get a position as a maid in my house. Don't you dare lie about my husband," Rebecca growls.

Rebecca pulls the knife out of Betsey and plunges it into her twelve more times.

I'm hugging my own body tightly. The unimaginable pain that Betsey withstands leaves me breathless. Betsey was innocent, but had been found guilty and sentenced to punishment by the wife of a rapist.

The injustice overwhelms me.

My mouth drops open, and I cover it with my hand. "This is horrible. Why didn't anyone try to help Betsey? Why didn't any of her friends try to protect her?"

Gwen shakes her head. "It wasn't like that in those days. The other slaves were afraid for their lives, and Bernie didn't care what his wife did to Betsey. There were plenty of other women slaves he owned. He raped them whenever he wanted."

"They are both the rottenest people I've ever seen," I snarl.

Gwen and I just sit together. The horrible images play over in my mind. I want them to stop, but I can't stop seeing them. "That was a barbaric way to die."

Gwen huffs. "That wasn't the worst of it. Watch . . ."

Betsey is laying in the dirt. The blood from her stab wounds is pooling around her body. We can see the sharp rise and fall of her chest. She isn't dead. Betsey is breathing hard. She moans and groans with each breath of air that is taken in and released.

Rebecca turns to the other slaves watching. The other women are crying. Several men look angry; the veins in their temples are engorged and their necks are pulsing or twitching.

Rebecca raises the bloodied knife into the air. "Not one of you is to talk to her. Nor will you sit with her and hold her hand. This woman is a whore and needs to be treated as such. She is to die alone. That is final. Anyone who tries to comfort this woman will have the end of this knife shoved through their flesh and straight into their heart."

Gwen and I stare into each other's eyes. Our tongues are tired. We have nothing left to say.

"All of you gather closer," Rebecca demands. "Get a good look at this . . . this dirty whore."

A large group of slaves gathers around Betsey. Rebecca steps forward and kicks Betsey in her bare chest.

Rebecca screams, "Let it be known to all of you who stand here! Any prostitute who succumbs to lewdness will not occupy, inhabit, live, or sleep in any house, room, or closet on this property."

Gwen and I sit back. My rage mingles with sadness. I flex my fingers and grab a handful of rocks. I stand and throw them at a nearby tree as hard as I can. "Your and Betsey's stories are the most outrageous things I've ever seen. Here I am, feeling sorry for myself, and the two of you have been through hell."

Gwen stands next to me and lobs stones at the tree. "We all suffered in death, including you. That's the point in me showing you what happened. That's why Betsey agreed that you should see it too. Betsey understands human suffering and pain. The thing that's so amazing about Betsey is that through all of her suffering, she still knows how to love."

I scowl at Gwen. "I don't think I could ever love a single thing again if those things ever happened to me."

"I wish you could see that you and I aren't that different. We both suffered a traumatic death. I'm trying my best to help you learn what Betsey taught me."

My curiosity is piqued. "Just tell me. What did Betsey teach you?"

"That good always wins over evil. Always. And that there's always a price to pay for ruining someone else's life."

I look down at my feet.

Gwen puts in an effort to make me smile. She says, "I still think you'd make a great guardian, even though you can be really feisty."

Her lighthearted comment cools some of my anger and shock. It helps me relax.

I gently glide my hand over Gwen's forearm. "I hope someday I'll get to meet Betsey. I'll get back to you on the guardian thing. I'm not sure I'm built for it."

While it thrills me to fantasize about helping dead people move beyond everything that happened in their lives, I'm not sure it is something I can actually handle.

The one thing I'm sure of is that I want to meet Betsey, not only because she helped Gwen, but because I want to meet the woman who can still love after being so deeply hated. I can't see myself ever doing the same.

Chapter Thirty-Six

M y death was premature and unfair, that's a fact. But I'm trying my best to move past this hollow feeling that's taken up residence in my heart.

"I'd like to see when things got really bad for me. Once I couldn't be cured."

Gwen swipes the hair from her face, pulls the hair to the side, and braids it. "Of course. Let's watch."

We are in my bedroom in Limbo. I wiggle deeper into the soft cushion of the sofa where we're sitting, and we focus on the scene in front of us.

Mama is sitting at the dining room table. In front of her is a big plastic container with a red plastic lid.

I amble into the room. "Hi, Mama. What's that?"

Mama puts her hand around the plastic container. "This is your special medicine. I made it myself. You know, a little of this and a little of that. This is what's going to solve all of your health problems."

I watch Mama open the container. She digs a silver tablespoon into the white substance and mixes three heaping tablespoons into my liquid dinner.

Mama gives it a shake. Then she looks at me. "You want to shake it up? For good luck."

A grin spreads across my face. "Yeah, I'd love that," I say.

I take the bag in two hands—shake, shake, shake—and I hand the bag back to Mama. I am still beaming.

"I love when we do stuff together," I tell my mom.

After five days of taking the magic medicine, I can barely speak. Mama rushes me to the emergency room. My legs and feet look as though they are filled with air. My swelled feet don't fit into my shoes, so Mama wedges socks onto them.

Mama pulls up to the emergency room. Ava is next to me, stroking my hair. Mama locks us both in the car and runs inside. Within a minute, people are at the vehicle with a gurney. Mama unlocks the doors. Ava cries and screams my name. The hospital people remove me from the backseat and place me onto the stretcher.

Inside the emergency room, I remember my thoughts were hazy, and I fought with all that I had to focus on what was happening. Then I go unconscious.

I see a doctor rush into the bay where I am laying.

"Mrs. Roslin, I'm Dr. Greene. I've taken a look at Molly's chart and placed a call to Dr. Becker. I think Molly has something serious going on. Her blood pressure is dangerously high. I suspect her kidneys have gotten worse, which is causing water backup to her heart and lungs. We're going to need to make some decisions. Dr. Becker said he'll be here in the next thirty minutes."

"Oh, no. Oh, please, Dr. Greene, you have to help my girl," Mama whines and adds in a few sniffles.

"Try not to worry," Dr. Greene assures her. "Molly is in good hands. You're already aware that Dr. Becker is the best kidney disease specialist in Philadelphia."

She acknowledges with a curt nod of her head.

"What will you do until Dr. Becker gets here?" Mama asks.

"We'll give her some IV fluids. I want to try to flush her system so we can get things moving again. I'm going to get Molly set up, and once Dr. Becker gets here, we'll figure out our next step."

After the doctor leaves, Mama leans over my gurney and whispers in my ear, "Don't worry, Molly, you'll get through this without a problem. A few tests, some new medications, and you'll be good as new."

My eyes are closed. I still haven't regained consciousness.

From Limbo, nothing can prepare me for what she says next.

Mama whispers, "Think of this as a little vacation. I do. We'll spend quality time together. And even though I'm not a fan of hospital food, it'll be nice not to have to cook and have the nurses fuss over us. I'll enjoy being taken care of for a change."

Gwen interjects, "Bad things are going to happen to your mom someday. She deserves everything she gets."

It is good to hear Gwen say that my mother will get hers. But I'm not sure I believe her. "Mama will not pay for anything she's done. She is too smart to ever get caught."

Chapter Thirty-Seven

$\mathbb{W}$ hile I'm in the hospital, I go from mild improvement to drastic decline.

After my being there for more than a week, and doing well for two consecutive days, Dr. Becker walks into my hospital room.

"Hello, Molly."

"Hi, Dr. Becker." His demeanor has changed. He seems more serious than usual. I grab my hospital bracelet and twist it around my wrist.

Dr. Becker makes eye contact with Mama. "Good to see you today, Rona."

"Oh, same here, Dr. Becker. I always know that Molly is much safer when you're around."

Dr. Becker looks down at his brown leather shoes. "Listen, I have something that I'd like to talk to you about."

The doctor raises his eyes to meet Mama's, and she stands from her chair.

"What is it?" she asks, alarm in her voice.

"Molly's kidney disease has worsened. They're only functioning at about forty percent. We need to start her on dialysis. It's the logical next step while we wait for a donor."

Mama places her hand over her mouth and nods.

"Rona, I know this is upsetting for you, but we still have time to find a donor. Molly will have her first dialysis treatment later this week. We'll see how she does, and if everything goes okay, she can get out of this place a couple of days after her first treatment."

"Of course. If that's what you think needs to happen, then that's what we'll do."

Dr. Becker gives Mama a polite smile, then turns his attention to me. "I want to explain what we're going to be doing, okay?"

My hands wrap on the metal railing of the bed in a death grip. "Will it hurt?"

The doctor pulls a chair up next to me. "No, it won't hurt. What we're doing is putting you on a machine that will clean all the bad stuff out of your blood."

I instinctively move away from the doctor. "Where do you hook the machine up to?"

Dr. Becker leans toward me and takes my hand. "We'll do minor surgery to make a bigger blood vessel for you. It's called a fistula. But we'll give you medication to make you very comfortable, and you won't even know we're doing it. After that's in place, you might feel a small stick through your skin when we hook up the dialysis, but nothing too awful."

The tension in my shoulder's melts away. "Do I only have to get my blood cleaned one time?"

"That's the tricky part. You'll need to have it done twice a week. We'll give you the treatment overnight. What that means is every week you'll be in the hospital for four days and get to go home for three days."

My breath catches in my throat. "For how long?"

"At least until you have a transplant."

I cry, and Mama comes closer and rubs my arm. "It's going to be just fine. Right, Dr. Becker?" Mama coos.

He nods. "We'll do everything to make it as easy on you as possible."

"But I don't wanna be in the hospital that much. I'll never be able to go back to school."

Dr. Becker stands and pushes the chair back against the wall. "Let's take this one day at a time. I promise you, I'll be working very hard to get you back to school."

Mama stops rubbing my arm, and her eyes narrow into tiny slits, but she remains silent. I see it now but didn't back then. Dr. Becker has just crossed an invisible line with Mama. Nobody gets to say when I do or don't go back to school except her.

At the moment, I must have felt the fury rolling off of my mom. I sit up taller in my bed. My shrill voice vibrates in my own ears, "I didn't mean what I said about school. It's more important that I get well again. Mama gets all of my schoolwork from my teachers. She makes sure I stay on track with the other kids in my grade. It's not so bad, and Mama makes learning fun too."

Mama puts her hand over mine. "You're such a sweet child."

The doctor moves to the door. "Yes, you have a wonderful mom. Your dad is pretty terrific too. You're a lucky girl."

Dr. Becker, like all the other medical people, has been fooled by my mother. Mama is a master manipulator. She can trick anyone into believing anything. She is stealthy and confident and absolute in her decisions about my medical care and Ava's too.

There were lots of times, especially in the last year of my life, when I tried to be part of my own medical care by thinking about things I'd like to ask the doctors and nurses. But when I tried to speak up, I could feel the weight of Mama's stare, and I would fall back into my role as the quiet, sick child. It was my own fear, turning my back on my basic human instincts that landed me at death's door.

Chapter Thirty-Eight

G wen and I continue to watch the vision. I have been receiving dialysis for several months when, one morning, Mama waltzes into my hospital room happier than usual.

"Good moooorning, Molly," she sings.

I press the button to lift the back of the bed. "Morning, Mama. How come you're so happy today? Did Dr. Becker find a kidney donor for me?"

Mama glides up next to my bed. "Oh, no, honey. It's nothing like that, but it is excellent news."

I watch her expectantly. "What is it?"

"Well, I've arranged a family vacation."

I stare at her blankly. My lips are moving but the words aren't forming. I take a deep breath. "Oh. That sounds great."

"It's more than great. It's exactly what our family needs. We need to get away for a while. But wait! Here's the best part. We're going to Disney World, and I contacted them, and they're going to treat us like VIPs. We won't have to wait in any lines, and I'm sure there'll be all kinds of special treats for us. Isn't that wonderful?"

My smile looks forced, like I'm smelling a pile of poop. "Yeah, that's really great. When are we going?"

Mama sits down, pulls a candy bar from her purse, unwraps it, and takes a big bite. I stare at it.

"We're leaving right after your treatment next week," she says.

I keep staring at the candy bar, my eyes pinned on it like a fly to a garbage can.

"Well?" Mama asks.

"How long are we staying?"

"A week."

"What about my dialysis?"

"I already took care of that. Dr. Becker arranged for you to have treatments in the mornings before we go to the park."

149

"But I get my treatments at night because they work better. That's what Dr. Becker says."

Mama shoves the last piece of candy into her mouth and crumbles the wrapper in her hand. "I understand that, but he said it'll be fine for a week."

Mama goes home early so she can, as she states, "make all the perfect arrangements."

In the early evening, Dr. Becker comes to check on me. "How are you feeling?"

I shrug. "Tired, I guess. So . . . my mom told me about our trip."

"Oh, good. I think it's wonderful that your family will get to spend time together doing something fun."

I look away from Dr. Becker.

"Is something wrong, Molly? Are you worried about something?"

I shake my head. "Not worried, but I'm so tired all of the time and even though I wanna go on vacation, just thinking about it makes me want to hide under the covers. Plus, Mama says I'm getting dialysis while we're in Florida and they don't even know me there."

Dr. Becker pulls a chair up next to my bed. "Look, Molly, I know you don't feel good and it seems like a lot to take in right now, but once you get to Florida, you'll change your mind. If it helps, I went to medical school with the doctor who will oversee your dialysis while you're there. He and I will be talking so there's no need to worry."

I turn onto my side and stare at the doctor. "Can I tell you a secret?"

"Sure, you can tell me anything."

"I don't like that my mom plans everything," I confide in him. "She does things and doesn't even ask if I want to do them. She doesn't ask any of us, not even Daddy. Like this trip. I'm sure it'll be fun, but why can't she ask if it's something I wanna do? She makes all the decisions for everything and sometimes I just wanna be part of it. You know, treat me like I have an opinion."

Dr. Becker gives me a sympathetic smile. "You know, that's a pretty normal thing for moms. They like to take care of their family, and sometimes they can get caught up making everyone happy, and they forget that others have opinions. Especially a mom with a sick child. Your mom is trying to make everyone happy. I think you should go on vacation and expect to have a ton of fun. How's that sound?"

I look away and shrug. "It's not fun being showed off like a freak 'cause I'm sick." I brush strands of hair from my face. "She tells everyone about me, and it makes me uncomfortable. They all look at me weird. I hate it."

"I'll give you that, Molly. Your mom does want everyone to know how strong and brave you've been."

"Yeah, but then they feel sorry for me and look at me like I'm damaged."

Dr. Becker stands and takes my hand in his. "You, Molly Roslin, are not damaged. You've had your fair share of challenges, but you're far bigger than your illnesses. You're bright and funny and pleasant to be around. You remember that."

I tighten my grip on the doctor's hand. "Thanks, Dr. Becker."

I remember that night, while the dialysis machine was running, I shut the television off and laid in the darkness. I focused on the hum of the equipment keeping me alive. I thought about the upcoming trip and decided that Dr. Becker was right and that I'd bring my best game, my best attitude, and I'd try to enjoy our family vacation.

Chapter Thirty-Nine

"**S**o did you have a good time on vacation?" Gwen asks.

"Well, it was exhausting. We were treated like celebrities, and Mama savored every moment. After that vacation, she made it her sole purpose to be the 'guest family' at as many events as possible."

"Oh, that's sounds . . . weird," Gwen says.

"It was! Without talking to me, she went to the school that I used to attend and got me a part in the school play. I played the role of a handicapped child who sat in a wheelchair. I had three speaking lines, and when I say three lines, I mean three sentences. Mama made me practice those three lines so I would sound authentic. She criticized me for weeks:

"For goodness sake, Molly, speak louder. No one will be able to hear you."

"Molly, you're playing a handicapped child. Stop smiling."

"For heaven's sake, Molly, you need to show more sadness in your eyes."

"Stop touching your hair when you say your lines, Molly."

"Molly? Do you have any idea how hard it was for me to get you this part? I spent hours on the phone with people. And then I had to visit with the principal to make sure she was in agreement after convincing the teachers running the production. It's practically a personal favor to me . . . all the other kids had to try out, but because of me they gave you a part."

Watching from Limbo, I discover that Mama had told the principal I could die and she wanted me to have this experience. The woman stops at nothing to get what she wants.

"Mama was obsessed with the play, and she ruined every bit of my confidence. I'll show you what happened on the night of the play."

"Rona," Daddy says after Mama tells me again to make sure I say my lines right, "Give her a break. She's tired and doesn't feel well."

Mama spins on him. "You listen to me," she says, pointing her finger in Daddy's face. "I went through a lot of trouble to make Molly a part of this so that she could have a chance to do things other kids her age do. The least she can do is be grateful and try her best. It's three stinking lines."

I admit to Gwen, "When all was said and done, it was nice to be around healthy kids my own age. But everyone treated me like a celebrity and talked to me like I was a friend, and that part made me very uncomfortable."

Then we watch Mama tell the Pennsylvania Ballet the same thing about me to get us in a box that overlooks the stage. We can see everything. My parents could afford whatever seats they wanted. But it was how they treated our family that made all the difference for Mama. They paid so much attention to us. We were brought backstage to meet the prima ballerina. We took pictures with all the dancers . . . me in my wheelchair and Mama standing behind me smiling so broadly it looks like her face is about to rip in half.

To Gwen and me it is clear who is having the fun. Mama isn't able to contain her excitement. She flatters all of the hosts; she tells them how grateful we are that they've allowed me to be a part of something so spectacular.

"You look very uncomfortable at every event. Did you have any fun?" Gwen asks.

"I guess so. It was nice and all, but I was tired. Daddy knew how much it took out of me, and he was the one who sat and talked to me while Mama talked to whoever was fussing over her. I would've rather stayed home and watched a movie or read a good book. At least I would've been comfortable. I don't think anyone knows how uncomfortable it is to sit in a wheelchair for hours. It made my butt hurt, and then my back would hurt. It was lousy."

Gwen nods. "But if you couldn't walk, at least you got pushed around."

"Who said I couldn't walk? I could walk, maybe not fast, but I was able to get around. Mama was the one who insisted I use a wheelchair when we went out. At the time, I knew I didn't need it, but I always did what Mama wanted, whether I liked it or not. I mean, I couldn't walk around for hours, because I spent so much time in bed, but I was fine on my own."

Gwen and I share a peaceful moment. I never had a friend where the silence was almost as good as the talking. I can feel her love for me, and I hope she can feel mine for her. My mind wanders and I think that someday Gwen and I will part. I don't want to leave her.

"Will I see you again after I leave Limbo?" I ask her.

"Of course you will. I live where you're going."

"But you're always here with me."

"Yep, but after you move on, I'll go back for a while before I come back to Limbo."

"Will I have a house to live in where I'm going?"

Gwen shakes her head, but she's smiling.

"Then where will I live?"

"You'll live everywhere. It's like here but better."

My shoulders relax. "Right. That makes me feel better because I mean, who would I live with anyway? I don't know any dead people."

Gwen grins. "You'll be around people who love you even though you may not have met them when you were alive. You'll also meet other people who you are meant to be around. It's sort of like everybody is nice and happy. People laugh and do things they couldn't do on Earth."

"Okay, I can handle that."

My anxiety eased, I hunker down into a bed made of soft pillows. I want to sleep. It seems like it has been forever since I've closed my eyes. As I allow myself to drift off, I am overwhelmed by a sense of stillness that is magnificent.

Chapter Forty

I imagine that we're laying on a huge beanbag chair. It's super soft and comfortable and purple. It's big enough for Gwen and me to lie on together.

The temperature is perfect. I'm free. I wear soft cotton pajamas today, and I'm barefoot. See, everything I want, I have, no matter how simple or complex, like my perfectly built bedroom that repairs itself whenever I blow off steam and smash it to pieces.

I lean against the huge beanbag and paint my toenails hot pink. They look fabulous. I wiggle my toes when I finish. I smile. I lay back, satisfied.

When I was alive, Mama always painted my fingernails and toenails for me. Especially when I was in the hospital. I thought it made me prettier to have my nails painted. Now I suspect she did these things for me so the doctors and nurses would praise her about being a good mother. The things Mama did that made me feel good now make me feel used. I've realized that everything and anything Mama did was only to further her own selfish motives.

"Hey, Gwen. I met this girl when I was in the hospital. Her name was Joon. I'd like to go back and watch my time with her. She was so much fun. We did something really crazy."

Gwen gives me her undivided attention. "Really? Yeah, let's see it then."

I am in the hospital again because my kidney problem has worsened, even with dialysis. My health has been unstable, and Dr. Becker admits me for observation. He says once I stabilize I can go home.

I have been there several days when a commotion wakes me in the middle of the night.

I open my eyes, and two teenage girls are in the room. One is in the bed next to mine, and the other one is fussing around, moving a chair next to the bed.

Once the nurse and orderly leave our room, I make sure the girls know I'm awake.

"Hi," I say.

"Hi," the teen girl sitting in the chair calls back. She stands and walks over to my bedside. "I'm Joon."

"I'm Molly. Is that your sister?" I ask, pointing to the girl asleep in the bed.

"Technically, no. But we're just as close as sisters."

"Why is she here?"

"The house where we were staying caught on fire last night. She got burned a little and she's having a hard time breathing, so they made her stay."

"What's her name?"

"Lulu."

Joon stares at me for a while. She seems to zone in on the dark circles under my eyes.

"You're pretty sick, huh?" she finally says.

"Yeah, I am. I hate being sick."

"What's wrong with you?" she asks.

"A bunch of different things. Right now, my kidneys aren't working the way they should, so the doctor said I have to stay here for a while. I'm always at the doctor or in the hospital."

"Oh. Have you been sick since you were born?"

I shrug. "Nope. When I turned eight, I got sick, and it's been one stupid thing after another since then. I've had surgeries and taken lots of pills, but the doctors can never figure out what is wrong with me. Until my kidneys decided to give out."

"That really sucks. Being sick is annoying . . . that's what Lulu says when her kidney is acting up."

Lulu lets out a soft groan, and Joon rushes to her side. "Hey, Lulu. It's about time you woke up."

Lulu smiles weakly. "What happened?"

"Remember, the house caught on fire?"

Lulu grimaces. "Oh, yeah. What the hell died in my mouth?"

Joon laughs. "I think it's from the smoke you breathed in."

"Can you get me a drink?"

I watch Joon fill a cup with water from the pitcher on Lulu's table. "Drink slow," Joon says and presses the red call button for the nurse.

"I was mesmerized by them," I say to Gwen. "I could literally feel the love they had for each other. I yearned to have that closeness with a friend. I craved it."

A few minutes later, the nurse comes into the room. "Well, hello, Lulu. I'm glad to see you're awake. How do you feel?"

"My throat is sore, and my body hurts. Other than that, I can't stand the smell of smoke in my hair." Lulu looks Joon up and down. "And her hair too."

Joon smiles. "As soon as I go back to our penthouse, I'll shower and put on fresh clothes, Princess Lulu."

Lulu rolls her eyes. "You mean the Dumpster on Market Street?"

The two teens laugh at the private joke.

Before the nurse leaves, she checks Lulu's vital signs. She comes back a short time later carrying several towels and two pairs of clean scrubs. She sits everything on one of the empty chairs. Then she turns to Joon.

"There's a shower in the bathroom," she tells her. "You go first and then I'll help Lulu."

Joon's mouth drops open. "Me?"

The nurse nods. "You need a shower, right? So go on and do your thing."

Gwen and I watch silently as each girl goes into the bathroom filthy and emerges looking clean. I don't know why this was so interesting, but it is.

Lulu is back in her bed, and Joon crawls in next to her. The two girls curl up together. They're a perfect pair.

The next morning, as the sun shines through the window, I stretch my weak limbs and look over at Lulu. I catch Joon smiling at me.

"Good morning," Joon says and makes her way over to my bed.

"Hi."

Joon picks up the pitcher from Lulu's table. "Do you want some water?"

"Yeah, that would be great."

Joon grabs Lulu's glass and fills it. When she hands it to me, I just stare at her. I say, "Mama doesn't let me drink from someone else's cup. She says it could be really bad for me and that I could catch another disease."

Joon pretends to look around her. "Well, your mama ain't here, and other than a kidney problem like you have, Lulu doesn't have other diseases."

"Yeah," I mumble, "you're right."

I grab the glass from Joon and guzzle the water.

Joon turns back to Lulu. "I met Dr. Becker in the emergency room."

Lulu brightens. "What did he say?"

"Only that he is admitting you."

"I love Dr. Becker," Lulu says.

I raise the back of my bed. "Dr. Becker is my doctor too."

Lulu looks over at me and smiles. "Oh, yeah? Then you're as lucky as I am."

I smile back at her.

"How long have you been here?" Lulu asks.

I use my fingers to count the days. "Six days so far. I'll probably be here for a week or two this time."

Joon moseys closer and climbs onto my bed. I grab the sheet and pull it up to my chin. "What are you doing?" I ask.

"I was gonna lay in bed with you for a while," Joon says.

"Why would you do that?"

"Because you look like you need someone to lay next to you."

I stare at Joon blankly.

She says, "There's something sad in your eyes. Like you're lonely or something. So I thought I'd lay next to you for a while."

I give Joon a smile and move over to let her slip into bed next to me.

"So you've been here for six days already. That's the worst. It's like being trapped. How often are you here?"

"Whenever I get too sick for Mama to take care of me, which is a lot. Mama takes good care of me at home, but I think she likes it better when I'm in the hospital. She thinks it's safer for me. But that's okay because I don't mind being in the hospital like I used to."

Joon looks over at Lulu, raises her eyebrows, and turns back to me. "I don't get that," Joon says. "Being sick is annoying."

"Being sick is awful," I tell her. "But in the hospital, I get to eat. When I'm home, I can't eat at all. When Mama isn't around, the nurses give me things like graham crackers and ice cream. Mama would freak out if she knew."

Joon pulls up the blanket on top of my bed to cover us. "Ew, that's weird. What do you mean, she won't let you eat? Does she starve you?"

I lift my shirt and show them my feeding tube. "I eat through this."

Joon leans over and inspects the plastic in my belly. "Oh, man, that would suck so bad not to be able to eat. When I was little, my evil foster mom wouldn't let me eat. She starved me. It's horrible being hungry."

I scrunch up my nose. "Your foster mom starved you on purpose?"

"Yeah, she starved me on purpose. For some reason, she hated me from the moment I went to live with her. That's why I say she's a dirty, rotten bitch."

I give her a lame smile. "I'm used to not eating. But I still want to eat junk food. All. The. Time."

After watching a show on television together, Joon moves back to Lulu's bed, and as the morning fades into the afternoon, Joon dozes off. Her exhaustion from watching over Lulu the night before takes its toll.

I tell Gwen, "You have no idea how much I wanted to have a tiny bit of the friendship that Joon and Lulu shared."

"It does seem like that are very close," Gwen remarks.

We both turn back and watch just as my mother walks into my hospital room. She stops abruptly and glares at the two teens with her nostrils flaring.

Chapter Forty-One

Mama narrows her eyes as she observes Joon and Lulu laying in the bed side by side. She stops at my bed and kisses me on the forehead, but she never takes her eyes off of the girls.

"Good morning, Molly. Who is your new roommate?"

Lulu puts her index finger over her lips, signaling for Mama to be quiet. Mama's jaw tightens. Her lips pucker together, and she acknowledges Lulu with a brisk nod. Then she turns on her heel and trudges out of our room. There is a bewildered look on Lulu's face as the screech of my mother's voice is heard as she confronts the nurses about my new roommate.

When Mama returns, she pulls a chair up and turns on the television. Lulu lifts her head and looks over at us. She gives Mama a kind smile, but my mother ignores her. A few hours later, when Joon wakes up, Mama goes over to their bed.

"So, who are you two?" Mama says.

Gwen and I can practically see the frost rolling off of her tongue.

Joon pops up and offers my mother her hand. "I'm Joon, and this is Lulu."

Mama studies Joon's hand, the dirty skin, and the black embedded around the cuticles of her fingernails. Joon would've had to take several more showers to clean all the grime away. Mama gives Joon a limp handshake, nods at Lulu, and walks into the bathroom. Leaving the door open, Mama scrubs her hands with soap. I catch Joon's eye and mouth, I'm sorry.

Joon smiles and waves off my apology.

A few hours later, Dr. Becker comes in to see Lulu and me. When he leaves the room, Mama follows him into the hallway.

We can hear her from our beds. "I don't care, Dr. Becker. I want to stay here overnight with Molly."

"Rona, we've discussed this already. Lulu isn't a child, and she deserves her privacy. I don't have another room to move Molly into. Besides, Lulu is a really nice girl, and I'm sure Molly will enjoy having someone closer to her own age to talk to for a change. Not only that, but I want you to go home and spend time with Ava and Kurtis. Molly will be fine. Trust me."

The discussion stops for several seconds before Mama speaks again. "Fine, but I'm not happy about this."

"I know you're not, Rona. You're a good mom. Now, go home and be a mom to your other daughter. We have this here."

Mama stomps into the room and picks her coat up from the chair. "Okay, I'm going home, but if you need me"—Mama glares at Joon and Lulu with a pinched expression—"you just tell the nurse to call me, and I'll come right back."

"Okay, Mama."

Mama moves closer to Joon and Lulu. "Girls, Molly needs her sleep, so please be respectful and keep quiet so she can rest."

"Don't worry, we will," Joon says cheerfully.

The three of us say nothing as we listen to the click-clack of Mama's heels moving down the hallway until she is gone.

I turn my head toward Joon and Lulu. "Sometimes Mama isn't the nicest person. She's overprotective of me, and when that happens, she acts rude. I'm sorry if she hurt your feelings."

Joon chuckles. "That's nothing. Your mom was nice compared to the way some people treat us. You would think being homeless is contagious."

I swing my feet over the side of the bed and sit up. "You're homeless?"

"Yeah. It's not the greatest life, but it's a life," Lulu says.

I move to a chair next to Lulu's bed and sit. "Will you tell me what it's like? I've never known anyone homeless before, just what I've seen on TV. Do you have a shopping cart that you push around?"

Joon and Lulu snicker.

"No, we're fresh out of shopping carts. We keep our stuff in plastic bags," Joon explains.

"Wow," I breathe. "Will you tell me everything? I wanna know what it's like and how you live and where you sleep and everything. Is that okay? Do you think I'm weird for asking you to tell me about it?"

Joon pulls a chair up next to mine and sits down. "No, it's not weird. If more people were curious instead of judgmental, we'd all be better off. What do you want to know first?"

"I don't know. What do you eat?"

"Food," Joon says. The two teens laugh.

Joon explains further. "We beg for money so we can buy food. Cheap food. If we don't have any money we pick food from the trash . . . that's called Dumpster diving."

"Oh." I try to smile, but my expression is tinged with disgust. "Um, where do you sleep?"

"Depends. Mostly in abandoned houses and buildings. Sometimes in a church, and if we're really, really desperate, I mean it's gotta be so cold we'll-die-outside desperate, we'll stay in a homeless shelter. They're the worst."

"Why?" I ask.

Joon pauses. "Because they're dangerous."

"Dangerous, how?" I ask.

Joon takes in a long breath. "Well, lots of times people staying in the shelters steal your stuff. Some of them are really high or drunk, and they fight all night long."

Joon glances over at Lulu. "We have to go to the bathroom together because sometimes women get raped in shelters."

I stare at Joon. I wait for her to tell me she is joking. When she doesn't, I shake my head. "I . . . I could never do what you do. I would be too scared."

Joon smirks. "You get kind of used to it. Don't get me wrong, we never let our guard down, but it becomes like anything else . . . routine."

I shift in my chair. "How many friends do you have?"

Joon's eyes light up. "I don't know. Lots. But only two good ones. Lulu and a guy named Skinner. We all stick together. Look out for one another."

Joon leans into me. "But Lulu is the best friend I've ever had in my whole life. Do you have a best friend?"

I stare at my lap. "No. I had one friend, her name was Veronica. We were friends for a while, but then something happened, and I ended up stuck in bed. I thought we were best friends, but when I went back to school, Veronica didn't bother with me anymore."

We are all quiet for a moment. "Hey, how do you take a bath?" I ask.

Joon puts her hand over mine, and I look at the filth under and around her fingernails. "We don't take baths or showers. We wash in sinks in public bathrooms. There are lots of things that are hard about the life we live."

I look over at Lulu, who hasn't said much. She has fallen asleep. A slow smile builds on my lips. "Will you take me to the streets where you live so I can see it for myself?"

Joon slowly shakes her head. "I don't think that's such a good idea, Molly. You're sick, and besides, your mom would have me arrested," Joon says with a giggle.

I trace the black around Joon's cuticles with my index finger. "I'm very sick and probably going to die if I don't get a kidney soon. If I'm gonna die, don't you think I should be able to do something that I've never done before? You know, see things that I've never seen?"

Joon pushes my hair behind my ear. "You make a good point."

Joon is quiet for a minute. "Okay. Your nurse comes in at one a.m. We'll sneak out then. She'll come back at seven in the morning, so that'll give us five or six hours. Are you sure you want to do this?"

I give her a huge smile. "I want to do this more than anything."

Gwen grabs my hand. "Wow. Did you really go?"

"I sure did, and it was the best time I ever had. I'll show you."

Chapter Forty-Two

When the nurse leaves my room just before one thirty in the morning, I dress in my regular clothes and turn to Joon.

She looks back at me and grins. "You ready to go?"

My complexion is ruddy as I grab my coat. I stand near the door and bounce on my tiptoes. "Yeah, I'm ready."

"Are you sure you want to do this?"

I put my hands on my hips. "How old were you when you started living on the streets?"

"Twelve."

I zip up my coat. "Were you sure that you wanted to live on the streets?"

"Hell, no. But I didn't have any other choice. I ran away because my foster mom and brother were abusing me. Anything would have been better than the way I was living."

"Well, I'm twelve. The same age you were when you became homeless, and I haven't lived at all. So yeah, I'm definitely sure I want to do this."

Joon strolls over to me and grabs my arm gently. "You're a gutsy little thing, aren't you?"

I nod.

"Fine. Let's do this," she says.

While Joon walks up to the nurses' station, I go the opposite way. I avoid the elevator, as Joon had instructed; I stand just inside the stairwell and wait. A few minutes later, Joon pushes through the heavy steel door.

"All clear," Joon announces. "Now listen, we have to take it easy, and if you get tired or feel sick or anything, you have to promise to tell me."

"I promise," I say, raising my right hand.

At the bottom of the stairs, we exit off to the side of the lobby.

Joon glances at me. "Just act natural."

I lift my chin toward her. I'm practically glued to Joon as we walk out onto the city streets of Philadelphia.

After a minute passes, I say, "I've always been brought into the hospital through the emergency room. Seeing the city from the sidewalk looks so much different. There are so many . . . people."

"Yep, the city is full of them," Joon jokes.

"Where are we gonna go?"

Joon pulls the hood up on her thin coat and then she pulls mine up for me. "Don't worry. I have a plan."

"It's freezing. I don't know how you can sleep out here."

Joon grabs my hand as we walk. "Well, when you're on the streets without a place to stay, you can't really sleep at night. You keep moving, so you don't freeze to death. But there are a few places we can go."

We walk for at least twenty minutes before turning up a small alley. At the far end, I can see people standing around a fire.

I grip Joon's hand tighter. "Do you know them?"

"I'm sure I'll know someone."

"What if you don't? What if they hurt us?"

"Unless they're total assholes they won't hurt us."

The little color I have drains away from my face.

Joon studies my expression for a moment. "I'm only kidding. We'll be fine. For the most part, homeless people fight over food and stuff, we don't fight just because someone needs to stop by a fire and warm up. Unless of course, they're drunk, then that's a different story. Oh, and people will kill over booze." Joon doesn't smile.

I hesitantly walk with Joon. I grab onto the sleeve of her coat and pinch the fabric with my fingers. She keeps moving up to the group of people gathered around the fire.

"Hey, Harry," Joon says. "How's it going?"

I let out a huge breath.

The guy gives her a wave. "You know, it's going okay. I heard there was a fire in the place you were living in. Everybody make it out?"

"Yeah, Lulu's in the hospital, and we all got some cuts and burns, but we're fine."

The boy standing next to Harry asks, "What? Am I invisible?"

"No. Sorry, Rudy. How are you?"

"I'm good, thanks for asking," Rudy says. Then he looks at me. "Who are you?"

"Molly."

"How long have you been out here?"

I glance at Joon nervously. "Um, a couple of days?"

Rudy grins. "Are you asking me? I thought I asked you the question, Molly. Where did you find this one?" he says, turning to Joon.

"Don't be a dick, Rudy. You're making her nervous. Remember when you first got to the streets and how scary it was and you're a boy? Try being a girl on the streets. Like she said, she's been out here a couple of days."

Rudy presses his hand against his heart, gesturing he is hurt. "Oh, come on. I'm just messin' with her. If she's gonna be out here, she better get used to it."

My eyes grow as I look at Joon and step closer to her.

A short while later, Joon and I leave the group and walk back up the alley.

"That Rudy boy wasn't very nice," I say.

Joon shrugs. "That's why we call him Rudy. You know, because he's rude. His real name is Matthew or something like that. Out here you gotta pick your battles and never let anyone smell your fear. Even if you're scared shitless you can't let it show."

I grimace. "Got it. Never show anyone my fear. That sounds simple."

Joon glances at me. I roll my eyes and we chuckle.

"Where are we going now?" I ask.

Joon crosses her arms over her chest to protect herself from the cold wind. "To show you some of Philly."

"I'm not sure if I should be excited or scared," I tell Joon.

"You should be both," Joon says seriously.

Chapter Forty-Three

I remember my body working against me as we walked in the biting cold night. The cold air seeped into my bones, and I felt as if I was freezing from the inside out. Every muscle grew stiff and I struggled to breathe. I did my best not to let Joon see me fighting to pull air into my lungs. She didn't seem to notice. She stays focused on where we were going. Besides, it didn't matter how bad I felt, I refused to give up and go back to the hospital . . . I wanted those five or six hours more than I ever wanted anything else in my life. Drive and determination saw me through the pain and kept me on the journey.

"Where are we going?" I ask in the vision.

"Train station," Joon says, waggling her eyebrows.

"Are we going on a train?" I ask her.

"Nope. The train station is where homeless people hang out. It's mostly warm in the winter, and there are lots of benches and bathrooms."

When we arrive at the station, there are very few people there. We take an escalator down to the train platform. At the bottom of the escalator, we turn right and keep walking. When we reach the end, we sit down and lean against the dirty tile wall. Soon two staggering teen girls approach us.

"Hey, Joon. Hi, girl. How are ya?" one girl says. She's wearing too much black eye shadow.

Joon stands and gives both girls a quick hug. "Hell, girl. You smell like old man booze. You're drunk."

"It's called whiskey, and it ain't old man booze, it's get real drunk booze. Besides, it's cheap," says the girl wearing too much black eye shadow.

Joon and the other two girls giggle, but I sit against the wall, my mouth hanging open and eyes popping out of my head.

Joon shuffles her feet. "Lulu and I were staying in an abandoned house, but it burned down. So we're looking for somewhere else to go. You know of anything?"

The drunk girl wearing too much black eye shadow sways. Then her upper body jerks forward at the hips, and she catches herself before she falls. "No, man. There ain't no place I know of. Whoooooo's your lil' friend?"

I stand quickly and speak with clarity. "I'm Molly. It's nice to meet you."

"Ha! Who's the princess, Joon?"

Joon takes hold of my hand. "Molly's a friend of mine. So back off."

Drunk girl wearing too much black eye shadow puts her arms up, palms facing us. "Hey. You know me. I ain't into starting no shit with nobody. I don't fight wit' nobody out here."

Joon's mouth goes slack. "I know, Stripes. Molly and me are just trying to spend a little time together. That's all."

Stripes grabs her friend's hand. "We'll catch ya later, Joon," she says as we watch them walk off.

Joon and I sit back down, and she opens her bag and digs through it.

"So, you were about my age when you started living on the street," I say. "What did you do when you first came here?"

Joon continues to dig. "I met a lady who helped me. Then I met other people along the way." She pulls out a pack of Life Savers from her bag. Joon picks lint and other crud from the one on top. "Want one?"

I take a piece of candy out of the roll and pop it in my mouth.

"The streets haven't been all that kind to me. I found myself in some trouble a few years ago. I've had friends die at the hands of pimps and assholes."

I clutch at my throat. "You know people who've died out here?"

"We all know people who died on the streets. The streets are brutal, and I know every day when I wake up it could be the last. I never know if I'll starve to death, get murdered, robbed, raped, run over by a car. Being homeless exposes me to bad shit every day."

"Weren't you ever so scared that you wanted to go to the police for protection?" I ask her.

Joon pops another piece of candy into her mouth and sucks on it. "Sure. Sometimes it gets so scary I wish there was someone I could run to, who would protect me from all the bad things. The reality is that it doesn't exist. The cops don't have the time. Plus, most of us are underage and can end up back in the system or with an abusive parent. Besides, there's a lot of good things about being out here too, like most everyone who lives on the streets is nice, and we try to help each other."

I lean my head back on the tile. "That must be nice. Having people to help you. I have doctors and nurses who try to help me, but they're paid to do that."

Joon smiles. "Yeah, it's pretty cool. We're like a secret community. Almost makes up for some of the assholes out here."

Joon gets up on her knees and looks me over. "How are you feeling?"

"What do you mean?"

"Well, I know you were getting tired, and that's why I brought us down here so you can rest."

I nudge her shoulder with my hand. "How did you know I was tired?"

"Because Lulu has the same problem with her kidneys as you and when she gets tired I can tell. You looked just like she does when she needs to see a doctor. That's when I know to push her to see Dr. Becker. You're both ridiculous thinking you can hide it from me. It's so dumb."

We both laugh. "Yeah, I feel more rested. Where are we going next?"

"To find something to eat. I'm starving," Joon announces.

"Do we have any money?"

Joon frowns. "Of course not. That's why we have to find something to eat."

Chapter Forty-Four

After we leave the station, we walk several blocks before Joon stops in front of a fast-food restaurant where we can see the people inside eating their food. They look like college students, their books spread around the tables, enjoying a meal with friends. Joon watches the people through the window and then she places her hands and the side of her face against the glass. I see tears roll down her cheeks.

"Why are you crying?" I ask.

"Sometimes it makes me sad to see what my life might have been like if my real parents hadn't died. Now that Lulu is so sick, I look at those people inside and realize I'm probably gonna lose the best friend I've ever had. I feel like I'm always losing things. You know?"

"Yeah, I do know. I've been losing parts of me for a long time too."

Joon turns and faces me. "Yeah, I guess you can understand."

Joon moves away from me and looks inside the trash can near the door of the restaurant. She pulls a bag from the bin. "Bingo! There are some French fries and a piece of burger."

She pulls out several fries and offers them. I grab three and shove them into my mouth. Then Joon hands me the small piece of hamburger, and I bite into half of it, giving the rest back to her.

As I chew the burger my eyelids ease closed. "Mmmmm," I say, "that's so delicious. It tastes like heaven."

Joon cocks her head to the side. "You really have been deprived. Come on. Let's keep moving."

As we walk again, I yammer about how delicious the fries and burger were. In midstride Joon stops suddenly, and it startles me.

"What?" I practically yell.

"I gave you that stuff to eat from the trash. I hope you don't get sick."

I smirk at her. "Too late for that, I've been sick for a long time."

Joon places her arm over my shoulder, gives me a quick squeeze, and we march on into the dark, cold night.

***

"That's some adventure you were on," Gwen says.

"Yeah, it was awesome."

"But you looked like you were really scared."

"Yeah, I definitely was. It wasn't a monster-under-my-bed scary. It was doing something unknown and being vulnerable. The craziest thing was, aside from the fear, I had never felt so alive."

Chapter Forty-Five

J oon and I walk and chat for another twenty minutes before she glances over at me.

"You don't feel good, right?" Joon asks.

I shake my head, and her eyes bug out.

"It's those fucking French fries!" Joon yells.

"No, it's not. My stomach is fine. It's my kidneys." I slow my pace and look at my new friend. "Is there somewhere we can rest?"

"Are you kidding me? No. We need to get you back to the hospital. I never should've taken you outta there."

I stop walking, cross my arms over my chest, and stomp my foot. "No! Stop! Coming out here with you is the best thing I've ever done."

I bite my bottom lip to stop it from trembling. Tears slide down my cheeks. "I've been so lonely. I know Mama loves me, but sometimes it feels like I'm being smothered. I have doctors and nurses who are constantly checking in, but I'm lonely all the time. Tonight I get to be normal, and I'm not ready to go back. Pleeease."

Joon scans me from head to toe, then clears her throat to break the spell. "I know what it's like to be lonely. I understand why this is so important to you. Here's what we'll do: we can make one last stop before we head back to the hospital. Deal?"

"Deal," I say.

Our eyes lock. "My father tells me looking into someone's eyes is a window into their soul."

"Oh, yeah? And what do you see in mine?" Joon asks.

"I see kindness and sadness and strength."

Joon looks away and puts her arm through mine to take some of my weight off my own legs.

When we reach the end of the block a car pulls over and stops beside us. The driver puts down his window. "You girls looking to make a little extra dough tonight?"

Joon's eyes narrow, and she glares back at him. "Piss off."

"You don't gotta play hard to get . . . I'm willing to pay."

Joon pulls her arm away from mine and steps closer to the car. "Listen, asshole, I said piss off. We ain't selling anything."

The man leans across the passenger seat and looks at me. "How about you? Just 'cause your friend doesn't want to earn some money doesn't mean you have to follow her lead. You gotta mind of your own. Right?"

I step to my right, so I am practically hidden behind Joon. She drops her bag to the ground, her feet are spread apart, and her hands ball into fists. The man chuckles. "You and your friend hiding behind you are two scruffy whores. Nobody's gonna want to tap those asses." Then the tires of his car screech as he races away.

Joon turns around and gently takes my upper arm in her hand. "You okay?" she asks.

"I'm fine. What was that all about?"

"He wanted to pay us for sex."

"Ew. Are you kidding?"

Joon lets out a loud breath. "I wish I were. I told you before, it is hard living on the streets. You put up with a lot of bullshit out here. You have to be willing to fight, because if you're not, people will tear you to shreds."

The air I am exhaling from lungs is visible in the cold night. My shivering turns into a full-body shake. My bright red cheeks look raw.

Joon and I continue to walk until we come to a convenience store. We go inside and Joon pulls a dollar from somewhere under her layers of clothing.

She buys a hot chocolate and hands it to me. "Here. Drink this. It'll warm you up."

I take the cup from her hand. "What about you?"

Joon waves me off. "I'm fine. I'm used to this."

I take a sip of the hot liquid and hold the cup out to Joon. "We can share it."

Joon grabs the cup and takes a big gulp. "Mm, that's good. See, you'd make it just fine out here."

I beam at Joon. "Really? Do you think so?"

Joon giggles. "Um, no. I was only kidding."

I hang my head.

Joon lifts my chin. "Hey, look. I was just messin' with you. I think you could do anything. You've got guts. You have a little bit of badass in you. But someone like you doesn't belong out here. You have parents that take care of you. The streets are only for the people that nobody wants to let in. We're like rabid dogs. People think we aren't human or that we're all crazy or drug addicts. Homelessness scares people who live in houses. The thing is, we're just regular people with nowhere to go."

I look down at my sneakers. "I wish there was something I could do to help you."

Joon hands the hot chocolate back. "It's not your problem, kid. Let's get going. Our last stop is somewhere special."

I smile. "Will we need a gun where we're going?"

"You're pretty funny," Joon remarks. "No, a gun won't be necessary."

As we leave the convenience store, I tell Joon, "Mama would be so angry if she knew I'd snuck out of the hospital to spend time on the streets of Philadelphia. But right now, what Mama thinks doesn't matter. All that matters is getting out of this cold and to our final destination."

Chapter Forty-Six

J oon and I walk hand in hand up a long cement staircase. I look up at the
building and admire the beautiful panels of stained glass lit from inside.
Joon pulls a large wooden door open and we step inside.

"Wow, it's so warm in here," I say. "So this is it? Our last destination is a
church?"

"Yep. It's really late to be showing up, but Father John doesn't turn anyone
away."

Inside the church, people are sleeping everywhere. There are old people, young
people, people in groups, and people all alone. I remember it was a beautiful and
tragic sight.

"This is incredible," I say as I look around at everyone. "I don't think I'll ever
forget this moment."

Joon gives me a look of understanding.

I say, "Among all this destitution, there's a sense of community. I can tell that
everyone here wants to belong, to have a place that feels like home. They want to
be with other people. It's so easy to see."

Joon takes my hand. "You see things clearly for someone who has never been
on the streets."

"That's true," I say. "But I'm no stranger to loneliness."

I follow Joon to the front of the church. We step through a doorway and into
a kitchen. A priest is sitting at a table with a cup of coffee in front of him and
reading a book. He looks up and stands when he sees us.

"Joon. It's wonderful to see you again. It's been quite some time. How've you
been?"

Joon walks up to him, and they embrace. "I've been good. I don't know if you
heard, but Lulu found out that her kidneys are failing."

"No. I didn't know. I'm very sorry to hear that. Where is she now?"

"She's in the hospital. We got caught in a house fire and she breathed in a lot
of smoke. But her doctor is more worried about her kidneys right now so he's
keeping her there," Joon explains.

The priest looks at me. "Who's your new friend?"

Joon turns. "This is Molly."

"Hi," I murmur.

"Hi, Molly. I'm Father John, and you don't have to worry, everyone is welcome here."

"Thank you," I say, eyeing the muffins on the counter beside him.

Father John follows my gaze. "Would you like a muffin?"

"Yes, please."

Joon and I sit at the table and Father John brings over two chocolate chip muffins on small paper plates.

I look at Joon and then down at the muffin.

"Are you sure you can eat that?" Joon whispers.

I lean into her and whisper back, "No. And I don't care."

My nose hovers above the muffin and I inhale its wonderful, scrumptious scent. Then, I peel back the paper and take a big bite as Joon and Father John watch.

Joon breaks the silence. "Molly hasn't eaten in a while."

"Yeah, I haven't eaten in like a long time."

"It's okay. You're welcome to another one when you're finished," Father John says, patting my hand.

"This is the first time Molly has ever been in the city without her parents," Joon tells the priest. "I was hoping we could grab some blankets and sit in the pews. We only have about an hour before we have to head back to the hospital."

"What hospital? What are you talking about?"

"Oh, sorry. Molly is Lulu's roommate at the hospital. She's been sick for a long time and is waiting for a kidney donor. She wanted to see what it was like to live on the streets, so we came out for a while."

The priest rubs his forehead with his thumb and index finger. "Joon, you know better than to do something like this. If Molly is ill, she should be in the hospital."

"Please, Father John," Joon moans, "I promised you I would never lie and that's the only reason I told you what we're doing. It's just another hour. What difference does an hour make?"

The priest bows his head. It looks like he was praying. After a few moments, he looks at me. "Molly, what you've done concerns me. If the hospital finds out you're missing, they'll be worried and call the police."

"It doesn't matter what happens," I tell the priest. "I've been sick for a long time, and I know my body is failing me. Joon gave me a chance to live for a few hours. It's been tough for me to be trapped in my house with no friends or anyone besides my family to talk to. I've had so many operations and procedures that I can't count them anymore. I asked Joon to bring me out, and even though she didn't think it was a good idea, she did it for me. All we want to do is hang here for a while and then I'll go back to the hospital. If anyone finds out that I left, it'll be my fault. What are they going to do? Punish me? I've been punished enough, and there's nothing anyone could do to me that could make me feel worse than my own body has made me feel."

Father John's eyes glisten. He sits quietly, contemplating.

"Okay," he finally agrees. "You two go grab a couple of blankets, but only for an hour."

Joon and I go back out to the central part of the church, and she turns to me. "Well, look at you getting bossy with a priest."

"Yeah, well. I'm tired of adults telling me what to do. Just because he's a priest doesn't mean he gets to decide."

Wrapped in scratchy wool blankets, Joon and I sit in a pew in the middle of the church. I stare at the altar.

"I wonder why God let me be so sick," I say without looking at Joon. Then, "It's so peaceful in this church. I love it here."

"Yeah, I always mean to come here more often, but then things happen. It's a nice place and Father John is the best," Joon tells me.

Behind the altar, there is a large cross. I stare at it. "Do you believe in God?" I ask Joon.

Joon stares at the cross too. "I didn't use to, but then Father John made me believe that He exists. I don't know what God is, but it makes me feel better to pretend that someone loves me."

I nod. "My parents believe in God."

"What about you? Do you believe in God?" Joon asks.

"It's hard to say. I want to believe there's something after I die, but I'm not sure. Like I said, if there is a God, then why make me suffer?"

"I think we all suffer in some way. Some people worse than others, but that's just life, I think," Joon says.

"Well, I know that I'm tired of being sick and that things aren't always what they seem; I had a teacher who said that to me once."

"How do you mean?"

"Well, take my feeding tube. Mama doesn't let me eat anything because she's protecting me from getting sick. But I ate tonight, and my stomach is fine. What if my mom doesn't know my body as well as she thinks she does? What if things aren't always what they seem?"

"I get it now. I think people thought I was happy in my foster home although I'm not sure why they would ever think that. Anyway, the things that were done to me inside my house couldn't be seen from the outside."

Joon looks over at me. "Did you ever ask a doctor if you could get your feeding tube out?"

"Mama will never let that happen. Never. Unless, of course, I get a kidney donor or make it to my eighteenth birthday. Once I'm eighteen, my mom can't stop me from doing anything."

I lie across the pew and look up at the painted ceiling. "Look how gorgeous those angels are."

Joon lies on the other side. "Yeah, they look happy and peaceful. It's like they're looking down on us."

"I hope you're right." I close my eyes and let the silence of the church fill me. "My body feels much better, my aches are almost gone," I tell Joon.

"That's good to hear," she says.

"This has been the most special night ever. I don't want it to end. I was thinking maybe I'd run away and stay with you until I die," I say, half serious.

Joon and I lie there until it's time to leave. As we get to the door of the church, Father John pulls us aside.

He looks directly at Joon. "You know, I never do this because I would have to do it for everyone," he says, handing her a twenty-dollar bill. "But in this case, I would feel much better knowing Molly took a taxi back to the hospital."

My eyes turn soft and fill with an inner glow. Father John opens the church door for us, and there is a taxi waiting at the bottom of the steps. "I called the taxi for you," he says.

Joon hugs the priest and thanks him for being so "cool." Then I step up to him and wrap my arms around his waist. "Thank you for not making me leave. Being here makes me feel great."

Father John places his open hand on my back and smiles sheepishly.

"And thanks for not making me walk back." I give him a weak but gratifying smile.

"You're welcome, Molly. I'll pray for your good health."

As I walk down the cement stairs, I grab Joon's hand. "I had a really great time. Thank you for sharing it with me."

Joon grins, but she can't hide the sadness in her watery eyes. "You got it. Let's get back before they find you missing."

Chapter Forty-Seven

G wen leans back on her elbows. "That was a really nice thing that Joon did for you. It was kind of risky. Were you happy to get back to the hospital?"

I shoot Gwen a mischievous smile. "Yeah, kind of. The streets can be terrifying. I really missed Joon after Lulu was released from the hospital."

I close my eyes and imagine Joon with her long, blond hair and crystal blue eyes. I remember how her smile could light up my day. It's nice to remember her.

I glance at Gwen. "Joon was the kind of person you'd consider yourself lucky to have met. She was just . . . special. You know?"

Gwen nods.

I sigh. "You know, Mama didn't like Joon or Lulu because they were homeless. She told me they were both degenerates. I was so mad at her for judging them like that. Joon was awesome, the complete opposite of Mama. All Joon wanted to do was love and be loved. It was that simple."

I think about Joon and Lulu . . . they were a team. A wave of sadness washes over me for all that I missed out on in my short life. The twosome may have had nothing and been homeless, but they were the luckiest girls I'd ever met.

I smile at Gwen. "Joon was like an old soul. Lulu knew she was going to die, and sometimes she got really depressed. When that would happen, Joon would climb into her bed and hold her while she bawled. That used to make me cry too."

"Because you knew Lulu was going to die?"

"Yeah, but also because they were so close and I didn't have anyone like that in my life. It opened my eyes to something else I was missing. You know, a best friend that would do anything for me. It makes me feel kind of selfish now."

Gwen rests her head on my shoulder. "You're not selfish, you're twelve. Anyway, I'll be that friend. I promise I'll never leave you."

I give Gwen a tight hug. "Thank you."

Gwen yawns loudly. "Let's watch the rest . . . I wanna see you sneak back into your room. Then I'm gonna get some sleep. Dead people get tired, too, if you haven't noticed," she says with a smirk.

***

Joon and I get out of the taxi a block away from the hospital entrance. We walk into the lobby and slip inside the stairway. I look up at the stairs and what lies ahead of me.

I grab Joon's arm. "Maybe we should just take the elevator."

"Are you kidding? We'll definitely get caught," Joon says. Then she looks closely at me. "You're too tired?"

"I'm too weak. How about if we just take it one step at a time?"

I hold onto the railing and take one step. Several minutes later, we have climbed ten steps.

Joon puts her hand on my lower back. "Okay, so we have to climb four stories. At this rate I estimate that we'll be there in about six and a half weeks."

Joon and I laugh. Then I sit down and shimmy backward on my butt up to the eleventh step.

Joon puts her hands on her hips. "Oh, right, I see. Well, by my new calculation, this will only take us three weeks." She goes down two steps and keeps her back to me. "I'm gonna give you a piggyback ride. Get on."

"You can't carry me all that way."

Joon shoots me a cynical look over her shoulder. "There are a lot of things I can't do, but carrying you up these steps isn't one of them. And you need to hurry up before we both turn into pumpkins."

I stand and hoist myself onto Joon's back. She rests at each new floor we climb, but she gets us to our destination. I squat in the stairwell as Joon goes to make sure we can sneak back into my hospital room.

"Okay," Joon says. "All of the nurses are at the station. I'm gonna distract them, and you hustle into your room. Ready?"

I wave her off. "How about if I sleep here for a couple of hours first?" I joke.

Joon gives me a stern look. "Get ready, here we go."

Joon takes off for the nurses' station as I duck down the hallway, past sleeping kids, and into my room. I jump into bed as quickly as I can and pull the covers over me.

All the while, Lulu is watching me.

"Where have you been?" Lulu asks.

"Um. Um. We went out for a while," I tell her.

Lulu pushes herself up on her elbows. "We who?"

"Me and Joon?"

"Joon smuggled you out of the hospital?"

Lulu sounds angry.

"Joon didn't smuggle me out. I asked her to take me, and so she did," I explain.

Lulu lays flat on her back. "That's my girl."

"Wait. You're not mad?"

"Nah. Why would I be mad? I've met your mother, and I don't think you'll be doing anything adventurous with her anytime soon."

Joon waltzes into the room, interrupting our conversation. She looks from me to Lulu. "Did Molly tell you what we did?"

Lulu beams at her. "No, but she did tell me you took her outta here for a while. That was pretty freakin' cool of you."

Joon hops on the edge of Lulu's bed. "Well, I'm a pretty freakin' cool chick."

Lulu grabs for Joon's hand. "Was it fun?"

Joon smirks as she looks over at me. "Ask Molly."

I pull my arms from under my blanket and gush about the things we did. While I am gabbing, Joon moves off of Lulu's bed and over to mine. She is next to my bed and watching me closely.

"What?" I ask impatiently.

"Um. Molly. The nurse will be here soon. Do you think maybe you should put your pajamas back on? She might think it's odd you're wearing street clothes."

I look down at myself and laugh. "Guess what?"

"I can hardly wait for you to tell me," Joon responds.

"I still have my sneakers on too."

I push the covers back and swing my feet over the side of the bed, then pause for a moment and close my eyes. My hands are gripping the edge of the mattress. When I open them, Joon is holding my shoulders to steady me.

"Here. Let me help."

A few minutes after Joon helps settle me into bed, the nurse comes in, just like clockwork, to check on us.

***

"That night with Joon was the last time I enjoyed being alive," I tell Gwen.

Gwen shimmies closer. "I'm happy you had the chance to explore the world a little . . . even for a short time."

I stand and look around Limbo. "It's so wonderful here."

"Yes, better than anywhere on Earth," Gwen adds.

"Can I show you one more thing that happened?"

"Yes, of course," Gwen says.

Chapter Forty-Eight

I'm lying in my bed the next morning and Lulu is in hers. Joon wakes and we both watch her saunter to the bathroom.

When the bathroom door closes, Lulu says, "Joon's the best thing that ever happened to me. I don't know what I'd do without her. She promised to take care of me, and she does. Joon never breaks her promises."

"That's nice," I say to Lulu.

She inhales and rolls to face me. "No, I mean, for real. There was this one time with a homeless woman named Rita. Well, Rita and Joon barely knew each other, but for some reason she trusted Joon. Anyway, Rita asked Joon to hold her money for her because her boyfriend was trying to steal it and she didn't have a good hiding place. She told Joon she'd catch up with her when she could to get it back. Rita made Joon promise not to spend the money."

My eyes are wide as I listen to Lulu. "Did Rita come back for the money?" I ask.

"Well, wait, I'll get to that. So it was ridiculously hot out and hard to find food in the Dumpsters that wasn't spoiled. Joon and I went a couple of days without eating hardly anything at all. We were so hungry we would've done anything to eat. So I told her we should borrow the money she was holding for Rita, that we'd pay it back. Joon was like, 'No way, I made that lady a promise and I won't break it.' If she finds me today and wants the money, I gotta have it for her."

"Wow, were you upset? Since you were so hungry?"

Lulu shakes her head. "Oh, hell, no. I was really proud of Joon. It was right then that I knew I could trust her to always keep her word. And guess what else?"

"What?" I ask with anticipation.

"Rita found us the next day, and she was looking for her money. So Joon gave it to her. Rita turned around and gave Joon twenty bucks for keeping her word, and we got to eat."

Chapter Forty-Nine

G wen and I stop watching my vision. I ask, "Do you remember the journal that my dad gave to me?"

"Yeah, you called it Alice. Right?"

"That's the one. Well, I didn't write in it a lot, but when I did, it was important. Anyway, I didn't know what I was going to do with it, and so I decided to ask Joon to keep it for me. I made her promise me that if I ever died, and she found out about it, she'd give the journal to my dad," I explain. "Let me show you."

It's the morning of Lulu's release from the hospital, and Joon bounds into the room with a cheery hello.

"Can you leave now?" Joon asks Lulu.

"Nah. I have to wait for Dr. Becker to come to see me. Then he'll let me go," she explains.

I interrupt them. "I wish you weren't leaving. I like having you guys around."

Joon walks over to my bed. "Yeah, you and me had some great times together. Your mom is kinda weird, but you're a cool kid."

"My mama is a helicopter—she hovers." I grow quiet for a moment. "Can I ask you to do me a favor?"

Joon looks at me with a quizzical expression. "Sure. If I can help you, I will. What do you need?"

I reach under my pillow. "I want you to keep this for me," I say, and hold up the journal for Joon to see. I thrust it toward her. "If anything happens to me, I need you to give it to my dad. It has all of my last wishes."

Joon gives me a curious look. "Why your dad?"

"Because you can't give it to my mom. She won't talk to me about dying. I can talk to my dad about anything. He's a really nice person. He'd want to know my wishes. You know, like who should have my stuff."

Joon takes the journal from me. "How will I know if anything happens to you? We'll probably never see each other again after today."

"You can ask Dr. Becker. He'll know."

"What if he doesn't?" Joon asks. "What if I never hear about you again? Then what?"

"If that happens, then you can read it. But if you do find out I died, I wrote my address on the inside cover so you can bring it to my house. But remember, you can't give it to anyone but my dad. Make sure you tell him I only want him to read it."

Joon holds the journal against her heart. "Fine. I promise I'll try not to fuck this up."

I giggle. "I love how you talk; you're so funny." I pause for a moment, looking at the older girl. "Thanks for doing this for me. I don't have any friends, and there's no one else I can trust with my journal."

Joon gives me a dazzling smile. "So you decided to trust me, who you've known for less than a week."

"Yeah, that's what I want. I heard from someone that you always keep your promises," I say, glancing over at Lulu.

Joon leans down and hugs me. "Okay. Sure."

"You promise to keep it safe and not lose it?"

Joon brushes my arm with her hand. "I promise."

"And you can't read it. Okay? It's for my dad."

"Yep, got it."

"Unless you have to read it, like I said before."

"Yep, I got that, too."

I lay my hand over my heart. "Thank you, Joon."

"You're welcome." Joon kisses my forehead. "You're gonna get better. I just know it."

I look up at the ceiling tiles and exhale. "Do you think so?"

"Yeah, I do," Joon says.

Dr. Becker walks into the room, and the girls turn their attention to him.

"I see you've enjoyed Joon's and Lulu's company," Dr. Becker says to me.

"Yeah, they're great," I say.

Gwen asks, "Do you think Joon gave your journal to your dad?"

"If Joon found out I died, she did. Lulu said Joon never breaks her promises. I would be very happy if I knew she did."

"Joon is awfully special," Gwen admits.

"She really is. I learned a lot from her in a short time. She taught me that fleeting moments of joy can mean more than a lifetime of mediocrity. My time with Joon finally gave me something in my life worth remembering. I consider myself lucky to have been loved by Joon and Lulu, even if it didn't last that long."

Gwen rolls onto her side. "That's so true. It's the smallest things that people do for each other that mean the most. Now it's time for us to rest because there's that other thing I need to show you."

I let out a loud sigh. "Fine."

Chapter Fifty

T he next morning, Gwen and I are sitting at a picnic table covered with a
 beautiful white cloth. There're fruits, pancakes, eggs, and lots of bacon on
the table. I fill a plate and eat.

"You and me both like the same food," Gwen remarks, crunching on a piece of
bacon.

"Yeah. There are soooo many foods that I love. So I figure, what the heck, may
as well imagine them so we can feast on them."

"I was wondering. What happened with Joon and Lulu after you left the
hospital? Did you stay in touch with them?"

I shake my head. "There wasn't a way for me to keep in touch. Even if there was,
Mama would've never allowed it. I told you. Mama didn't like them."

Gwen and I watch my old life while we eat breakfast.

The weather is no longer cold. It's the middle of summer and I am laying in my
bed with the covers draped over me. There is no sound except for the hum of the
air conditioning cooling the house.

It's been nearly five months since I've seen Joon and Lulu. I have continued my
dialysis treatments. It's a grim time for me because I'm not getting better.

Gwen looks over at me and disrupts the vision. Her eyes are set hard. "It's time,
Molly."

I glance at her and raise my eyebrows. My thoughts seize. Gwen sugarcoats
nothing. I worry about what she wants me to see; she's made it clear it will be
important.

"Please," Gwen says softly.

"Sure. This is going to upset me. Right?" I ask her.

"Right."

I follow Gwen down a narrow path of dense, brittle weeds that have grown far
above our heads. I can't see where we are going, and that makes me both spooked
and tense. The path branches off in various directions. We keep going straight.
The trail finally opens to a remote river. It's gloomy here. There are no flowers.

The sky is covered by murky gray clouds, and there's mud everywhere. The river water gushes with ferocious strength. It looks dangerous. The sound is deafening.

I scream over the sound of the water, "Where did this water come from?!"

"I brought it here with my thoughts!" Gwen yells back.

Gwen takes my hand. "We need the power of the water for you to see the present. Once you learn to focus, you'll be able to see the present from anywhere. But this is where you begin."

We are both watching the brown water whoosh by, and the riverbanks are overflowing. Then we see my mother. She's with Ava.

"Mama, I've been sick since Molly died. When am I gonna feel better?" Ava cries.

"I don't have an answer for you. But what I can tell you is that I won't stop trying to figure out what's wrong with you until we get an answer," Mama says.

Hearing Mama's words to Ava is like having an icepick stuck in my spine. Her assurances bounce around in my head and conjure up the same dreadfulness that I had being sick all the time.

Watching Mama and Ava together, I can see that my sister has the same symptoms I started with: vomiting, diarrhea, weakness . . . things hard to diagnose.

Mama is sitting at the kitchen table and reading a book. Ava screams from her bedroom, and Mama races up the stairs. Inside my old bedroom, Ava is sitting in her bed, and there is blood everywhere. It runs down her chin and soaks the top of her nightgown. The sheets are covered in the deep red, sticky liquid. It is a gruesome scene. Something straight out of a slasher film.

I cringe at the agony on Ava's face. I jam my hands into my armpits. I hear myself whimper. I look at Gwen, and she's blinking rapidly. We are both stunned by the way Ava is shrieking, as though her pain is too unbearable.

Mama grabs Ava by the shoulders. "Calm down, sweetheart. It looks worse than it is. It's nothing to be alarmed about."

My sister looks at Mama. Ava's eyes are swollen. She continues to wail. Tears run down her small cheeks.

The helpless look on Ava's face sends a stabbing pain through my gut. I want to take Ava in my arms and rock her. I want to assure her she's loved. I need her to know that I'll always miss her. I want to protect her from whatever is happening.

Mama lifts Ava up and places her on the floor. Then she strips Ava's bed of the soiled linens. My mother works without emotion.

Mama places Ava in a warm tub, kneels next to her, and washes her hair and body. Ava looks up at Mama; her eyes search my mother's face. I'm startled by the dark circles around Ava's eyes and her pale complexion.

My heart thumps in my chest. I have never been so helpless. Tears form in my eyes as we stare at Ava from Limbo.

Mama helps my sister out of the tub.

"Ava? How do you feel?" Mama asks.

Ava holds her head. "My brain hurts."

"You have a headache?" Mama asks.

"Yeah. I want to go back to bed."

Mama carries Ava into the bedroom and lays her down. "Now you stay right here," she instructs, pointing her witch finger at the bed.

Ava lays her head down on the pillow. "I miss Molly," she says.

There's a stab of pain in my heart, and I cover it with my hand.

Before Mama leaves the bedroom, Ava gets up and heads toward the bed that was once mine.

Mama watches for a second, then steps in front of her. "No, Ava. You need to sleep in your bed. This is Molly's bed, remember? She wouldn't have liked you sleeping in it."

I pull in a jagged breath. "That's not true!" I yell. "You can sleep in my bed!" I scream from Limbo. Ava can't hear me, but I wish she could.

My little sister nods at my mother as tears roll down Ava's round, colorless cheeks.

After Mama tucks Ava into her own bed, she goes downstairs to wait for my father to come home.

To my delight, that night, after Mama is asleep, Ava defies Mama and lays on top of my bed and covers herself with her favorite blanket.

Chapter Fifty-One

G wen and I gawk at the vision of the next morning. We watch Mama feed Ava oatmeal with spoiled eggs.

I watch Mama open a folder on the kitchen counter and write things on the paper inside.

"My mom is making fake medical records about Ava. I bet she did the same thing about me," I say.

Several hours later, she has Ava in the car as she rushes my baby sister to the emergency room.

From the backseat, Ava complains, "I hate going to the hospital. Why do I have to go there all the time?"

"Because you're sick a lot, Ava," Mama snaps.

Gwen's eyes drop as she nods.

Mama is in the ER with Ava again. She speaks to the doctors and nurses with ease, showing just the right amount of emotion. Even from Limbo I see she is skilled in the art of deception . . . a believable storyteller.

Days later, when Ava is brought home, she is laying across my mother's lap in the backseat of the car. My father is driving. He's squinting his eyes, and the small lines of concern on the corners are more pronounced.

Then I see the feeding tube poking out from under Ava's shirt.

My eyes pop open, and my jaw clenches tightly as I listen intently to Mama.

"It must run in the family. Good thing I already know how this feeding tube works," Mama says.

Daddy looks in the rearview mirror at Mama. He remains silent and continues driving.

"Why doesn't my dad do something?" I ask Gwen. "He must know this isn't normal."

Gwen doesn't answer.

Mama strokes Ava's hair as she whimpers.

Daddy looks in the mirror again. "Is she okay?" His voice fills with deep concern.

"She's doing just fine," Mama sings. Then she looks down at Ava. "Aren't you, sweetheart? Tell Daddy you're going to be better in no time."

Ava lets out a soft moan.

"I think she's still a little groggy," Mama says casually.

Gwen rubs my back. "Looks like your dad is worried about Ava."

I tell Gwen, "He's definitely scared. I have to figure out how to help her. I don't think you understand what it means that Ava has a feeding tube."

Gwen squints at me. "I think I have a pretty good idea."

My shoulders slump forward. Gwen is right. I'm overwhelmed, I'm not thinking rationally. Truthfully, I'm in a full-fledged panic. I have a ball in my belly that's working its way up to the top of my throat. My legs bounce uncontrollably, and I jump up from the log we've been sitting on. Leaves and twigs snap under my feet.

"What am I going to do?!" I scream, flailing my hands toward the sky.

"There's nothing you can do. I'm sorry. I needed to show you what's happened to Ava so you can fully understand that all the things your mother did to you were real."

I spin on Gwen and jab my index finger at her. "No! You showed me so that you can make me feel horrible! Why would you let me see that if there's nothing I can do to change it?"

Gwen's voice remains calm. "You can be angry with me all you want. But the truth is you should be angry with your mother. She's the one who betrayed you. She's the one who's torturing Ava now. She's the one who killed you."

I know it's true. Mama killed me. I don't know exactly how yet, but I know she did it. I want to scream at the top of my lungs. I want to let my father know Mama is a liar. I wish so hard I could tell him that Mama murdered me. I want to tell him there is nothing wrong with Ava. It's too late for me, but not Ava. She can still live.

Gwen walks away from me, and I follow. I do not want to be alone.

"Gwen, wait up."

She stops. I run toward her and fling myself into her arms. A loud sound escapes me and I feel flooded with sorrow.

When I open my mouth, unspoken truths pour out of me. "I was blind. I thought my mother was perfect. But she isn't perfect. She's much less than perfect. Mama sits on the side of evil, and I spent my whole life trying to please the devil. All I've done is put my sister in harm's way. I have to fix this."

Gwen tightens her embrace. "You cannot hold yourself responsible for your mother. You were a kid yourself."

"You're not hearing me. I need to help Ava. What can I do to help my sister?"

Gwen looks down at the ground and gently shakes her head. "You can't help her from here. We can't affect life on Earth from here."

"There has to be something. Please, think. I'll do anything to make Ava safe."

Gwen looks into my eyes. "It hurts my heart so much to see you suffer."

I have no words to describe the hollowness that fills me.

Gwen lifts my chin. "You'll find out everything that happened to you . . . and what's happening to Ava."

I want to fast forward through the time I have to remain in Limbo. Watching what happened to me is devastating; watching the same things happen to Ava is like being burned alive. But I can't wait any longer. I take several long breaths to calm my nerves.

"I don't care what Mama has done to me anymore. I want to see what my mother is doing to Ava. You and I have to find a way to help my sister. Doing nothing is not an option."

Chapter Fifty-Two

Gwen and I watch my mother put away groceries. She's humming as she takes out a carton of milk and places it in the back of a corner cabinet.

I grab my stomach. "Oh, no, Gwen."

Gwen's eyes are downcast.

I wish I could enter the scene and confront Mama, but I'm helpless. Instead, I stand and pace in the grass. When I stop, I am standing in front of Gwen. I'm holding the base of my throat with one hand, and my other hand roughly combs through my hair.

My hands clench into fists, as if they have a mind of their own.

"Mama is going to make Ava sick again. She'll kill her just like she killed me." I grind out the words through gritted teeth and with spittle flying from my mouth. "I can't believe my healthy little sister is going to die."

Gwen stands and places her hands over my fists. "Yes. Your mom murdered you. I'm angry for you. It's hard to watch her deliberately do hurtful things to you, and now to Ava. It's even harder to understand why. We know your mom craves attention from people, but still, to do what she's done and continues to do is pure evil. Even if she is sick in the head."

Gwen goes quiet and lowers her head. "I'm not making this any better for you. I'm trying my best to be helpful, but I'm having a hard time controlling my own rage."

"I get it. Everything you say is true. I know now that my mom is evil." I cross my arms over my chest and suck in as much air as I can to calm my anger. "Let's go back and watch this bitch."

The next night, Mama pulls the spoiled milk from the back of the cabinet. She opens the lid and takes a whiff, then crinkles her nose. She holds her breath while pouring the rancid milk into the feeding bag, then pours in liquid acetaminophen. Three days later, after a steady diet of the rotten milk and children's pain reliever, Ava looks close to death.

After two more days with heavy doses of the milk and acetaminophen, my sister turns gravely ill, and they are off to a different hospital. In the emergency room, Mama describes her symptoms to the doctor.

Mama sits on the edge of the chair next to Ava's bed and holds her hand. "Well, at first, I thought it was just an ear infection. She complained about it hurting, so I took her to the doctor, and he gave her an antibiotic."

"Liar!" I scream. Gwen jumps from my sudden outburst.

"She's a liar!" I yell while pointing at the vision.

Gwen stares at me with a deer-in-the-headlights look. I settle myself down and listen to Mama tell the doctor more lies.

"I thought the antibiotic was working and then, all of a sudden, she had all the classic symptoms of the flu: high fever, stiff neck, and a chronic headache, so I figured it wasn't an ear infection. But then this morning she woke very confused and couldn't tolerate light. About an hour ago, she had a seizure. That's when I was sure it was something else. In fact, I'm worried she has meningitis. It all adds up and makes sense to me now."

The doctor frowns at Ava, who is laying in the bed. Her tiny figure looks like a small mound of rags. His eyebrows knot together. "You could be right. I'll run some other tests first, and if we don't find anything, then we may need to consider doing a spinal tap."

Mama places her palm on her own cheek. "Yes, yes, I know. It's terrible, and I hate to put Ava through such a painful procedure."

Mama shakes her head slowly, as if she is struggling with what to do. "But I think it's the only way to figure out what's wrong with her," she says.

The doctor nods. He turns to the nurse and whispers instructions. When he turns back to my mother, she sniffles and wipes her hand across her cheek.

Ava looks tiny and wrung out. She looks from Mama to the doctor. Her eyes are glassy. "Mama?"

"Yes, Ava. What is it, honey?" She leans closer.

"You said it'll hurt. Will it hurt bad?"

Mama glances up at the doctor and nods. "A little bit."

Tears trickle from the sides of Ava's eyes.

The doctor puts his hand on the tissue-thin hospital gown covering Ava's delicate shoulder. "Don't worry. I'm going to give you something to help you relax."

Ava's bottom lip trembles. "When will you give me something?"

The doctor lets out a soft sigh. "As soon as the nurse comes back," the doctor promises Ava, patting her arm.

After the doctor runs tests on Ava, he keeps his word and gives Ava medicine in her IV, and her face goes slack. Her eyes ease closed, and there is a slight smile on her lips. They move her to a brightly lit, sterile room.

The nurse says, "The doctor is going to give you something to numb you, sweetie. Try to hold still."

The nurse lays Ava on her stomach and holds her arms as the doctor inserts a needle into her spine. Ava flinches and grunts as the needle breaks her skin.

Ava opens her eyes for a moment, then closes them again.

As the doctor pushes the needle in further to remove spinal fluid, Ava's eyes snap open, and she releases a piercing scream. "Ow, ow! It hurts! It hurts!"

"It's going to be okay," the nurse coos, to calm her.

"No," Ava cries. "Stop! It burns!"

The procedure lasts for almost twenty-five minutes, an eternity for something that looks this painful.

Because of how much Ava screams and cries during the spinal tap, the doctor gives her a little more of that "something" to relax her when he finishes. This time Ava drifts off to sleep completely.

When she wakes, she struggles to string her words together.

"My back hurts!" she cries.

"Yes, honey," the nurse says. "But not for long. I'll give you something for the pain."

The doctor turns to Mama. "We're going to admit her. She's going to need antibiotics for a bacterial infection."

"A bacterial infection? From what?" Mama's mouth hangs open, waiting for an answer.

"It's hard to say," the doctor tells her.

The doctor doesn't know the cause of the infection, but Mama knows. Gwen and I know now too.

The harmful things Mama put into Ava's body have compromised her immune system. The acetaminophen and the rancid raw milk did further damage to her vulnerable health. Ava stays in the hospital for two weeks because Mama continues to bring syringes of the bad milk mixed with acetaminophen. She injects the concoction into her feeding tube when no one is watching. Ava's body finally wears down and, after more tests, the doctor discovers a problem with her liver.

I look over at Gwen. "My mother is tearing Ava's body to shreds. It's all happening so quickly. I was sick for years, but my sister is dying in weeks."

"Yes. Your mother has learned how to prolong the agony. She can make Ava very sick, and let her get almost well again. She repeats the pattern. She has learned the right formula . . . from practicing on you."

I look out over a lake I've brought to mind. "My mom murdered me." I let those words bore in further, into my core.

Gwen doesn't respond. I don't need her to comment. I am grateful for her silence.

As Gwen and I continue watching, some days Mama doesn't infect Ava, and my sister feels a little better. Then Mama knocks her down again.

This shouldn't surprise me. I'm now learning Mama's pattern, the way she works and operates, the shrewd, sneaky behavior she has honed to a science. I can tell that Mama enjoys the art of the game by the way she smiles and the noticeable bounce in her walk every time Ava becomes sicker. Ava is merely a puppet in her play, just like I was. Our roles in this dark, twisted drama depend on her perverse desire for attention and control. It's the most sickening thing in the world to watch a parent bring their child to the brink of death and back again and again.

I fear Mama will kill Ava, and it causes me great pain that there's nothing I can do to stop her. But I'm not willing to give up yet. No, not yet.

Chapter Fifty-Three

The only thing on my mind is my sister. I'm consumed with worry about her well-being. I wish there were something I could do to help.

Gwen and I watch Mama in her car. She leaves the hospital after she is told Ava's liver isn't functioning properly. She's humming "Zip-a-Dee-Doo-Dah." Mama parks the car and enters the public library. She moves around the bookshelves like a spider, her fingers lightly running across the spines of books, making their way to eat the fly caught in its web.

I watch over Mama's shoulder as she reads about liver disease. She flips the page, and there are two lists: things to help with the disease and things to avoid. Mama's finger scurries down the page, and she places her long, manicured, cherry-red fingernail at the top of the list of things people with liver disease should avoid. From her purse, she pulls out a small pad and pen and writes five words: no sugar, fried food, and salt.

Mama stares at the written words. She smiles to herself.

"Such an easy list," she whispers.

My mom closes the pad and holds the small book to her heart before placing it back in her purse. I want to pull the pen from her hand and poke it into her eye until I skewer her pea brain.

At home, Ava is bedridden. She has been given the sentence of the same life I left behind. Her life is passing her by, and all I can do is watch from a distance.

***

I take a deep breath. "Gwen, I have to tell you something, but I'm afraid you'll think I'm nuts."

She stares into the beautiful night sky. "You sound so serious. How bad can it be?"

"Bad. After being in and out of the hospital so many times, I used to wish I would get cancer and that it would kill me."

"What? Why?"

My belly cramps and a loud sigh escapes my throat. "Because the kids in the hospital who knew they were dying of cancer would get their treatments and go home. My mom would tell me when they died. She'd say I should feel lucky that I didn't have anything that would kill me. But I didn't think I was lucky. Sometimes I would feel jealous that they were going to be free from all the suffering. That's nuts, right? That there were times I thought being dead would be easier than living."

Gwen pulls a soft blanket over her shoulders. "Not at all. Nobody wants to live their life in pain. Can I tell you a secret?"

"Yes! Tell me something so I don't feel like such a freak."

"When I was in the concentration camp, there was this guard. He was a lot older than me, like as old as my dad. Anyway, he would stare at me a lot, and it made me really nervous."

I rest my head on Gwen's shoulder. "Because you thought he was gonna kill you?"

"Nah-ah. He was different. The way he looked at me made me feel icky. Anyway, one night he woke me up and told me I had to follow him to the building where we sorted clothes. He said I needed to work through the night. I knew he was lying to me, but I couldn't say no. My mom woke up and, out of panic, asked the guard where he was taking me. He let go of me and punched her twice in the face. He broke her nose. Then he dragged her to the middle of the floor, where everyone could watch, and kicked her a bunch of times in the chest and stomach."

I'm observing Gwen. In all her calmness, her elbows are pressed tightly against her sides.

Gwen explains, "The guard grabbed my arm and dragged me outside. He took me to the building where we sorted clothes that were stolen from us. We called it the death mill. It was an awful place. A lot of the clothes were taken off of dead people that they'd murdered. It smelled like vomit and shit and piss and fear and misery. Every time I was assigned there, I had to sort through piles of clothes. Some of the shirts and pants were crusty with blood. Some had bullet holes in them. That building was a reminder that my life no longer belonged to me."

Gwen stops talking to collect her thoughts.

"Once we were inside the death mill, he grabbed my other arm and put his nose against mine."

The image of Gwen and the Nazi soldier appears. Gwen looks like a different person. She's filthy and wears what looks like a burlap sack. Her hair is chopped close to her head. Her eyes are sunken and flat. The dark circles under them make her look sickly.

"If you make a sound I will kill you," he says. "Nobody will care either. You pathetic people live and die at our mercy, my mercy, so don't fuck with me."

Gwen whimpers.

"Take your clothes off."

Gwen tries to pull away.

"Stupid girl!"

The guard backhands Gwen, and she falls to the concrete floor. The horrid, sordid man rips the shabby cloth from Gwen's body.

I gasp. I can see all of her bones. Not just her ribs, but also the bones in her arms and legs. Her kneecaps and ankles would have been exposed entirely but not for the thin, gray skin that covered them.

The sight of Gwen makes me want to run away, but I count to ten in my head. I want to be strong for Gwen . . . the way she has been strong for me.

When the guard turns Gwen around and pushes her face-first over a table, I can see every vertebra in her spine. I can actually count them. I am so distracted by how Gwen looks that I am taken by surprise when the guard tears her saggy, blackened underwear from her bottom, presses his hand down hard on her spine, and rapes her. I hold my breath the entire time.

I hear Gwen pull air into her lungs. I look over just as her shoulders fall forward. Her spine is bowed, and her sobs break free.

I throw my arms around her. "Oh my God, Gwen. You're okay. It's all okay now."

Gwen cries and cries and cries. "It hurt so much. It was like he was shredding my insides to pieces. But it wasn't just physical pain. I couldn't sleep. I was afraid when I had to leave my bunk, and I barely talked to anyone. I couldn't accept that I had no choice, no say, and no ability to stop anything bad from happening to me."

I know nothing about the pain she describes. I've had other pain, but the pain that comes from being tortured and raped is impossible for me to imagine.

"Did you tell your mom?" I ask her.

"No. I couldn't do that to her."

Gwen looks into my eyes and I can see she is distraught.

"I'll show you what happened next," she says.

When the guard finishes, he throws her clothes at her. She tries to wipe the blood from her thighs as she quickly dresses. He grabs her under one arm and marches her back to the bunkhouse, where she stumbles to her bunk. The heavy steel door slams shut behind her.

Gwen says, "The sound of the lock being thrown behind me was like fireworks going off in my ears."

Gwen climbs into her bed, and her mother climbs in next to her.

Gwen's eyes are red and swollen. Her mother holds her gently, and asks, "Where did that guard take you?"

"To the place where we sort the clothes," Gwen says in a shaky voice.

Gwen is laying on her back. Her mother is looking into her eyes as though searching for something she lost. Gwen looks away.

"I couldn't let her see the pain and humiliation of what the guard had done to me," Gwen tells me.

I nod. I'm no stranger to humiliation.

Her mother asks, "Did he do something to hurt you?"

Gwen looks around in the dark at the other bunks filled with dying women and young girls. She moves in closer to her mother and whispers, "People talk. We don't know what they'd do to save themselves. So please, please don't ask me about it anymore."

Gwen's mom holds her daughter for a long time while they both cry. Then her mother pulls back and looks into Gwen's face.

"Okay. We'll not speak of it ever again," she says.

The brutality of Gwen's story terrifies me. It wasn't that I didn't know things about sex. When I was alive I had read the book Where Did I Come From? Mama had bought it for me when I asked her about babies. But the kind of sex Gwen endured was mean and violent, nothing at all like what I'd learned.

I stare at Gwen, looking for signs that she was raped and tortured. I don't know what I expect to see. That's the thing about being abused, I'm realizing. People look okay on the outside, but inside they are fighting the demons left behind by abusers. A battle that must be won.

I lean back on my elbows; I'm mentally drained, yet grateful I didn't experience what she went through.

"That was the worst thing that happened to me in the concentration camp. It was even worse than dying."

"I can see why," I say.

Gwen rubs her temples with both hands. "That guard came for me every night for a month before I was murdered."

I shrink away from Gwen in horror.

"Sometimes he'd beat me after he was done. Other times he would put his 'thing' in other places. I wanted to be dead, just like you did. When he was doing it to me, I envied the other prisoners who were taken away and didn't come back. I would imagine they had escaped and had freedom, or they were slaughtered. Either way, they didn't have to face our cruel reality any longer. You and I are a lot alike. Just like you, I welcomed death over the suffering of him raping and beating me repeatedly. It's hard to admit that because I wanted so much to survive. In the end, death was my ultimate companion. Sometimes people can push you to the point of thinking that living is too hard."

The air hangs heavily between the two of us. I want to say something intelligent and meaningful to make Gwen feel better, but instead we both escape into the dense, darkened silence.

I say sheepishly after a while. "So I guess I'm not so weird thinking about death that way."

Gwen wipes tears from her cheeks. "Nope, you're not so weird. We've both seen the mean-spirited, bloodthirsty belligerence lurking deep inside of the human spirit. That's our connection."

"I wish it could've been different, for both of us. But I'm glad we're connected. I don't know that I could do this without you," I murmur.

Gwen and I take in the quiet beauty of the night. Then, without talking, we lie under our blankets and hold onto each other until we both drift off to sleep.

Chapter Fifty-Four

Liver damage means Ava will remain ill and at my mother's mercy. This makes my mother capable of subjecting Ava to painful and unnecessary medical procedures, along with giving her new medications in clinical studies.

I think, Mama must be thrilled that Ava has a real illness.

Dr. Becker is the same doctor who treated me for kidney problems; he was also a specialist in liver failure. The team at Dr. Becker's office was always happy to see Mama. They showered her with tender smiles and embraces. Now that this is Mama's second child with a grave illness, it is a windfall for her. To sum it up, Mama has hit the disturbed-mother-who-makes-her-kids-sick-and-gets-away-with-it lottery.

I watch Ava over the next several weeks. She ages quickly. She moves slower. She takes twice the time to do simple things like brushing her teeth or combing her hair.

However, Ava hangs onto every tiny bit of independence, such as walking or going downstairs to get herself something to drink. She pushes her body as far as it can go, right to the brink of exhaustion. I know this because it's what I did too.

Ava's failing liver isn't her only problem. She is plagued by fevers, exhaustion, and diarrhea brought on by the things my mother sneaks into her feeding bag. Ava spends most of her time in a bed, whether at home or in the hospital, just like I did. Mama has destroyed Ava's good health. My sister's condition is similar to what my own condition had been during the months leading to my death. The remainder of my sister's life is in my mother's hands, still stained with my blood.

Gwen and I watch as the weeks race by. Mama doesn't quit. She won't leave my sister alone. Ava has no peace. But Mama enjoys an abundance of empathy and sympathy from others. Mama thrives while Ava dies one lethal dose at a time.

I turn to Gwen. "If someone doesn't do something soon to help Ava, she's going to end up here, and as much as I want to be with her—and believe me, I really do—I think she deserves to live a long, happy life."

Gwen pushes a few stray hairs out of her face. "I wish there was something we could do for her, I really do, but I can't think of anything. I have a burning desire to stop your mother from causing more harm. She deserves to get caught."

Gwen and I watch more.

Ava is at home, and Mama is in the bathroom with her. She is making my sister pee into a plastic cup. Ava is weak from excessive doses of liquid acetaminophen. She's having a hard time staying upright on the toilet as my mother shoves the cup under her.

"Mama, can you give me the medicine to make me sleep? I'm so tired, but my body hurts too much, and I can't stay asleep," Ava says.

I raise my hands above my head to stretch my tired back. "When I was alive, sleep was my friend . . . my best friend in the whole world. Sleep took away my misery. Now it's Ava's friend too. That breaks my heart."

Mama helps Ava back to bed and tucks her in. "I love you so much, Ava," she whispers.

A sweet smile plays on Ava's lips at the sound of our mother's voice as she pushes liquid sleep aid into her tube. My little sister knows that a release will follow and soon she'll have a short reprieve from her suffering.

Gwen and I watch Mama walk out of the bedroom. She's back in the bathroom. Mama lifts a sewing needle and sticks it into the tip of her finger. She presses, and her blood pools on the tip. Turning her finger over, Mama lets several drops of blood drip into Ava's urine sample. When she is satisfied, my mom twists the lid on and gives the urine and blood a quick toss . . . shake, shake, shake, the act of deception complete. Ava's yellow sample turns dark pink.

I stop watching because I think about the times when I had blood in my urine, too.

"I bet my mom did the same thing to my urine samples. I definitely had blood in my urine . . . several times," I say to Gwen.

"Yes. I'm sure that's exactly what she did."

The next day they're back in Dr. Becker's cheery office. Mama leads Ava over to a high-back chair and lays a blanket she brought from home over her. A short time later, Dr. Becker strolls in. I notice that when he smiles at Ava, his eyes smile too. He is a nice man. When I was alive, I didn't even hate having to go to the hospital to see him.

"Well, look who's here," Dr. Becker sings as he takes a seat behind his desk. He's looking directly at Ava, almost as if Mama isn't in the room. My mom fidgets in her chair, an expectant smile from ear to ear as she appears to anxiously wait for Dr. Becker to fuss over her. He doesn't. I like him even more.

My sister gives the doctor her best smile, but it's weak. I can see that from Limbo.

"Hi, Dr. Becker. Did you find something to make me better?" Ava asks.

Dr. Becker breaks his eye contact with her and looks down at his hands. "No, Ava, not yet. But there are things we can do to make you more comfortable."

Dr. Becker finally looks at Mama. "There was blood in the sample you brought in today. I'm a little worried about that."

Mama gasps, and her mouth gapes open. She's a lunatic. I know that now.

Ava sits across from the doctor, staring at him with wide eyes. "Dr. Becker, don't do any more tests on me. Okay?"

"I won't, Ava. Not right now, anyway. You'll need to give us more urine samples, but that was easy, wasn't it?"

Ava's head bobs up and down.

I know from my own experience that medical testing is as about as enjoyable as I imagine swallowing crushed glass would be. My life was hard enough without the painful poking and prodding. I know the same is true for Ava. But there comes a point when you learn to tolerate the things you hate because you have no choice.

Mama and Ava are in the car after leaving Dr. Becker's office. My mom turns to Ava in the backseat.

"You listen to me, Ava," she growls. "It is not up to you to decide to tell Dr. Becker that he shouldn't perform tests on you. That's like signing your own death sentence. It could be one of those tests that heals your liver. When we go to see Dr. Becker, you are to keep your thoughts and opinions to yourself. Do you understand me?"

Ava looks like a wounded animal. Her eyes are downturned, and her bottom lip quivers.

"But Dr. Becker listens to me, Mama. He wants to know what I think," Ava says in a beaten tone.

Mama turns around fully and glares at her. Ava's eyes meet Mama's, and then quickly drop to her lap. "I'm sorry, Mama."

"You should be sorry! You have no idea what is or isn't good for you."

I scream at the vision. "But you know what's good for Ava. Don't you, Mama? You know exactly what's good for her, and you knew what was good for me, too. You're a fraud. You're a vile, twisted coward."

Chapter Fifty-Five

Ava rests in her bed while Mama is downstairs tinkering in the kitchen. She pulls a half full bottle of liquid acetaminophen from the cabinet.

Alone in the kitchen, Mama talks to herself, or maybe she is talking to the devil.

"You think you can ask Dr. Becker not to give you any more tests," she says. "Well, I have news for you, Ava. I'm in charge of what goes on here. You're just a child. You have no say in the matter. Now, I'll have to show you who the boss is around here. You're not as smart as your sister; she knew to keep her damn mouth shut and leave the medical decisions up to me."

I'd made it so easy for Mama to manipulate me. "I did everything my mother expected. She knew I would obey her, and she took every advantage. How could I be so dumb? Even Ava, who is younger than I was when it all started, knows enough to ask Dr. Becker questions."

"Ava is young, but she spent a lot of time with you," Gwen says. "She saw all the suffering that you went through. You told me that she was wise for her years. Maybe, because of you, she sees your mother through a different lens. Maybe seeing what happened to you will save her."

There's nothing I want more than for Ava to be saved, but the truth is, my mom is wickedly clever. Nevertheless, I hope Gwen is right. I hope Ava keeps asking questions of the doctors, the nurses, and Daddy.

Later that night we watch Daddy stroll into Ava's room.

"Hey, Ava. How are you feeling?"

"Hi, Daddy. I feel the same."

"I'm sorry to hear that, sweetheart." Daddy holds a small shopping bag. "I brought you a present."

Ava perks up. "You did? I love presents."

"I know you do," he says and hands the bag to my sister.

She pulls out a box. Inside, it holds a gold ring with a heart on it.

Ava places the ring on her finger and stares at it.

"I love this," she says, leaning over to hug my father.

Daddy holds her hand and looks at the ring. "This ring is very powerful. It's going to make you well and strong again. Whenever you feel sick, all you have to do is make a wish on the ring. And you know what I think?"

Ava's face is filled with awe. "What?"

"This ring," he says, touching it, "this is special. It's going to sound a little funny to you, but I think that Molly was right next to me in the store when I bought it."

"She was?" Ava asks with her mouth slightly open.

"Yes, ma'am. I was walking back to work from lunch. I turned the corner and there was this jewelry store, and in the window, there was a big poster. It said Jewelry by Molly. Well, it turns out there's a woman who makes every piece by hand, and her name is Molly. When I saw that sign, I marched into that store and told the man behind the counter that I needed a ring for the most special girl in my life."

"That's me!" Ava sings gleefully. "I'm your most special girl. Right, Daddy?"

"Yes, princess, you are."

Ava admires her new ring. "Daddy, Molly was special too. She was the most special girl to me."

My father inhales sharply and he grows misty-eyed. "Yes, baby. Molly was your most special girl."

"She was your most special girl too. We can both be your most special girl."

Ava pouts. "I love Molly a whole lot, and if she was here, you would've bought her one of these rings too. Just like mine, so we could be the same."

"That's right. You're a smart girl."

Daddy looks away and wipes a tear rolling down his cheek.

"I miss her," Ava says.

"I miss her too, baby. I miss her very much," Daddy says.

I hunch over with my arms wrapped tightly around my knees. I wish I could somehow make my presence known and physically connect with my father and little sister.

Gwen touches my shoulders. "Your dad and little sister love you so much. You will live in their hearts forever."

The love I have for my sister and father is so big it would be impossible to measure. I wish I could tell them to run . . . because now I know better, now I know the truth.

Chapter Fifty-Six

For the next hour I replay a hundred times the scene of Ava and Daddy talking about how much they love and miss me. It gives me happiness and pain. I can't help but dwell on being separated from both of them. I wish I could stop, but it's so hard to let go of things I can't have, things that were stolen from me.

I need to take my mind off of things. I nudge Gwen. "Let's play basketball."

Gwen jumps up and grabs my hand. "Yeah, that'll be fun. You can teach me how to play."

I imagine into being a basketball court in the middle of the ocean at Cape May beach, combining my two favorite places into one. The water is blue-green, calm . . . soothing. The sky is clear, and the sun warms my skin. I dribble the basketball and then I show Gwen how to do the same. Not once does the ball leave the court and go into the water. It's like we're surrounded by an invisible force field.

We play for hours, and when we're done, we jump into the ocean water. We swim with colorful fish tickling our feet. Then we float on our backs for a while.

I close my eyes and listen to the peaceful whir of the ocean below the surface. It is a light and pleasant hum. "I haven't played basketball since forever," I say to Gwen.

We make our way closer to shore. Gwen stands in the water and places her hands under the back of my neck and knees, holding my weightless body. "You're really good. Now I know why you beat all the boys."

I put my arms around her neck. "Yeah, I might've been a great athlete. I bet I could've played on the varsity team in high school if I had lived."

I dunk my hair in the water. "I was a good student, too. I always got As. My mom and dad bought us books all the time. I loved reading. It gave me an escape from being sick. I can't even count the number of books I've read."

"Reading was one of my favorite things, too."

"I've been thinking about my feeding tube. It made it so easy for my mom to kill me. It'll make it just as easy for her to kill Ava."

Gwen weaves her fingers through mine. "She can't hurt you anymore. That has to make you happy."

I pull my hand away gently and wrap my arms around myself. "I mean, yeah, I'm happy Mama can't hurt me anymore, but I'm dead." I take several deep breaths. "If someone doesn't figure out that my mother is demented, Ava will be here soon. I don't want her to die."

We leave the water and sit on the beach. I lay on my back and grab handfuls of warm sand, letting the grains flow between my fingers. I like how it feels. "Do you think my mother is going to kill Ava?"

Gwen lies back next to me. "I don't know, but I sure hope not."

I close my eyes. I wish I had known that Mama was a monster before she killed me; maybe I could've stopped her.

I hate myself for leaving Ava to battle the demon-mother I failed to slay.

Chapter Fifty-Seven

I've taken some time to myself, time to be alone. I imagine I'm back in the city of Limbo. I'm hanging out at a picnic table, staring at the clouds. The soft white puffs contrast brilliantly against the turquoise sky. It's so beautiful; everything is perfect here. A soft breeze lifts my hair and I remember why I'm here. I look for Gwen but don't see her anywhere.

"Gwen, where are you?"

Gwen appears next to me.

"Where have you been?" I ask.

"I went to visit my mom."

I look into her eyes. "Are you okay? Did something happen?"

"No, I'm fine. I wanted to spend some time with her."

"Are you sure nothing's wrong with you?"

Gwen smiles, and her eyes get misty. "No, nothing is wrong. Sometimes I wish I hadn't died. I think I would've been a great mom. I love kids."

I put my arm over Gwen's shoulder. "I know. As nice as it is here in Limbo, it makes me sad to think about all the things I won't be able to do."

"Anyway," Gwen says, "going to see my mom makes me happy. She knows how to cheer me up just by being herself."

We are silent a moment and then Gwen nudges me. She pulls out orange nail polish, spreads her fingers apart on the picnic table, and paints them.

"That's a pretty color. Can I use it when you're done?"

"Sure thing," Gwen says.

I smile. "I love that we can paint our nails in Limbo. It's very cool."

Without looking at me, she asks, "Do you want to see what's happening now?"

"Ugh. Yeah. I guess so."

Gwen smiles. "All right, let's get to it then."

Mama pulls into the driveway. She is returning with Ava from having blood tests, something Dr. Becker wanted to be done every few weeks.

A cheerful-looking woman rushes up to my sister. "Hi, Ava. How are you feeling?"

Ava glances at the woman, then back at my mother. Ava's limbs hang loose. She looks into the woman's face with a blank expression.

Impatiently, Mama huffs, "For goodness sake, Ava. This is Mrs. Turk. She just moved in across the street. You met her the other day. She asked you how you're feeling."

Ava gives Mrs. Turk a bewildered look. "I'm okay."

Mama gives Mrs. Turk a hug and whispers, "Forgive Ava. She's been through a lot, and sometimes the pain medicine makes her goofy."

Mrs. Turk shakes her head. "I don't know how you do it, Rona."

Mama pulls back slightly to look into Mrs. Turk's eyes. "I only do it because there are people like you to help me. I don't know what I would've done if you weren't around to keep me company when I'm not at the hospital. Not to mention all those dinners you've sent over for Kurtis and me."

Mrs. Turk smiles. "It's nothing. Honestly, I'm happy to help. So are the other neighborhood mothers. In fact"—Mrs. Turk leans in closer—"we bought you something special."

Mama puts her hand over her heart. "Oh, that wasn't necessary."

"Don't be silly," Mrs. Turk says. "We all agreed that you needed something nice to cheer you up."

After Mrs. Turk leaves, Mama helps Ava into the house and gets her settled in bed. She stands over my sister and smiles. "So, what do you think the women bought me? I bet it's a full spa day. Oh, maybe they bought me tickets for dinner and a show or one of those lovely Tiffany friendship bracelets. Who knows? It's so exciting, isn't it?"

Ava stares at Mama with pitiful, sunken eyes. "Mama, my side hurts, and I have a headache again. Can I have medicine?"

"Of course," Mama answers mindlessly. My mother goes into the bathroom I once shared with Ava and brings back a bottle of pain relievers. Surprisingly, she gives Ava a cherry-flavored pill and lets her chew it. Then Mama goes down to the living room, puts her feet up, and turns on the television.

A little while later, the doorbell rings. My mother opens the door, and a man is facing her with a large bouquet of flowers. Mama gasps. It's hard to tell if she's pretending to be happy or surprised.

Taking the flowers, she closes the front door behind her and looks at the bouquet.

"Are you fucking kidding me?" she sneers. "This is the big surprise you cheap bitches got me? Some damn flowers?"

Gwen looks at me. We both wear an expression of disbelief.

Mama takes the flowers into the kitchen, opens the trash can, and throws them away, vase and all. With her hands on her hips, she paces the kitchen, stomping from one side to the other. Back and forth, stomp . . . stomp . . . stomp until she stops abruptly. She stares at a plaque on the wall that reads, Live for Today. I can see the fury building inside of her. Mama snatches the plaque and hurls it across the room, where it splinters into pieces.

I'm nervous for Ava because I know from watching my own past that her fits of rage are often followed by acts of cruelty. But she manages to rein in her anger until later that night, when my father gets home.

"You know what, Kurtis?" she asks as soon as he takes off his shoes. "Did it ever occur to you to do something nice for me? I'm here all damn day, stuck in this house with your sick daughter, and all I get from you is a, 'Hi, honey' when you come home. Did you forget I recently lost a child? How about I get a job and you stay here and deal with this shit?"

My father rushes forward with his arms open to her. "Oh, Rona. I know that you're still grieving for Molly. We all are, and you're not alone. I didn't know you felt this way."

Mama twists away from my father. "No, you wouldn't know anything about how I feel. I'm tired, Kurtis. We have another sick child laying upstairs."

Daddy tilts his head. "Where is this coming from? Is something wrong? Is Ava okay?"

"Is something wrong? Is Ava okay?" My mother sings back to him. "Yes, Ava is fine. I had a shitty day and thought that maybe, just maybe, you'd come home at a sensible time and take care of me for once."

My father releases a robust groan. "Rona, if you needed me home earlier you could've called me at the office. You can't wait until I get home and unleash your bullshit on me. Do you expect me to be a mind reader or something?"

"No," Mama says, glaring at him and pointing her finger in his face. "I expect you to be a good father and a good husband. You've turned out to be neither of those things."

"Rona, stop it! I lost a child too. And Ava lost a sister. We're all trying to move on without Molly here. It's not easy for any us."

"Yes, well, maybe if you spent more time with us, it would make it easier. But nooooo. You stay at the office day and night while I'm stuck here," Mama spits.

Daddy rakes his fingers through his hair. He takes several deep breaths. "Right, Rona. Because no one can parent as perfectly as you. Remember, you're the one who wanted to stay home to raise the children. You're the one who decided to drop out of nursing school. I was willing to work five jobs if I had to so that you could stay in college and get your degree. You made the decision to stop going to school. You decided that your career could wait. I never once asked you to stay at home. In fact, I begged you to finish school. I told you we could get a nanny, but you refused because there wasn't anyone on this fucking planet who could take care of your children the way you do."

"That's right! Imagine if some stranger had taken care of our dying daughter. You wouldn't be able to live with yourself!" Mama screams.

"We weren't here when Molly died! She was with a stranger, Rona. We, you and I, failed her!" Daddy hollers.

I put my hand over my mouth and turn to Gwen. I can't believe what I'm learning. "My mother told me she'd dropped out of college because of me. You heard my dad; it was her choice. She could've finished. She could've been a nurse. I always believed that I took her away from her nursing career. That's what she wanted me to believe so I'd be grateful to her. Mama never gave up anything because of me."

I look down at the charm bracelet that Daddy gave me as a birthday present. I touch the charms and shake my wrist to hear them jingle. "None of us really knew Mama. She let us see a person who is way different than the woman she is. My little sister and father are doomed."

My mother murdered me, and now she's going to murder again.

Chapter Fifty-Eight

G wen and I are standing in the middle of a cobblestone street looking up between the buildings at a planet. The same as I looked at the Moon from Earth. The difference is that this planet is much closer than the Moon was to Earth.

The planet above me is green. There are mountains and trees and bodies of water. It is a remarkable sight.

I turn to Gwen. "This place is unbelievable. How is it possible that we can see that planet from here?"

Gwen chuckles. "You know how it works. Because you imagined it. That's where your soul will go to rest; your thoughts create your surroundings."

"Well, that's weird. I wasn't thinking about seeing a planet."

"Maybe not exactly. But maybe you were thinking about having lived a different life. Somewhere away from where you were on Earth. In that case, the planet could appear because it's different from what you experienced on Earth. See what I mean?"

"Yeah, I guess so." A thought occurs to me. "So, if that's true, then I can imagine that my mother is a good person. And Ava is happy and healthy. That she doesn't have a feeding tube. Which means I can save her from here. Right?"

"No, remember I told you it doesn't work that way," Gwen explains. "In Limbo, you can have anything you can imagine, but you can't change what happened to you or what's happening to someone who's still living."

I move off the street and sit on a curb. "That's just stupid."

Gwen plops down next to me. "Remember when you first got to Limbo and you didn't want to see the things your mother was doing to you? Well, it's the same thing. You can imagine that Ava is perfectly healthy, and that's what you'll see, but it won't make it true. I think that would defeat the purpose of understanding your life and your family. Don't you?"

"Yeah, you're right, but it makes it harder for me to know what's happening to Ava," I say.

My eyes sting from tears.

"I left my sister in the grips of my psycho mother," I say finally. I feel overwhelmed with guilt. "I'm sorry, Ava. I'm sorry. I'm sorry."

Gwen grasps my shoulder. "You're not responsible. You didn't do this to Ava."

"You don't understand. I left her alone. I know you say that it's not my fault, but if I had been smarter, paid more attention to what was happening, I could have stopped Mama."

"You didn't know what she was doing."

"But I knew other things and I didn't tell anyone. The way she sometimes lied to the doctors. The way she was angry when things didn't go her way. I should've told my father." I hang my head in shame.

"What is it, Molly? Tell me."

I shake my head.

"You can tell me anything," Gwen says.

"It's nothing that's going to help Ava," I tell her. "But when I was alive, there were times when I'd get this weird sensation . . . you know, that something seemed wrong. I couldn't put my finger on it back then. I told myself it was all the medication that made me feel that way. It's hard to admit to myself, and even harder to tell you, that I had bad feelings. Especially in the last months of my life. If I had only told someone . . ."

I need a change of scenery. Gwen and I walk to a beautiful lake. She takes my hand in hers, and we sit together watching the sunset over the water. I expect the tranquil setting to calm me, but instead my insides are twisting, and my chest burns as I think about Ava, all alone, in the hands of a killer.

Chapter Fifty-Nine

S ometimes it's hard for me to get Mama's face out of my mind. Not the face I've been seeing in my visions of the past and present, but the face that reflects her true character. In these fantasies, her beauty has faded, her charm is distorted, and I know I'm seeing her for the first time as she is.

Mama's once comforting smile is replaced by a mouth filled with razor-sharp teeth. Her soft brown eyes are two red-hot coals. Her rich eyelashes are centipedes with long legs that wiggle like the snakes of Medusa's hair. Thin, black veins run from her cheekbones to her chin. Mama is ugly. She is wicked, the kind of woman who would make her children sick to death. When the image takes hold, I have to squeeze my eyes shut to block it out.

"Gwen, let me show you what happened before I died."

I take Gwen to a farmhouse that overlooks a field of tall grass where horses graze. We are sitting next to each other on a porch swing.

In those last months, I had five more harrowing, near-death illnesses brought on by Mama that deliver me to the emergency room, and a few hospitals stays. My kidneys were doing most of the dirty work for her, until out of nowhere I developed clotting and infection of the vascular access, the tube where I got my dialysis. A few days later, I had an infection in my bloodstream and I had to stop dialysis for a while.

Sitting next to Gwen, I twirl my hair nervously. "I don't know what's worse .. . that I'm dead or knowing I'm about to watch myself die."

I feel my anger take hold. It didn't need to be this way. I was a perfectly healthy kid, and, well, it didn't need to be this way.

I summon a scene from the past.

I am back home, laying in my bed. I am emaciated. I can barely see my form under the covers. My oily, mangled hair is matted to my head. I am the sickest I've been in four years. I am too ill to get out of bed to shower or use the toilet. Mama gives me sponge baths when she has time and brushes baby powder through my hair to absorb the oil, but nothing replaces the clean feeling of soap and water.

I am on my back, staring blankly at the ceiling. The skin around my eyes is dark. My lips are cracked and flaky. My skin is draped over the bones in my face and head. My jawbones protrude, and my eye sockets are grotesquely sunken in. I am reduced to a skeleton covered in gray, dry flesh.

Gwen turns to me. "You look so sad. It makes me want to reach back in time and hold you."

"I had no idea I looked that bad. Hours had turned into days, and before I knew anything, my body shut down. I can't believe how horrible I looked."

I fall silent. I have a profound empathy for the girl lying in bed, alone. It's as though I'm watching someone other than myself. I don't recognize that girl. I don't want to know her pain and suffering.

I sit next to Gwen, trying to pull from her strength. I was defenseless. Watching a child die is the worst terror known. Especially when that child is me.

"I hadn't been out of bed, ya know? I hadn't looked in a mirror for eleven days. Probably better that way," I add.

Gwen turns her head away from me, but I know she's listening. After several seconds she faces me. "Molly, you're a warrior. Under those circumstances, you were fearless. Your mother is a disgrace to humankind. Your blood was still dripping from her pitchfork when she started the sick cycle of abuse over again with Ava."

There's nothing more I can say; Gwen has summed it up perfectly.

We watch for a while longer; I'm still in my bed. I don't move other than to adjust my body now and again. Time moves slowly.

Gwen turns to me. "What are we watching? You've been by yourself. You're barely moving."

I cock my head to the right and squint at the images of the past. "I was alone."

"For how long?"

I look Gwen square in the eyes. "For the most part . . . days. I was alone when I died. It was as if I didn't even matter to anyone. Like I never existed. Mama was busy. And my dad, he came into my room every night to sit with me for a few minutes. But I doubt he knew at that moment that I was going to die. I think for my dad this was just another illness that I would overcome eventually."

We watch again.

I'm on my back. The covers on my bed are twisted. I'm shivering, but too weak to untangle the covers.

"Hi, Molly," Mama says as she enters my room.

My eyes follow her as she approaches me. "Mama, something's wrong."

"Oh, sweetheart. I know it feels that way, but you're going to be fine."

I swallow hard. "Where's Ava? Why isn't she sleeping in here with me?"

"Well, given this bad spell you're having I thought it would be best if Ava slept in the spare bedroom. I want to keep things quiet so you can get the sleep that you need," Mama says.

"I don't wanna be in my room alone anymore."

Mama brushes my greasy hair from my face. "You're not alone, silly. The sitter is right downstairs."

"I want you to stay with me," I plead. Tears stream down my face.

"I know you do. I really wish I could, but you know that Ava needs my attention too."

That night, when Daddy comes home from work, he sits with me. He strokes my hair. "How are you feeling?"

I look into his eyes but don't speak.

"Molly, I know you're nervous, but I spoke to your mom, and she said this is temporary. She told me Dr. Becker said this is to be expected and that in a few days you'll bounce back."

Gwen and I know my mother hadn't talked to Dr. Becker in weeks, and I hadn't been to see him in more than a month.

I flinch.

"Are you in pain?" Daddy asks.

"Yeah," I murmur.

"Let me get your mother," Daddy says and leaves my room.

"Gwen, I need a break. It's too depressing."

Gwen nods. "Do you want to talk about it? What it was like?"

I give Gwen a halfhearted shrug. "I guess so. One hard thing about my death is that I didn't have closure. I should've been surrounded by my family, weeping at the side of my bed. No one was there to hold my hand and tell me not to be afraid. No one stroked my hair while telling me how much they loved me and how much I'd be missed. I had none of that. I wanted my family around me so much it hurt. I wanted to say good-bye to each of them. I wanted to tell them how much I loved them and that I would miss them all so much."

I pause and place my hand on my forehead. "Ava was taking ballet and jazz lessons. Mama was out of the house with her every day. A teenage girl named Maria was paid to stay with me. Mama would come home in the late afternoon and stay in the kitchen to make dinner. She lost interest in me once she understood I would die."

Gwen and I see Maria. She's downstairs on the phone "babysitting" me.

I'm in my bed. I've peed on myself again.

"Maaarrr . . ." I try to call. But it is like the words clumsily tumble from my lips.

Maria cradles the phone between her ear and shoulder. "Are you kidding me? Did she really say that she wants to be with Josh? Seriously. He's so out of her league."

"Maaarrr . . ." I try screaming again.

I tell Gwen, "Maria, my clueless babysitter, didn't know I was too fragile to yell for her. She couldn't have imagined how hard I'd hoped that she'd come to my room and sit by my side, so I didn't have to be alone."

I'm lying on my side, staring at my night-light. My nightgown is uncomfortably bunched around my waist. I'm shivering, not from fever, but because there's no fat left on me to stay warm. I'm gasping for air . . . sucking in . . . panting out . . . sucking in . . . panting out. I look around. My eyes are large and wild. I look like my bones have been molded into the fetal position.

I fill in the blanks for Gwen. "In the beginning, as my body shut down a little at a time, it hurt. It was sort of like when you first put your feet in the ocean. The water is icy cold, and it hurts, but after a while your toes and ankles go numb, and you inch your way out farther into the waves until the water doesn't feel cold anymore. That's the way the pain was when I was dying, except it lasted a lot longer than it takes to edge into the ocean."

I cringe, thinking about the loneliness and physical pain I experienced during those last hours. "All of my joints were swollen. My skin was itchy, and I was too lethargic to scratch . . . that in itself was torture. I forced myself not to think about being itchy. That was really hard."

I hang my head, feeling the weight of all that happened. "I had sores in my mouth, and it was difficult to swallow. My hands shook and, no matter how much I tried, I couldn't make them stop. Sometimes my body would twitch uncontrollably. I had a constant headache. I was isolated in my room and wanted so much for someone, anyone, to come and hold me while I suffered. That was the worst part for me, not wanting to live, but being scared to die, and longing for someone to be there to say good-bye to me, to witness it."

It's dusk. I am in my bed. I take short, quick breaths. As the hours pass, my breaths became fewer until the sound of my breathing was like shallow hiccups. My eyes dart around the room and then I am crying. My sunken chest heaves as I sob. My head turns to the side to gaze at the clock where the nightstand sits. It was 7:56 p.m., and in that moment I close my eyes for the very last time.

I stop watching to tell Gwen what is happening, to tell her how I was feeling. "I remember those last moments. I cried for all that I had endured; all that I had lost; and, most of all, for the loneliness that had taken up a home in my soul. Once I closed my eyes, everything faded, and my brain stopped working, and I woke up here."

I rub the back of my neck for self-comfort. "I can say it now without breaking down into a blubbering puddle of snot and tears, but back then, the thought of death terrified me. I was scared to leave that world behind me even though my life had been so pathetic . . . so wasted. It was sad to think about people going on without me . . . to think about all the things I would miss out on."

"The end of your life was tragic," Gwen says.

"In those final days, I wondered who I would've married, what I would've named my children, what my husband would've looked like. I didn't know what it felt like to make love, to be a teenager, to be in love with someone. To have my heart broken by my first crush and to dance with my father on my wedding day. I realized that I'd never know Ava's children, and they'd never know me."

Gwen picks at the blades of grass near her feet. "You know, you've had a rough journey. But mourning a future that won't happen is always the hardest part of dying."

"It's okay. Just you being here with me is enough." I shake my head softly. "The safest place in the world for a child is with their mother, right? That's what moms do; they protect their children with their own life if they have to. Why couldn't that be true for me too?"

Gwen turns and lies on her belly in the grass. "Unfortunately, we don't have control over our circumstances. I didn't ask to be born during the genocide of my people. It just happens. It's how we deal with it that's important. It's important to remember what was good about our lives. You have so many things to be happy about."

"You're kidding me, right?" I ask.

Gwen adjusts her body. She can't seem to stay still. "Nope. I'm not kidding you. Think about it. You had your dad and Ava. You had Joon and Lulu. You had Dr. Becker and Rainey. You had people who loved you and that you loved back. That's what you need to think about when you remember your life. You experienced many good moments and many good people that had nothing to do with your mom."

Gwen gives me a weak smile.

I consider her points. "You're pretty smart for someone who died, like, over fifty years ago."

"Yeah, well, you'll be this smart too if you become a guardian," Gwen says.

"You know, I would've never imagined the inside of Mama's chest is nothing but an empty cavity where her heart never grew. I've learned a big lesson since I've gotten here . . . that people are not always what they let you see; in fact, it's what we don't see in a person that counts the most. Whether it's good or bad." I rub my eyes and stare at the ground below my feet.

"You look tired, but we've almost seen it all," Gwen says. "Let's watch the rest."

I look into the clear sky and close my eyes momentarily. When I open them, my deathbed is before me again.

Chapter Sixty

D addy gets home from work late and walks to my bedroom. I'm lying on my side facing away from the door. He creeps across the floor, trying not to startle me. He eases himself onto the bed beside me.

"Hi, honey," Daddy whispers. "I missed you today. I wanted to come up and say hello."

Daddy kisses the back of my head, then strokes my hair. "Your mom told me you're getting better. I'm a firm believer in the power of positive thinking . . . and I'm praying every day for your recovery."

My father bends over and takes off his shoes. He places his socked feet on my bed. "Anyway, I'm up for another promotion at work." He pauses and loosens his tie. "I think I'm going to turn it down, though. I want to spend more time at home. I want to spend time with you and Ava. You're both growing up so fast."

My dad traces his index finger around my ear. "I know that you've been sick for a long time, and I want to be here to help take care of you. I told your mother, but she has other ideas. She worries about all of us and wants to make sure we have the money we need to take care of you girls."

Daddy leans in and whispers into my ear. "But I make plenty of money already, and this time I'm going to put my foot down. I already told my boss that I need to be home more, and he understands. He said, 'Kurt, do what you have to do. When I was a kid, I was sick a lot and having both of my parents around was the best medicine.'"

Daddy stretches his arms over his head and exhales loudly. "Anyway, my boss and I agreed I'll keep my current job and I'm even going to work from home a day or two a month."

Daddy runs his fingers through the ends of my greasy hair splayed across my pillow. "I'm telling your mother in the morning. You know, to avoid a scene tonight. I know your mom wants me to make more money, but she wants me at home more too. So I thought I'd wait until the morning, not to worry her before bed."

My father flings his feet over the bed and places them on the floor. "I'm going downstairs to eat dinner, but I'll be back. Can I bring you something to drink?"

Silence.

"Hey, Molly. Would you like a drink, baby?"

More silence.

"Molly?"

More silence.

Daddy grabs my shoulder and turns me onto my back. He looks into my still face. "Molly? Can you hear me?"

He bends over and leans in closer. "Molly!"

He grabs my hands. "Wait! No! Molly! Open your eyes!"

Daddy slams his ear on my chest and listens for the beat of my heart. He is met with more silence . . . the kind of silence that makes you want to reverse time, a silence that instantly makes you question how you can go on . . . how you'll take your next breath.

Daddy stands next to my bed. He administers CPR. He doesn't know I've been dead for more than two hour.

Everything happens in a blur.

Daddy screams for Mama. She bounds up the stairs like a gazelle. Then she's next to my bed.

"Rona! What's wrong with her? You need to do something!" Daddy screams.

Mama drops to her knees next to my bed. She's holding my wrist, then groping it to find a pulse. Daddy paces back and forth behind her. Ava appears in the doorway.

"What's wrong?" Ava whimpers.

Daddy grabs her up and races down the stairs. He hustles into the kitchen and snatches the telephone. He dials 911 as Ava buries her head in his chest.

"Nine one one. What's your emergency?" the operator asks.

"My daughter. It's my daughter Molly. She's not breathing!" he screams into the telephone.

After more questions, Daddy places Ava on the sofa. "Stay put. Don't move. Okay?"

Ava nods and collapses sideways on the sofa, curls up, and cries.

Daddy runs upstairs.

Back in my bedroom, Mama is holding me and humming softly. She looks up at my father as he approaches.

"She's gone," Mama tells him. Daddy is too distraught to notice that she sheds no tears.

Daddy climbs onto my bed with me and takes my body from my mother. He looks at her. "Ava's downstairs. She needs you."

Mama slowly leaves my bedroom.

Daddy and I are alone. He's holding my lifeless body. He's sobbing.

"Oh, Molly. Oh, please wake up. Please, God, give me a miracle and let her wake up."

Daddy rocks back and forth as he holds me in his arms. His tears soak my gray skin.

Mama is in the living room with Ava. She calls two neighbors, and word of my death moves at the speed of light. The next-door neighbor is in the house before the ambulance arrives. Mama makes crying noises and sniffs and produces real tears. She pretend cries well . . . Mama has learned to cry on demand. Everyone is in shock and they can't tell she's faking, but Gwen and I can.

After the ambulance has left our house, the coroner arrives. The tall gentleman has to pry Daddy's arms away from me. Daddy follows him and another man who move my body downstairs.

"Wait!" Daddy shouts outside my bedroom door. He grabs a clean blanket from the linen closet. "I need to wrap her in this blanket. She's always cold. I don't want her to be cold anymore. Do you understand?!" he screams hysterically.

The larger of the two men looks at my father with deep sadness. "Yes, sir, we'll do whatever you'd like us to do to keep your daughter comfortable."

Daddy lifts his head and looks at him with wild eyes. His head drops suddenly. A sob breaks free, and he leans into the stranger, who holds my father in his arms while Daddy sobs. The man gives Daddy some time, then pulls away from him. "What else can I do to help?"

Daddy wipes his nose on his sleeve. "You'll make sure you bathe her. She hated feeling dirty. My wife gave her sponge baths, but they weren't enough."

"Of course," the coroner says definitively. "I will make sure the water temperature is just right so that she's good and warm."

"Yessss!" Daddy cries. "She was so cold."

Daddy shakes his head back and forth. He looks at the man who has come to take me away. "This is real? She's dead?"

"Yes, sir. She's gone. I'm very sorry."

Daddy follows the men carrying me out to the vehicle that will take me away. He stands next to the driveway after they have pulled away. Then he hunkers low to the ground and stays there watching the taillights until I am gone.

Everyone has left our house. Mama is on the sofa with Ava. The television is muted and gives off an eerie glow. Daddy is up in his and Mama's room, sitting on the edge of the bed, still in his suit from work. He eventually gets up and walks into my bedroom. He kneels next to my unmade bed, grabs my covers, and pulls them to his chest.

"I'm so sorry, Molly. I'm so sorry you were here all alone. We had no idea that you were going to die. None. I'm sorry for everything. I will never get over this . . . ever. Mama and Ava will never be the same again. Our family is changed forever. Without you here, there will always be a part of me missing."

Daddy weeps until his body gives way, and he lies on the floor next to my bed until he falls asleep.

***

I look at Gwen, and she looks back. "Oh, Gwen. My death broke his heart. I wish I could go back and hold him. To tell him how much I love him and that he was a good father."

Gwen grabs onto me. "You all lost so much, but you'll live on in your dad and Ava's hearts. You'll be with them always."

I bury my head in Gwen's chest. "I don't wanna be here. I wanna go back to him and Ava!" I roar.

Gwen tilts my head up and looks into my eyes. "Just like on Earth, you can't go backward . . . you can only move forward from here."

Chapter Sixty-One

My father's grief unnerved me. I am helpless in my ability to get him through the stark realization that I am never coming back. To watch him mourn over me is sad and despairing. I wish that I could console him and let him know that I'm doing okay now . . . to soothe both of us.

I'm sitting in a forest of dead trees, but I don't know how I got here. The ground is dry and cracked. Quickly, the sky changes to dark purple, and black lightning cracks across the sky. My body is shaking, and I can't control it.

"Molly!" Gwen yells over the raging wind.

My head snaps up, and I reach for Gwen's hand. "What's happening? I'm scared."

Gwen grips my hand tighter and screams over the unbearable noise. "What's around us is a reflection of your soul! It's what's inside of you!"

I lower my head. My heart seizes in my chest. "Oh, Gwen, I can't stop thinking about the warning signs that I ignored."

Gwen moves in closer. "There were no warning signs."

"About a week before I died. Mama came to my room later than usual, and she sat on my bed and hugged me like she did every night of my life. I was very frail, too tired to keep up any kind of façade. She leaned in and gave me a hug, and when she did, I could feel her disease. It was the same hug as always, but that time I knew it wasn't real. Her embrace was practiced, and her stiff back and rigid arms betrayed her. I knew something was wrong with her."

"That's not a warning sign. That was an instinct, and it was already too late," Gwen says.

I nod, but it's difficult for me to accept this. I still feel at fault.

The black sky opens and dumps rain on us. Not regular rainfall, but a storm that smells like garbage and rot. Gwen pulls me forward, and we take shelter in a small, run-down shack she has imagined. There are large openings in the old, rotten wood where the windows are missing. The rain pelts us as we sink lower to the splintery, wooden floor.

"Let it go!" Gwen screams over the thunder and pouring, foul-smelling rain.

I gaze into Gwen's eyes. My new reality makes my head spin. The walls look like they're pressing in on us.

Gwen grabs my shoulders and shakes me. "Let it go. You were fooled, tricked, taken advantage of by your mother. She knew everything she was doing to you. If you want to move on to a better place, you need to leave all those dark feelings here. It's time to drop them and move on."

After watching my father grieve my death, Gwen's words are much more meaningful. I can no longer give my mother a pass or blame myself. I finally realize there was no way I could have known or understood what Mama was doing to me—and now that I see things for what they are, I have finally found acceptance.

I open my arms and wrap them around Gwen. As we embrace, my tears flow, and my body trembles.

When we part, I feel as though a weight has been lifted. Slowly the rain stops, and the sky turns blue and sunny again. I have survived the storm.

***

Gwen and I walk to my beach in Cape May and sit down. Finally, she speaks: "You'll be leaving Limbo soon."

I tilt my face toward the sun and smile. "Yeah, I know. I hate for this time to end now because you won't be with me every day."

Gwen raises her eyebrows. "What are you talking about? We'll be together forever. I already told you."

I nudge her gently in the ribs with my elbow. "Do you promise?"

Gwen makes an X over her heart. "I cross my heart."

Chapter Sixty-Two

It has been two and a half months since I died. Gwen and I are watching Joon. She is sitting on a curb outside of my house with her friend Skinner.

"How long have we been waiting?" Joon asks.

Skinner lifts his wrist and glances at his watch. "Just over two hours."

Joon runs her fingers through her long, greasy blond hair. "I hope he gets home soon."

As if on demand, Daddy pulls into our driveway.

"Here we go," Joon says, walking the long driveway toward the car.

Daddy gets out of the car and looks at Joon and Skinner suspiciously, taking in their dirty, tattered clothing. Daddy adjusts his stance, his feet spread apart, back erect, like he is preparing for a fight.

"What do you want?" Daddy's voice is deep and stern.

"My name is Joon. We met once for a few seconds. When your daughter Molly was in the hospital. My friend Lulu was her roommate."

Sadness flickers across Daddy's face. "Okay. So what do you want?"

Joon holds up my journal, the same leather-bound book he gave me to write down my thoughts.

"I went to visit Dr. Becker recently. He told me that Molly died. Molly gave me her journal. She asked me to give it to you if anything happened to her. That's why I'm here. Molly said, well, she said that she wanted you to have it. She . . . she said it was important to her that she leave something behind."

Daddy reaches for the journal. He flips to a random page and tenderly traces his fingers over the words I wrote. His stiff back softens. His eyes brighten, as though he has just seen an old friend.

"I appreciate you bringing this to me. Thanks."

"Sir, Molly said it was important for you to read it by yourself," Joon explains.

She shoves her hands into the pockets of her stained jeans. Her voice cracks. "Molly said it would upset her mom too much, and she didn't want to put her through any more pain."

Daddy turns the journal over in his hands. Then he leans into his car, pulls out his briefcase, and sticks my journal inside.

"Did she say anything else?" he murmurs.

"Yeah, Molly said that she really loved you. She loved her whole family. She wanted you to know how lucky she was to have you," she says. Joon pauses and wrings her hands together. "I was really sad to find out Molly died. She was a nice kid. She was funny. She was smart, and we laughed a lot together. I just want you to know I'm sorry she died."

Daddy clutches his briefcase tighter. "Thanks . . . I appreciate that." He looks Joon up and down. "Do you need money to get back home?"

Joon shakes her head. "No. We're fine. I hope you'll find comfort in whatever she's written. She said her final wishes are in there."

"You didn't read it?" Daddy asks.

"No. She asked me not to."

Daddy gives Joon a sad smile. "Thanks. And good luck . . . to both of you."

Inside the house, Daddy kisses Mama and goes up to their bedroom, locking the door behind him. He pops open his briefcase and pulls out my journal. Sitting at his desk, he turns to the first page and reads:

I'm Molly. Daddy gave me this journal so I can write down everything I'm thinking. I will call you Alice. I promise to write to you as much as I can.

Daddy smiles and moves his fingers along a brown ribbon attached to the journal. It's the page I wanted him to read first so he could understand why I needed him to have my journal:

Dear Alice,

I'm in the hospital, and I met two girls, Joon and Lulu. I like them both a whole lot. I will give Joon my journal before Lulu leaves the hospital. I want her to give it to Daddy. I pray every day that Joon will keep her promise and if I die she'll give this to Daddy.

*

Dear Daddy,

If you're reading this then I want you to keep my journal to yourself. I don't want you to show Mama because I know if anything happens to me, she will be very, very sad.

I'm very alone with my thoughts. I have no idea if I will die, but something inside is pushing me to write this. I wish I knew what was going to happen to me. If I die will I go somewhere different?

I know I'm not getting better. When I asked Mama if I would die, she told me to stop asking silly questions. Mama said that any day now, I'll be well again. But I know my body, and I know it's getting worse.

My dad flips back to the beginning and reads through the pages. He looks mesmerized by all that I have to say. All my silly thoughts. All my hopes and dreams. Then his eyes widen when he gets to a more serious entry.

*

Dear Alice,

I wish Mama's special medicine would work. I've never wanted something so much in my life. Mama and I were sure it would make me better. Even though her special medicine might not be working, I'm super happy that she came up

with something on her own. Every time I see her reach for
the plastic container in the cabinet above the stove and mix
that magic into my bag, I remember how lucky I am that she's
my mom.

I don't want to hurt her feelings by telling her the medicine
doesn't do anything good for me. I think she knows her
special medicine isn't working, but neither of us talks about
it. Somehow, it's easier not to talk about bad things. Mama
and I love being together, but we aren't anything alike, and
that makes it hard to talk to her sometimes.

My father stares at the page. His index finger slides back to the top, and he reads
the entry over again. His forehead creases; he looks confused. Daddy turns the
page.

*

Dear Alice,

When Mama came to the hospital today, she was pissed off.
She told me it was because she hated having Joon and Lulu in
the room with us. Like I told you yesterday, it's funny how
Mama and me are so different. Joon and Lulu are the best
things that have happened to me in a long time, probably
ever.

When I told Mama the girls were really nice and didn't
bother me, she told me she was also disappointed that Dr.
Becker wasn't doing more to help me get better. Today, she
doubled the dose of her special medicine. We're both hoping
it works for me.

238

After Mama unhooked my bag from the feeder and added all the special medicine, she led the two of us in prayer that God would make the medicine work.

Mama is doing everything she can to heal me. I hope her plan works.

Daddy closes my journal. A sob breaks loose from Daddy's throat as he speaks aloud. "Losing you was the worst thing that has ever happened to me. If I lose Ava, I won't be able to go on."

He slumps over and allows his tears to pour out of him. He hugs himself and rocks gently back and forth.

Once he has composed himself, he creeps into my old bedroom and lies in bed next to Ava. She shimmies closer to him, and he draws her into him as they fall asleep.

I stand and turn to Gwen. "My dad is so sad. It looks like his heart is broken."

"He's grieving the loss of his daughter . . . whom he loved more than anything."

"I wish he knew what my mom did, and what's being done to Ava."

Gwen is quiet, as if she's reflecting on my words.

The long stretch of silence between the two of us is more than I can take. I struggle with the sad images of my father. I want to rush back to him and tell him that I'm okay now.

I pull my hair to one side. "So Joon actually went out of her way to bring Daddy my journal. I almost wish I hadn't sent it to him, though."

Gwen looks at me questioningly. "Why? I know your dad is heartbroken, but he also looks relieved to see the journal that belonged to you. I'm sure knowing what you were thinking at the end of your life means a lot to him."

I fidget with the hem of my shirt. "I know all of that, but he was so sad. I think my journal made things worse for him. It seems selfish now that I'd want him to read it."

I rest my back against a tree. "It gets worse. The next entry, the last one I wrote, it's going to destroy him."

I cross my arms over my chest. I'm consumed with guilt and shame. When I wrote in that stupid journal, I thought it would be great for Daddy to hear from me if I died. Now I know it was a stupid decision that made me feel special when I was alive. Dumb. Dumb. Dumb.

I adjust my body and lean against Gwen. She holds me as we prepare to see my last journal entry.

Chapter Sixty-Three

It's morning, and through the lonely hours of the night, I forgive myself for causing my father more pain. Gwen is next to me. She scoots closer, and I give her my attention.

"What?" I ask.

"Are you doing okay?"

I nod. A powerful surge of courage runs through me. "Yeah, took me all night, but there's nothing I can do about it. I gave Joon my journal, and she gave it to my father, just like I asked her to. I don't want to wait anymore. Let's watch him read my last entry."

My father is in his and Mama's bedroom, sitting at the desk. He gently brushes his hand over the leather cover and opens it to the next and final journal entry.

Dear Daddy,

If you are reading this, then I'm dead. I hope there is a heaven or some better place where I'm at now. I know you think we go somewhere when we die. I've never wanted to believe that more than I do right now. If there is another place I go after I die, I hope that I'll see you all again someday. I need you to know how much I love you and Mama and Ava. I hope you'll never forget me and that I'll always be part of your life. My biggest fear is that I will be forgotten. Now, to the reason for this entry.

Dr. Becker is discharging Lulu from the hospital today, she's my roommate. Since I need to give this journal to Joon before they leave, I wanted me to say a final good-bye . . . just if what I think will happen, does.

My kidneys are in bad shape. Daddy, I'm so tired. It's too hard to fight anymore. Mama says I'll be fine, and I hope she's right. I wish I would get better so I'd have something to focus on. But I know in my heart that there's no real answer about what will happen, whether I will live or die.

I know how hard you and Mama tried to make me happy. I want you to know that all those nights you spent with me playing cards, reading, or just talking, made me so happy. If I have to leave here, please give Ava lots of attention. You and Mama have spent so much time taking care of me. I think she'll need you more than ever.

Mama will need your attention too. She hasn't been herself lately. She's been agitated, and snapping at me for the littlest things. I haven't seen her smile or laugh in weeks. When she comes to the hospital, she sits in the chair next to me and hardly listens to anything I say. I think maybe Mama's sad or something. I hope you'll be able to make her feel more herself again.

I'm afraid of the future and what will happen to my life when I go home without a new kidney. If I can get better, that would be my dream come true. I hope and pray that a year from now I'll have a new kidney and get to start my life over. I love you, Daddy. I've always loved you, and I'll love you until the day I die (which I hope is when I'm really, really old).

Hugs and kisses,

Molly

Daddy closes my journal and presses the book to his chest. He closes his eyes and lifts my journal to his nose, taking in a long whiff of the leather. A single tear slides down his cheek. He raises his hand and brushes it away.

"Don't worry. I'll take good care of Ava, I promise," he says aloud.

Daddy opens a desk drawer and places my journal under a pile of papers. He walks over to his bed and stands.

Daddy falls to his knees and looks to the ceiling. "Oh, Molly, I wish I could turn back time . . . I should've spent more time with you. I should've demanded more from the doctors. I didn't know you were going to die . . . I swear."

Daddy softly shakes his head. "I've noticed a change in your mother before you died, too. I suppose in her heart she was sad because she may have suspected you wouldn't survive. I think she kept it a secret because she didn't want to worry me about something I couldn't control. Your mom seems fine now. She'll never get over losing you, and she's taking good care of Ava."

It's hard to watch my father grieve me, to see him so vulnerable and broken.

Daddy turns around and sits on the floor, leaning his back against the bed. He slows his breathing. "Your mom and I have been arguing a lot since you died. Mostly about Ava's feeding tube. I swear, sometimes she seems addicted to it. I want it taken out like Dr. Becker suggested, but she won't even consider it. I'm still working on her, though."

***

"Gwen! Did you hear what he just said? He fights with my mom about getting Ava's tube out. Maybe she's going to be okay," I gush.

Gwen pats my hand. "I hope you're right."

"You don't believe my dad's gonna save Ava. Do you?"

Gwen lowers her eyes. "I don't know. I think he'll have a hard time convincing your mom to have the feeding tube removed. And as long as Ava has the tube, your mom can do whatever she wants. I don't see her giving up that control."

"But do you think there's a chance that my father figures out what my mom is doing to Ava?"

"Look, I know you want a definitive answer. It's hard to say. I honestly don't know whether he'll figure it out. But if he does, I'm sure he'll do something. He loves you both too much."

I look down at my hands. "I don't think anyone could ever stop Mama."

I want Gwen to tell me I'm wrong. She doesn't let me down.

"Your dad will do anything to stop your mother. This I know."

Chapter Sixty-Four

After Daddy composes himself, he stands and goes into my old bedroom, where Ava is lying in her bed. She is ashen and slight.

"Hi, Ava," Daddy says, sitting on the bed next to her.

Ava gives him a weak smile. "Hi."

"What are you doing?"

Ava points to the bag of liquid food. "Mama just gave me a new bag. She put special medicine in it."

Daddy's back straightens. "Oh, yeah? Special medicine. The medicine she keeps in the cabinet over the stove?"

Ava nods. "It doesn't work that good," she whispers. "It didn't work for Molly either, but she never told Mama."

Daddy's eyes dart to the bedroom door. "Honey, I have to run downstairs and grab something. I'll be back soon."

As I watch with Gwen, my breath flows in and out of my lungs rapidly.

Daddy leaves my old bedroom and goes to the kitchen. He marches over to the stove and opens the cabinet above it. He pulls out the container of special medicine. He removes the lid and smells what's inside. Then he wets his finger and sticks it into the crystals. When his finger hit his tongue, he gags.

Mama walks into the kitchen and sees him. "What's wrong? What are you doing?" she asks.

He stands upright and holds the container out for her to see, then rushes toward her.

"Rona! What did you do? This special medicine . . . the one you gave Molly and are now giving Ava . . . its salt!"

Mama's face drains of color.

Daddy steps in closer. "Did you kill Molly with salt?"

Mama shakes her head in disbelief and takes several steps back from my father. Her hand jerks to her neck.

"I have no idea what you're tal . . . tal . . . talking about," she stammers. "You're wrong about everything."

"Oh, dear God. You did. You killed her. How long did you poison her? What else did you do to Molly? Huh? You killed her, and now you're trying to kill Ava."

Mama's eyes shift around the room like a caged animal looking for an escape route.

"I did no such thing!" she screams. "You're fucking crazy!"

Daddy takes a couple of steps forward, closing the distance between them. "You're a fucking liar!" he roars.

Daddy lunges at my mom. He tackles her to the kitchen floor and puts his hands around her throat. Mama tries to pry them off, but his anger makes him too powerful. She kicks her legs, which only makes my father tighten his grip. Her eyes bug out of her skull, and her face turns bright red. Finally her lips turn purple, and I am sure he will kill her.

I know it's wrong, but I wish he does kill her, to avenge my death. Hate for my mother and love for my father converge inside of me.

"Daddy?" Ava's voice shrieks from behind him.

My father turns quickly and looks at my feeble baby sister. His hands detach from around my mother's throat. When he stands, Mama rolls onto her side, coughing and gasping for air.

Daddy rushes to Ava and quickly opens the small backpack that holds what is left of her liquid dinner. He shuts the feeding valve off. Then he picks Ava up, grabs his keys, and walks out the front door. He drives at high speed to the hospital.

Daddy rams through the emergency room doors with Ava in his arms. "Dr. Becker! Get him right now!"

When Dr. Becker finally enters the bay where Daddy cradles Ava on his lap, he looks at my father with grave concern.

The doctor pulls a chair close to Daddy. "What's happened?"

Daddy looks up at the doctor. Daddy's face is wet with tears and his eyes are red and puffy. "It was my wife. How could she do this? How didn't I know?"

"Kurt, you're not making any sense. Has something happened to Rona?"

Daddy shakes his head. His chest heaves as his sobs break loose. Dr. Becker whisks Ava from my father and hands her to the nurse standing inside the bay. "Take her next door. I'll be there in a few minutes."

The doctor kneels in front of my father. Daddy is shaking and bawling. He bellows a sound I thought was reserved for animals.

Watching him sends a bolt of fear through me. Does he think Ava is going to die? I reset and bite back my own fear as Gwen and I watch my father.

"Kurt. Talk to me. Is Rona okay? Did something happen to her?" Dr. Becker asks.

Daddy reaches over and grabs Ava's half-full bag from the floor. He hands it to the doctor.

"What's this?"

"It . . . it . . . is . . . Avaaaa's," he cries, and rocks on the hard plastic chair.

Dr. Becker takes the bag and studies it. He squeezes the liquid inside the bag as though it is a foreign substance. Then he turns to Daddy with a blank look. "I don't understand."

With shaking hands, Daddy grabs the bag from Dr. Becker. "Salt. Rona was putting salt in her bag. I think . . . I think . . . she killed Molly. Rona told the girls it was special medicine that she made. Molly wrote about it in her journal. A girl named Joon, she said she knew you, she brought me Molly's journal. Then, tonight, when Ava told me she was getting Rona's special medicine, something clicked, and my instincts told me to investigate."

"Joon?" Dr. Becker says in a daze.

Dr. Becker lets out an audible breath. "Oh, dear God." He takes Ava's feeding bag from my father and turns to walk away.

"Wait!" Daddy yells.

Dr. Becker turns back. Daddy's eyes are glowing, like fire and brimstone. "Ava had half of the bag tonight. I don't know . . . I don't know how long this has been going on."

The doctor pats my father's shoulder. "Kurt, just stay here. I'm going to help you and Ava, I promise. I'll have the nurse bring Ava back in. Okay?"

Daddy nods and mindlessly rakes his fingers through his hair. The nurse brings Ava back in and places her on the bed.

Ava whimpers.

"What is it, Ava? Does something hurt you?"

"Noooo. I'm scared."

"There's nothing to be afraid of. I'm staying right here with you. I'm going to take good care of you."

Ava peers up at my father and smiles.

Daddy slips onto the hospital bed next to her, and she snuggles into the nook of his arm and rests her head on his chest. As I watch my father and sister, it hits me that I've saved my little sister by having Joon bring my journal to Daddy.

Relief washes over me and a soft moan escapes my lips. "My mother has been caught. She's been stopped. Ava will live," I say while hoping that my broken heart can begin to heal.

Gwen and I move toward each other to embrace, as tears of relief run down my face.

Chapter Sixty-Five

D r. Becker admits Ava to the hospital that night, and late the next morning, he checks on her. Daddy is asleep in a chair next to her bed, having refused to leave her alone overnight.

"Kurt?" Dr. Becker says.

Daddy's eyes snap open, and he sits up straight.

"Good morning."

Daddy looks at the doctor. "Dr. Becker. Thanks for coming by."

Daddy turns to Ava." How are you feeling today, sweetheart?"

"I'm tired is all."

Daddy kisses Ava's forehead.

"Dr. Becker, did you hear anything from the lab?"

The doctor nods. He takes Ava's hand in his own. "Hey, Ava. Your dad and I need to talk for a minute. I asked one of the nurses to bring you some ice cream."

Ava's face lights up. "Really? Did Mama say I can have it?"

My father's jaw clenches. "From now on, I'm in charge, Ava. Mama won't be telling you what you can and can't have anymore," Daddy says, keeping his voice low and gentle.

In the hallway, Dr. Becker explains there was a high level of salt in Ava's feeding bag.

"Look, Kurt, the psychological problem your wife has is challenging to detect. She fooled a lot of people, including me. Rona is a very sick woman. Given the level of sodium in Ava's bloodwork, I called the police, and they'll be coming down here to talk to you this morning."

The doctor hesitates for several seconds. "I'm sorry this happened to you and your family. Right now the best thing you can do is take care of Ava. I suspect the police will arrest Rona today."

Daddy shoves his hands in his pockets. "Dr. Becker. Why? How? I mean, why would a mother harm her own children? Rona never showed any signs of hatred toward Molly or Ava. She's bossy and demanding, sure, but I never suspected she would hurt either of them. Honestly, that was the farthest thing from my mind.

Now I have to live with the knowledge that I let my wife kill my daughter. I don't even know who Rona is."

As Daddy's words sink in, I realize that Daddy too has to question everything he thought to be true. Oddly, this comforts me. I am not alone in being fooled by Mama. Daddy wonders about the same things that have brought me anguish since I learned the truth about my death.

At this moment, I know that I did the most critical thing right . . . the innocent words in my journal saved Ava. I feel vindicated. I no longer died it vain—I died to save my sister.

"You know," Gwen says, "if it weren't for Joon living up to her promise, this could've all turned out differently. She's a good person. And it's obvious she loved you very much."

Gwen takes my hand in hers. "How do you think your mom is going to react?"

I shrug. "Oh, she'll be mad as a hornet. I don't know how these things work, but maybe she'll be sent to prison."

"Yeah, I bet she will be."

I look into the sky. "I guess it's her turn to feel pain. I'm happy that she's been stopped. Whatever happens to Mama now is because she brought it on herself."

Gwen rests her forehead against mine. "Well, just think. You saved your sister, and your mom will never be in charge again. You're a hero."

"You mean I'm a dead hero."

I let that sink in. It's a bittersweet moment for me. My sister will thrive again, and I can only hope my mother will pay consequences for her actions. It's not hatred that I feel so much as indifference.

I shake off my thoughts, look at Gwen, and give her a victorious smile. "I saved my sister."

The two of us sit and take in the beauty around us.

"My time in Limbo is almost over."

Gwen leans into me. "It wasn't so bad, right?"

"Are you kidding? It was the worst." I giggle. "No, I guess it wasn't so bad but only because everything turned out the right way."

I draw in a long breath. "I'd like to see what happens to my mom."

Gwen raises her eyebrows. "Are you sure?"

I nod and rest my head on my friend's shoulder. The journey to this point has been painful and joyous. It was challenging to learn the truth about my life, and it's liberating to let it go.

I saw things differently when I was alive, through a lens of trust. Now I see things for what they are and how they've always been. It's a huge difference.

I can only hope that Mama will have remorse for what she did to Ava and me.

Chapter Sixty-Six

Mama sits in the back of a police car, her arms behind her back, wrists bound by handcuffs. She stares out of the front window. Her eyes are narrow, and her jaw is set firmly. The anger smolders around her nose and mouth.

The police car pulls into the back lot at the station, and as an officer guides Mama out, she looks around, as if expecting to be greeted by reporters eager to hear her story. She looks at the police officer with a scowl, in her "I'll fuck you up" way.

Mama jerks her arms away, trying to break free from the officer's grip. "Where are the news people? I need to tell my side of the story. This is all a big lie made up by my husband. I swear to you. Before my older daughter, Molly, died, my husband and I were having marital problems because he was cheating on me," Mama says.

Mama tries to stop walking, but the officer pulls her along.

She seethes, "Are you listening to me? My husband has been trying to take our younger daughter away ever since my older one died. He's a liar!"

Mama looks up at the tall officer, who doesn't return eye contact. Her face turns bright red, and she speaks through clenched teeth. "You're working for him, aren't you? How much did he pay you to set me up? Huh? How much?"

The officer finally looks down at Mama with his flat brown eyes. "Ma'am, I don't know what you're talking about, but I would suggest you save your story for your lawyer."

Mama tries to twist away from the officer again, but she's no match for him, and he effortlessly pulls her toward the entrance doors. Inside the police station, Mama is fingerprinted, strip-searched, and placed into a holding cell with another woman.

My mother glares at her cellmate, who glares back. The woman sneers at Mama and says, "Keep looking at me like that, and I'll come over there and kill ya. Hear me?"

Mama turns away, but Gwen and I can practically see the steam oozing from her forehead. When Mama turns back toward her cellmate, the woman is standing next to my mother. She grabs the collar of Mama's shirt and lifts her. The woman puts her nose against my mother's, and for the first time ever, I see fear pass in my mother's eyes.

"When I ask you a question, I expect an answer," Mama's cellmate fumes.

The woman jacks Mama up against the block wall. "What's wrong? Cat got your tongue? If you ain't gonna use it, how 'bout I just rip it outta your mouth?"

Mama's eyes bounce around the cell. "I . . . I didn't mean to offend you. I lost my daughter recently," she says, squeaking out a tear.

The woman bangs Mama's head against the wall. "Bitch, I don't give a shit why you're here. You think I ain't got my own family problems? You think you're the only woman who lost someone? You need to think again. You can save your tears for someone who fucking cares."

The woman shoves Mama one more time into the wall as she releases her shirt. "If you give attitude to the bitches on the inside, they'll eat you for dinner . . . probably breakfast and lunch too."

The woman howls in laughter in a way that makes my blood run cold.

Mama gets onto her cot and puts her back against the wall. She doesn't take her eyes off of her cellmate.

My mother is trembling. Her knees are against her chest, and her arms are wrapped around her legs.

I'm scared for her, but I don't tell Gwen. I know Mama doesn't deserve my sympathy, and I certainly don't forgive what she did, but it's hard to watch anyone look paralyzed with fear. But I am not coldhearted like Mama, that's the difference.

I lay back on the blanket Gwen and I have spread under us. "Let's take a break. I'd like a little time to process things."

Gwen lies back next to me. "Do you want me to go?"

"No, I want you to stay with me."

Gwen rolls onto her side and faces me. "Are you okay?"

I'm looking into the smooth blue of the sky above me. "Not really. I want my mom to pay the consequences for her actions, but I'm kind of nervous for her."

Gwen sits up abruptly. "Molly, you can't be serious. Your mother killed you. She didn't think at all about the suffering she caused you. I'm not saying you should hate her or anything. I'm saying . . . well . . . I'm saying you shouldn't feel bad because she has to pay for a serious crime that she committed . . . against you."

I grab Gwen's hand and interlace our fingers. "That's the problem. I do hate her for killing me, but I feel bad for her too 'cause she's my mom. Does that make sense?"

"Kind of. I can't imagine what it'd be like to find out my mother hurt me on purpose to get what she wanted from other people. But at the same time, you can't be so hard on yourself. I think you're one of the strongest people I've ever met. To go through everything you did and still have even an ounce of kindness for your mom makes you a super special person. Right now, I think you're confused. But, with time, it'll all become clear."

"I wish you could've been my mom."

Gwen frowns. "I never made it past fourteen, so I would have no idea how to be a mom."

Gwen lies down next to me. There's a chill in the air, and goose bumps rise on our arms. I picture a soft, warm blanket so I can pull it over the two of us. Once we settle, we both close our eyes and allow sleep to carry us away. I'll face whatever comes next when I wake.

Chapter Sixty-Seven

Shortly after Mama is arrested, the district attorney files murder charges against her for my death. Since there wasn't an autopsy performed on me after I died, there is no substantial evidence to use in the trial. But the district attorney had still filed every charge he could against her hoping to get a murder conviction.

The trial lasts for three weeks. Mama appears to thrive on the media frenzy that buzzes around her, keeping her the center of attention. Throughout the trial, she turns to the cameras with a frown or watery eyes.

The prosecution accuses my mother of being a calculated child killer who researched, planned, and executed my death and attempted to murder Ava in the same manner. The prosecutor was right: Mama did those things.

Mama's attorney argues that she has a disease called Munchausen syndrome by proxy, a mental illness that comes with severe emotional challenges.

The prosecutor argues that even if Mama did have a disease, she's demonstrated that she has the ability to reason. He fights for my mom to be held accountable for her actions and receive the maximum sentence.

In the end, the jury doesn't find sufficient evidence to convict Mama of my murder, which disappoints me, but she is found guilty of endangering a child, tampering with medical records to deceive doctors, and child abuse with the intent to kill for what she did to Ava. Mama cries out in protest, proclaiming her innocence.

Her tears have no effect on the judge, who sentences her to ten years to life in prison with the possibility of parole after serving seven consecutive years. Daddy literally jumps from his seat when the judge is done speaking. My father's face is red, and the lines around his eyes have deepened. Daddy yells, "Ten years is not enough time! She needs to rot in prison. She should be convicted to life without parole. She killed my daughter!"

The guards silence him, of course, but the judge is lenient on Daddy, given the circumstances.

Mama doesn't even turn to look, but the corners of her lips curl into a smile.

I assume that Mama is thrilled that she has won. She will go to prison, yes, but she'd gotten away with murder, and that must make her feel victorious.

"My dad is right, Mama should never get out of prison," I say to Gwen. "Ava will be a teenager if she gets out in ten years. What if she tries to see her again? What if everyone forgets what she did by then?"

Gwen shakes her head. "Your dad will never forget that you're gone. You see those embers glowing in his eyes? That's the sign of red-hot vengeance."

Seven years in prison, if she gets out early, doesn't seem like enough time. I lost my entire life at her hands, and Ava suffered irreversible damage to her liver. It seems unfair, but everything that's happened has been unfair.

Mama didn't succeed in killing Ava, but it still seems like she's won.

***

I've chosen to sit next to a stream. I am deep in a forest with towering trees, and the smell of pine awakens my senses. It reminds me of Christmas. The sound of the water running over the rocks is soothing. The day is warm, and sunbeams poke through the foliage, making beautiful patterns of sun and shade over the forest floor. Above the trees, the sky is turquoise. A soft breeze caresses my body as I wait for the final curtain to come down on my life on Earth. I imagine there are soft quilts and fluffy pillows all around me, and I sink into them. Gwen lays down and snuggles against me.

"It's so peaceful here," I say to Gwen, watching white rabbits hopping on the other side of the stream.

"Yeah, you have a wonderful imagination. I love it."

We take in the glorious sights, sounds, and smells of nature. I relax. My body, mind, and spirit are one.

"Well, today should be interesting," Gwen remarks.

I nod and suddenly sense my adrenaline. "We can only hope. She got away with murdering me. Mama has a huge personality. I bet all the other women in prison will love her."

I pause and look at my hands, happy that they are a healthy color and not that horrible gray I last saw when I lay in my bed, waiting to die.

Gwen snuggles in closer, more for my benefit than hers. I think she wants me to know I'm not alone and that I'll never be alone again. I'm grateful.

Mama's ankles and wrists are shackled as she shuffles into her new home for years to come. As the guard guides her to the cell where she will live, the other inmates scream at her.

Mama doesn't flinch. Instead, she holds her chin up, puffs out her chest, and walks fearlessly. She makes eye contact and smiles at several women who are watching her closely. She stands before her open cell and looks in. The guard nudges her forward, but Mama plants her feet firmly on the cement floor as she faces her confinement.

Mama's cellmate is a woman covered in tattoos. She stands and gives my mother a toothless smile. "Welcome home, sugar."

Mama looks at the guard, who gives her a shrug in response. Then she gives Mama a slight push into her cage, shuts the barred door, and walks away.

"I'm Sadie. You got the top bunk," the large white woman covered in ink says.

Mama wrinkles her nose as she assesses Sadie's tattoos, which creep up her neck and face. Instinctively, Sadie reaches up and covers her neck with her hands before averting her gaze.

"Hello," Mama begins with a tight smile. "I'm Rona. I don't mind sleeping on the top bunk unless, of course, you'd prefer it."

Sadie seems to think about it for a moment. "Nah, I'm good down here."

"You have such beautiful hair," Mama says. "I'd love to braid it for you."

Sadie's hand moves from her neck to her long, frizzy hair. "Oh, yeah? Okay, I'd like that."

Mama looks at the top bunk and back at Sadie. "I guess I'll climb up and take a little rest."

Sadie shrugs as Mama climbs the metal ladder welded to the bed frames.

When she reaches the top she kicks her shoes off over the side. Then she leans over the top bunk and looks down at Sadie. "I need to get a few hours of sleep, so try to be quiet."

Sadie's mouth flails open as though she's going to say something.

Mama's eyes narrow, and Sadie lowers her eyes to the floor and nods.

Mama lays back, crosses her arms over her chest, and smiles.

Chapter Sixty-Eight

Gwen and I are numb as we watch Mama flourish in prison. She has taken on the unique role of mother-slash-teacher to the other inmates. They go to her with questions about their legal cases, raising children, dealing with the guards, and even home remedies. She is book smart and can learn effortlessly from reading, so she has made herself a needed member of the community.

Because Mama wasn't found guilty of actually murdering me, she is able to explain her "period of confusion" when it comes to Ava.

Mama sits in the common room of the prison. The television plays in the background and a dozen women sit around listening intently to her story. "I never did anything harmful to my daughters. That sonofabitch bastard husband of mine made up this whole big lie. He has a girlfriend, you know. He's had one for years. Oh, I pretended not to know anything about it, but I knew," she says.

"Well, honey," one of the older women says, "your husband is gonna rot in hell for what he's done to you. Don't you worry one bit."

Mama uses a tissue to dab at her eyes. "I'm so lucky to have all of you as friends. I'll tell you, out there, in that shit world, everyone always believes the man over a woman. It's an awful truth. So I'm happy we as women can stick together."

The women nod and mumble their agreement.

I stop watching and address Gwen. "I'm ready to move on to my final resting place. I've seen it all now. How does it work?"

"You'll go to sleep now, and when you wake I'll be able to tell you if you're ready. Remember, you can't bring anything bad to where you're going. Once I know for sure all is good, you'll go right away," Gwen says.

That night, I lay in my oversize bed and think about my life and my family as I drift off to sleep.

When I wake, it is still dark and Gwen is beside my bed and gently shaking me. "Molly. Molly. You need to wake up. Something important is happening."

My eyes flutter open. "What is it?"

"There's something you need to see."

I hope it's nothing to do with Ava. I bound out of bed and imagine the familiar bench in the park where I played basketball when I was alive. I look ahead of me.

Mama is on the top bunk. She's moaning.

"Is she having a bad dream?" I ask Gwen.

"Nope. Look closer."

Mama is holding her stomach. She's rocking from side to side.

"Sadie," Mama says with a gasp, "I need a doctor."

Sadie storms the cell bar door and yells, "Help! Rona needs help!"

Soon guards are running toward Mama's cell. They talk to Mama while she is doubled over, clutching her stomach and moaning. Her movements are jerky. She looks to be in agonizing pain, but I don't feel sorry for her.

A guard gets on her radio. A gurney appears. They're moving Mama from her cell and pushing the gurney quickly to the medical care center. A nurse waits with Mama while the ambulance pulls up and she is taken to a hospital.

Gwen and I watch inside the emergency room. The guards handcuff one of Mama's wrists to a bar on the side of the bed, and her other hand is clamped over her mouth. "I'm gonna throw up," she says with a grunt.

The nurse gives Mama a pan as she hurls.

After the ER doctor completes a physical exam, Mama has an X-ray, a CT scan, and an ultrasound. All the while, she complains and questions everything they do.

The doctor walks into the bay for the second time where she's laying. "Hi, Rona. I have your test results."

"Oh, Dr. Elliot, thank God! What's wrong with me?" She is panting.

"Well, I'm fairly certain you have a bowel obstruction. We're going to give you a barium enema to get better images of your intestines," Dr. Elliot explains.

"Really? Do you have to? That sounds awful," Mama whines.

"Well, it's not very pleasant, but it usually lasts no longer than forty-five minutes, from start to finish. A technician will be in for you soon and we'll get started," he says.

"Wait—can you give me something for the pain?" Mama wails.

"No, not just yet. Once we get this procedure done I'll give you something. I need you awake. I want you to hang on and it'll be over before you know it," Dr. Elliot says.

"Hang on? That's easy for you to say. You're not the one in pain," Mama barks.

The doctor pats her arm, like he would a child, and leaves the bay.

The barium enema looks excruciating. Mama is on a table in a small room. She lays on her side as the doctor inserts a tube into her rectum and the barium fills her intestines slowly. Mama's yelping like a dog being stepped on.

"Stop!" she yells. "You're hurting me! Stop it! Something's wrong!"

But the doctor reassures Mama all is fine as he gets the images he needs to make a good diagnosis.

I tell Gwen, "My mom is freaking out over one medical procedure. I was never allowed to complain in front of her. She called it bellyaching. I'd get in serious trouble for that. Now, look at her, crying and screaming. She's so pathetic. That test was nothing compared to some of the tests I had to do because of her."

"Yeah, I think it's interesting how she gets upset when she's treated the same way that she has treated you. She's a coward and a complainer, that's for sure."

Gwen reaches for my hand and squeezes it as we wait for the doctor to deliver Mama's test results.

Chapter Sixty-Nine

Dr. Elliot enters the ER bay. His brow scrunches as he approaches Mama's bedside.

"Dr. Elliot, finally. Please, give me good news and something for this damn pain."

Dr. Elliot says, "I've ordered pain medication for you, and the nurse will be here with it soon. We have the results of your tests. Rona, you do have a bowel obstruction. It's pretty bad. There are a few things going on. You have a large hernia, but I can also see that your bowels are twisted. That needs to be fixed right away."

Mama covers her mouth with her hand. Genuine shock registers on her face. "What? That can't be, Dr. Elliot. You must've read the results wrong."

Dr. Elliot shakes his head. "I know it's not what you want to hear."

Mama flinches and lets out a sharp yelp as she curls in the bed. "Look, I can't take this pain anymore!"

"Rona, we need to take you to the operating room. Now. So we can fix what's going on. I'm very concerned," Dr. Elliot says.

"Yes! Immediately. I'll be getting out of prison when I'm forty-one years old. I'll still be a young woman with my whole life ahead of me. I have a daughter, she'll still be young, and she needs a mother."

The doctor turns to the nurse who enters the room. "Cindy is going to give you something for pain. We'll be moving you to the OR within the hour."

Mama squirms on the bed.

"It's not so easy being at the mercy of other people," I say to Gwen. "I guess Mama's getting a taste of what it's like not to know what's gonna happen."

When the surgery is complete, Mama is put into a hospital room. Dr. Elliot looks tired and worn out by the time he goes to check on her.

"Hi, Rona. How are you feeling?"

Her eyelids are heavy. "A little groggy," she answers. "How did everything go?"

Dr. Elliot frowns, but Mama's eyes are closed. "Well, better than I had hoped. There was a portion of your intestines that were twisted. Unfortunately, they were that way for too long and they died."

Mama's eyes open and she looks at the doctor. "What?"

"There were complications. I removed the obstruction and fixed the hernia, but there was a portion of your intestines that was dead from being twisted, so I removed the damaged area and reattached it, which was the right thing to do. Now, the downside is that I had to surgically insert a gastric feeding tube in your abdomen area. It's essentially a port where you'll need to be fed through for now."

As the doctor gives Mama the information, I can see her eyes focusing on him. Until she is fully awake.

"What are you talking about? Why? I didn't give you permission to do that."

The doctor sighs. "I did it to save your life. You did sign the paperwork before we went into the OR, remember? To give us permission to take lifesaving measures."

Mama gives him a blank stare. "Well, what now?" she demands.

"For now, you'll rest. Tomorrow morning the nurses will feed you through your tube. You won't feel a thing."

Mama turns her head away from the doctor. "I know what a feeding tube is and how it works, Dr. Elliot, probably better than you do. I just can't believe you took the liberty to put one into me."

"You need to get nutrition, and that was the only option. You'll need time to process. The bottom line is you would've died if the dead intestines weren't removed. This may not be for forever. Our goal would be to have you eating normally again," Dr. Elliot explains.

"You don't know shit," Mama grumbles. "You can cram food into your pie hole. How the hell am I supposed to manage this in prison? Thanks for nothing, Dr. Elliot. What a mess you've made of everything."

Dr. Elliot moves toward the door. "I'll be back to check on you later."

"Don't bother," Mama spits.

Dr. Elliot keeps walking, without turning back.

***

"This is crazy," I say to Gwen. "Almost unbelievable to think that my mom now has to deal with a feeding tube. The restriction that comes with it is awful, and the one thing Mama doesn't like is not being able to do, eat, or say whatever she wants."

"Your mom deserves everything she's getting."

I agree with Gwen. I give her a smile and say, "At least some justice has been served, but it doesn't seem like enough. Mama thinks she's bigger and better than anything or anybody. But she isn't."

I hope this is a long, hard road for Mama. The same road she forced me to travel. I am surprised that Mama's suffering brings me joy. I almost feel guilty about it, too.

Chapter Seventy

Mama stays in the hospital for another ten days before they transfer her back to prison.

Inside the prison medical unit, the nurse discusses the plan for Mama's care. "You'll come here for your bags, and we'll put them in this backpack," she says, holding up a bland gray bag. "Then you'll join the other women in the cafeteria."

Mama scoffs. "You're kidding me, right?"

"No, I'm not kidding," the nurse says curtly.

"You expect me to strap on some liquid feeding bag and sit with the others while they eat? You're out of your mind," Mama barks with finality.

"Rona, you're are incarcerated and living in a prison. While I understand you may not like what's happening, it is not your decision. As I've already explained, you will come here, get your bag hooked up, and join the other prisoners in the cafeteria. Is there anything else you need to discuss?"

Mama glowers at the woman. "No. Certainly nothing I need to talk to you about."

A few weeks back at prison and Mama is miserable. Apparently, not eating puts her in a foul mood all the time. Finally, annoyed at the situation, Mama goes through the food line and eats again. She does this for three days, and then things change again.

One night after dinner, Mama is laying on her top bunk. She's so cold that Sadie gives Mama her blanket. Mama's breathing is rapid, and she's not making much sense.

Sadie puts her hand on Mama's forehead. "Shit, woman. You're burning up. I'll get one of the guards."

Mama growls, "Don't you dare. I swear I'll kill you if you tell anyone. Those idiots don't know what they're doing. They'll send me to that incompetent nurse. Just leave me be. I'll be fine. I know my body."

Sadie shrugs and lies on her bunk.

We watch my mom suffer through the night. She's completely out of it ten hours after she began feeling ill. By six o'clock the next morning, twelve hours later, Mama lays motionless on her bunk. Sadie gets up and uses the toilet. She looks at Mama, who's facing away from her.

Sadie gently pushes her shoulder. "Hey, Rona. You need to wake up."

Mama doesn't respond.

"Rona, come one. Get up. You're gonna hold up breakfast."

When my mom doesn't move, Sadie stands on her bunk to get a better look. She puts her hand over Mama's mouth and nose. Then she jumps from the bunk onto the floor.

"Guard! Guard! Hurry! She ain't breathing!" Sadie screams.

My own breath catches in my throat and my mouth drops open as I look over at Gwen. "What's happened to her?"

"I'm not totally sure, but it looks like she was sicker than she thought," Gwen says.

We are both mesmerized as the events unfold.

They rush Mama from her cell to a waiting ambulance. The emergency medical technician is on his radio with the hospital. "She doesn't have a pulse. A guard administered CPR until we got there, but he wasn't able to revive her. Her body temperature is ninety-five point five degrees. We'll be at the hospital in about ten minutes."

Mama is never revived. She died on the top bunk on top of a thin mattress inside her prison cell and wasn't discovered until it was too late.

My elbows are digging into my thighs as I watch unblinking as Mama's body is removed from the emergency room. She is fully covered with a sheet. I try to let the situation that just happened seep into my being.

"My mom is dead?" I say.

Gwen says, "Yes. She's dead."

I let out a loud breath before I get up and imagine I'm sitting in a warm and cozy wooded area. Gwen is next to me. I turn to her. "There's something else I need to know . . ."

Chapter Seventy-One

I take in the vastness of Limbo. I look over my right shoulder, then my left. My hands won't stay still.

"Are you okay?" Gwen asks.

"No, not really. I, um, now that my mom is dead, what'll happen to her? My stomach clamps down tight, full of worry.

Gwen casts her eyes to the ground. "You want to know if you're going to see your mom here in Limbo or where you're going next. That's what you're worried about, right?"

"Yeah. I don't want to talk to her ever again. I have nothing to say to her . . . definitely nothing nice."

"You can relax, Molly. People like your mom, who have black hearts, go someplace different. Your mom won't see anyone where she is."

"There's no way I'll 'bump' into her? You're totally sure about that?"

"Yep, I'm sure. Come on, I'll show you."

Gwen and I stare into a white cloud above us. The vision of Mama comes into view. We look closer, zooming in on her. Mama's in a small, dark, locked closet. It's a little smaller than a coffin.

"That looks horrible," I remark.

"It is," Gwen says. "For as long as she's in there no one will ever open her closet, and she won't be able to get out on her own."

Mama stands in the blackness alone. She's thrashing her entire body against the walls of the closet. She's making crying sounds between her grunts and groans. I can only imagine that she wants someone to save her.

I put my hand over my mouth. Watching her suffer is almost too much.

Gwen explains, "All the physical and emotional pain your mom caused you and others are what she's experiencing now. You can see the closet is so small, she can't even sit."

I turn my head to put my left ear closer to her sounds. "What is she saying?"

Gwen lifts her shoulders. "I have no idea. Your mom can't talk or hear anymore."

I look closely. Small gnats buzz around her, taking teeny-tiny bites from her flesh, but she can't lift her arms to swat at them. My skin itches from watching.

I imagine Mama is screaming inside her own head to be let out. Her rage is uncontained. I shiver knowing she won't get out anytime soon.

Gwen studies me. "Do you want me to tell you all about where your mom is?"

I scratch the tip of my nose with my index finger. "There's more?"

Gwen nods. I nod back.

"Well, your mom will go through a lot of appalling physical changes. They'll be drastic; she will become as ugly on the outside as she was on the inside when she was alive. She'll stay in that dreary place for a long time . . . ten years for every year she lived on Earth. She'll be trapped in her own twisted, thwarted mind. She'll be in a heightened state of fear, annoyance, and pain. Each day, she will believe her torture will end, but the end won't come for a long, long time. It's the worst kind of punishment."

"Will she have to stay for the whole time? And what happens to her when she's allowed to leave the closet?"

Gwen turns toward me. "How long she stays depends on her. If she's actually sorry for the damage she caused, which isn't likely because she seems incapable of feeling empathy for anyone, she'll be let out to a contained area where she will live among her own kind. There are a lot of mirrors around, so she will see how ugly she became while suffering in her closet. It's a constant reminder of her sins. Like the others she's doomed to live with, she will look like a decrepit creature. Her skin will bubble all over her body, her eyes will be all one color—flat black, and her teeth will dangle like rotted stubs from her gums."

Gwen pauses. We both look around at the tall grass and wildflowers. The sound of a stream trickles in the distance. It is peaceful.

Gwen clears her throat. "It's not a place like this. If your mom is released into the contained area, it's almost as awful as the closet. It's barren land where there's no day or night, no sun or moon, just dirt and dark gray skies. If she isn't released, she'll remain in her closet. Either way, it's hell . . . literally."

I take in all the colors and joy surrounding me. "That sounds terrifying."

Gwen shrugs. "It should be terrifying. She's getting what she gave. Besides, I don't think that's worse than her killing you. Do you?"

"No. There's never an excuse to murder someone. Especially not your own kid."

Gwen takes my hand. "Exactly." Then she smiles, and her whole face lights up. "Hitler got five hundred and sixty years in a place absent of peace and light and filled with pain. I don't feel bad for him. He's getting what he gave. On Earth we called it karma, but here we call it the Harvest."

"The Harvest? Why?"

"Because when we die, we get what we've planted and nurtured when we lived. And it doesn't matter if a person was rich or poor, ugly or pretty, popular or unpopular. The only thing that matters is whether or not they acted with good intentions. Period."

I think about my own life. I try to remember if I had ever been unkind. This unnerves me. I know I had bad thoughts about certain people, had even wished bad luck on them.

I confess, "There were people I didn't like. Some of my classmates, this mean nurse, and one or two doctors. I had wished I would never have to see them again. The way you describe it makes it sound like everyone has to be perfect, and nobody's perfect."

Gwen shakes her head. "No. Not perfect. We all have flaws; it's only bad for the people who hurt people, who have no empathy or sympathy for others, and who see people as objects. The ones who don't think about how their words or actions impact others."

"But Mama's lawyer said she had a disease. What about that?"

"Your mother's disease didn't stifle her free will. She knew right from wrong; otherwise she wouldn't have lied and changed medical records and brought you to different doctors all the time."

"I guess you're right," I say.

I reflect back to the morgue where an autopsy was performed on Mama. It was determined that her bowel had perforated and she had gone septic—meaning her body had poisoned itself to death. Mama was poisoned to death. Just. Like. Me.

I draw in a long breath. "Gwen, you see things with so much clarity. I don't know what I'd have done without you every step of the way."

Gwen shoos me with her hand. "We aren't finished yet. There's still one more thing left to do."

Farewell, My Friend—the Final Chapter

D addy and Ava are visiting my grave. The two are somber as they stand hand in hand staring down at the small tombstone with my name, date of birth, and date of death. Looking at my name engraved on the black granite gives my belly a burning sensation, as though I have a nest of angry hornets trying to get out. It just doesn't seem real.

But then I see Daddy's and Ava's faces, and a warmth spreads through me.

Daddy looks down at Ava, and she looks up at him. They share a smile. He holds out a charm bracelet he bought for her. Daddy lifts Ava into his arms. "You see this bracelet?"

Ava touches the small charms. "Yeah, it looks just like Molly's. How come you have it?"

Daddy looks at the bracelet, and his eyes swell with tears. "I bought it for you because one day when you get married, you'll wear this bracelet to remind you that Molly is there with you."

Ava's eyes are cast down upon my grave. "Molly protected me."

"Yes, sweetheart. Exactly like I told you. Molly made sure you'd be safe, and well again."

"I miss her, Daddy." Ava's lower lip vibrates, and she bursts into tears. She throws her arms tightly around my father.

"I miss her, too. But we'll make sure that what she did for you is never forgotten."

Daddy puts his hand over Ava's heart. "Molly will live in your heart forever. I know she's with you now, and she'll always be with you."

The two of them silently stare at the tombstone.

"Daddy?"

"What is it, Ava?" Daddy looks into her face. He was always one to really listen.

Ava focuses on my tombstone again. "Is Mama coming home?"

Daddy runs the palm of his hand over Ava's hair. "No, baby. Remember, I told you that Mama went somewhere for a long time because of what she did to you and Molly. Then something terrible happened to her belly and she died. She won't ever be back, and you never have to be afraid of her again."

"Mama got sent away because she made us sick when we weren't. Right?"

Tears spill from my father's eyes and slide down his cheeks. "That's right. You were never sick, and neither was Molly."

"Did you know Mama was making us sick?"

Daddy draws in a sharp breath. "No. I never knew," he says adamantly. "I would never let anyone hurt either of you if I knew, not even Mama."

"Okay, Daddy. I love you. I love Molly, too."

After watching the two people I love most in the world share this heart-wrenching moment, I know it is finally time for me to move on. My little sister is safe, and, as for Mama, justice has been served. I have found my peace.

I grab Gwen's hand and hold it gently in my own. "I'm ready to go now."

Gwen smiles and pulls me into her. We hug, and I am filled with joy and an overwhelming sense of gratitude. "I'll always remember this precious time with you."

Gwen holds my hand as we walk into the purple light. I see two figures before me. As I get closer, I instinctively know they are my father's parents, who died before I was born. Gwen releases my hand and I go to them, as though it is the most natural thing for me to do. They are familiar. I am finally home. I didn't imagine it would be so beautiful . . . perhaps I would've been less afraid to die if I knew the pure joy I would have here.

As I take my grandparents' hands, I remember back to my last hour of darkness. I had lain in my bed alone, gasping through my final breath, and I thought my life was over, but now I know it has only just begun.

Continue reading . . .

Chapter One: Tuesday

Read Paige Dearth's **RAINEY PAXTON SERIES**, A Little Pinprick, Book One. Rainey was born addicted to heroin. **Read a sample of A Little Pinprick here . . .**

Rainey Paxton was only a few hours old. The nurses tried to calm her as her tiny body twitched. Her wail was shrill and steady. Rainey Paxton was in pain, the sound and sight of a child born addicted to heroin.

Rainey weighed less than four pounds. Her arms and legs shook wildly. The baby couldn't sleep, couldn't be comforted. No amount of swaddling, stroking, humming, or cradling could soothe her.

For the first days of her life, she cried for long periods, barely ate because she couldn't keep still long enough to suckle, and vomited when she did eat. The piercing screams didn't stop, so she had to be isolated from the other newborns in the neonatal intensive care unit.

It wasn't a mystery why Rainey was the way she was. She needed a fix—the same drug her mother injected while she was in her womb.

A few nurses who nurtured the infant while she remained in the hospital gave Rainey the love her mother should have given.

One of those nurses, while holding the child, turned to a colleague. "And to think . . . this precious girl will be sent home to her parents soon—the people who did this to her. It makes me sick."

Chapter Two: Four Days Prior

M iranda clenched her jaw and panted through the next labor pain. Her water had broken thirty minutes prior and the contractions were coming more frequently. She knew this meant that the baby would be coming soon. Miranda's long dark hair was held back with bobby pins. The skin on her face was peppered with angry red sores, dug raw by her fingernails clawing at insects that weren't there, a result of hallucinations brought on by her addiction to meth and heroin. Her once-sparkling brown eyes were flat, and except for the bulge in her belly, her bones protruded through her scrawny physique.

Miranda looked over at her boyfriend, Peter. He had wavy blond hair and dull gray-blue eyes. The couple were sitting in their station wagon, an old jalopy a hair away from being just a pile of rusty metal. They were in the parking lot of Bedford Hospital. Heavy metal music with a screeching guitar and relentless drumming were blaring from the car speakers. With the volume set high, the windows vibrated from the bass thumping inside the smoke-filled interior.

Miranda, groggy from the heroin she'd taken earlier, threw her head back and belted a verse of unrecognizable song lyrics. Then she looked over at Peter again, while mindlessly shoving a few fingers inside the torn car seat to feel the cool metal of the springs. The smell of mildew from the leaky rear window was secondary to the rankness of old beer and stale cigarettes. The car's brake lights were duct-taped in place, something Peter was proud to have *fixed* himself.

Grinning at Miranda, Peter tapped white powder from a small bag into a spoon, then squirted water from the end of the needle into the powder and flicked his lighter to cook the mixture. Nodding, Miranda tied off her arm, using her free hand and her teeth to tighten the worn canvas belt. Then she turned the volume down on the radio, and watched her boyfriend expectantly. She wanted her last hit of heroin before going into the hospital.

"Hurry up, Peter," she said with a grunt. "Before I get another contraction."

Peter filled the syringe with the heroin solution, slapped the vein on Miranda's arm, and slid the sharp point under her skin and into her vein. He pulled back on the syringe, waited to see the blood flow into the needle, and injected the drugs. Miranda's shoulders twitched and her eyes rolled back in her head.

"Ahhhh," she groaned, laying her head back on the seat as her mouth dropped open and her slack tongue jutted over her bottom lip.

Peter smiled, knowing how good Miranda felt, and this built anticipation for his high, that would follow. "I'm gonna take you inside before I hit myself," he said. "I don't want you to have that kid in the car."

Miranda fumbled to light a cigarette, took a few sloppy drags, and nodded.

In the emergency room, Miranda's head hung, chin on her chest. Occasionally her head bobbed from side to side.

Peter looked at the intake nurse, "I'm Peter Paxton and this is my girlfriend. She's ready to have that baby," he said, anxious to get back to the car. The intake nurse, appalled, watched Miranda closely, concerned by the pregnant woman's condition.

"Mr. Paxton, she's really out of it. Do you know if she took anything?"

Miranda doubled over and grabbed her stomach as a hiss escaped her.

Peter ran his hand over Miranda's greasy hair. "Come on, babe. Just breathe through it."

His eyes were blazing when he dragged them back to the nurse. "No, she didn't take nothing. What's your problem? Can't you see she's having a baby? She needs you to help her. How about that? How about you do your job?"

Miranda lifted her head, eyes still closed, and let out a wail. "I need this baby outta me."

Pursing her lips, the nurse turned back to her paperwork and asked, "What's her name?"

"Miranda Andersen."

"Yeah, baby?" Miranda said, lifting her head half an inch. "What's going on?"

"Nothing. I'm just telling the nurse your name."

The nurse's lips pressed together tighter. "Mr. Paxton, it's important that we know if Miranda has taken anything . . . for the sake of the baby."

Racked with another contraction, Miranda doubled over and let out a throaty moan.

Peter forced a sigh as he looked into the nurse's eyes. He shook his head slowly in a show of disapproval. "Listen, my girlfriend is tired and in a lot of pain. That's it. Now let's get on with it unless you expect her to have this kid in the wheelchair."

The nurse's eyes narrowed and she turned her attention to the paperwork, jotting down a few more notes. She stood and pushed Miranda into the back, where she was transferred from the wheelchair to a gurney. After needing help to undress, Miranda was covered in blankets, and an oxygen mask was put over her mouth and nose.

With Miranda settled in, Peter went back to his car and mixed himself a brew of heroin and meth. "Something to lift me up but keep me grounded," he muttered to himself.

Forty-five minutes later, Peter stumbled back into the hospital to find that Miranda had given birth to a baby girl.

The medical team in the delivery room was heartbroken for the baby and repulsed by the lack of remorse Miranda and Peter seemed to have for what they had done to their child.

After the juddering infant was laid in her mother's arms, Miranda smiled and glanced up at Peter.

A smile played on the nurses' lips as she touched the baby's fingers. "She's beautiful. What's her name?" she asked, worried about the life the child would have with her parents.

"Rainey," Miranda said dreamily, then winced with pain.

The nurse lifted her eyebrows. "Rainey? That's unusual."

"Yeah," Miranda said, her smile growing. "Rainey ain't no ordinary kid. She's gonna bring me and Peter all kinds of good luck."

Peter chuckled as he rubbed his arms. "Girl, I love that name, and she's gonna love it too."

The delivery nurse leaned away from the derelict couple and stared hard at them. Her expression was mild but her body was rigid, arms crossed. She forced a smile. "Is there a significance to her name?" the nurse asked in the most pleasant voice she could manage.

Miranda's high was wearing off from the intense labor pains. She had a far away, dazed look when she glanced at the nurse, "You ever hear of the blues singer Ma Rainey?"

The nurse shook her head.

"She was born in Alabama. Beautiful black woman. Yeah, was known as the Mother of the Blues. You should check her out. Cool and mellow . . . when I'm high I love to lay back and listen to her voice. I'm telling you that woman sounds like an angel."

The nurse let her hands drop to her sides, trying to ease the tension that had built up in her shoulders. The medical staff had a hard time with drug-addicted moms. So many women wanted babies who couldn't have them, and then there were women like this . . . women who didn't deserve the miracle of motherhood.

The nurse looked at Rainey's tiny figure, then reached over and placed her hand on the baby's back and said gently, "A blues singer, huh? Well, Rainey sounds like a hearty name. However, this little angel is having a hard time, so she'll have to go to the NICU. It's pretty clear she's in withdrawal, but the doctor has ordered tests to make sure."

Peter glanced at the nurse with fiery eyes. "Our daughter will be just fine, okay? Right now, Miranda could use something to ease her pain."

"Sir." The nurse struggled to keep her tone even. "Clearly, your daughter is sick because Miranda took drugs while she was pregnant. There's nothing fine about that."

Miranda looked at Peter. "Geeze, babe, she's so uppity," she grunted. She turned back to the nurse. "Who the hell do you think you are to judge me? You don't know nothing about what I've been through."

Peter gave the nurse a strained smile and said, "Give us a minute, will you?"

When the nurse left the room Miranda kissed the top of Rainey's head while the baby wailed in her arms.

Peter grabbed Miranda's hand. "Rainey Paxton," he said letting the name roll off of his tongue. "She's beautiful . . . the most gorgeous baby I've ever seen."

Peter leaned in, kissing the tops of both Miranda's and Rainey's heads. "Miranda, you're so damn hot as a mom, I'd fuck you right here," he said, then pulled down the thin hospital gown and kissed her breasts.

Miranda giggled and pushed her greasy, tangled hair away from her face. "You have to stop it. They ain't gonna let us get it on in here—besides, I'm kinda sore down there. But I can't wait to get the fuck outta this place. It's like I'm in prison with all these wires attached to me and shit." Miranda pulled Peter close. "I need a hit, babe. The morphine they gave me earlier is wearing off."

Peter kissed the little craters on her cheek. "I don't think that's a good idea. Before the doctor left, I heard her tell the nurses she was gonna give you something to help you with withdrawal. So, I think you should hold off for a while. Besides, I only have a little H left in the bag."

The nurse came back to take Rainey to the NICU. Since Miranda couldn't shoot up drugs while she was in the hospital, her doctor gave her methadone to keep her from having withdrawal symptoms. This kept the cravings at bay, and her whining about pain to a minimum.

Within twenty-four hours of giving birth, while baby Rainey fought to detox, Child Protective Services was summoned, and two days after Rainey was born, Miranda left the hospital without her child. If she could prove that she and Peter could stay sober, they'd be permitted to bring Rainey home.

In the car, Miranda turned to Peter. "Look, man, we both gotta stay clean if we wanna bring the kid home." She opened a plastic bag and pulled out a box. "They gave me this stupid pump to use until she comes home. They won't let me feed her until all the dope is out of my system, and if I don't pump, my milk will dry up, and then we'll have to buy shit for her to eat."

Peter lit a cigarette and nodded. "Yeah, it sounds like a whole lot of stuff you gotta do, sucks to be you." He grinned. "Anyway, I found a clinic we can go to near our house. That dumbass doctor told me about it so we can get that methadone shit. But just one thing first." He reached into his pocket and dangled a small bag of heroin from his fingertips. "I say, one last party before we give it up for a while."

Seeing the small plastic bag, Miranda's body was awakened. Her arms tingled and her mind raced with thoughts of getting high. She smiled. "Oh, Peter. I love you so much," she said, taking the bag from him, "Okay, one last time."

Chapter Three

Rainey was diagnosed with neonatal abstinence syndrome and a cluster of other issues caused by illicit drug use by her mother. As a consequence, Rainey spent the first month of her life in the Neonatal Intensive Care Unit. She had frequent seizures while being weaned from heroin and meth. Gradually the baby grew stronger and gained weight.

By the time Rainey was healthy enough to leave the hospital two months later, Miranda and Peter had stayed clean, and after drug testing, were cleared by Child Protective Services. Though the baby might not have known the shift, she was soon taken from the sterile walls of the hospital with loving, round-the-clock care into a rundown home in the heart of Kensington, a small, dilapidated, drug-infested section of Philadelphia. Miranda and Peter lived on a block that had twelve row homes on either side of the street. They rented one of two on the entire block that hadn't yet been condemned uninhabitable by the city.

Peter and Miranda made a bed for Rainey from a pile of old clothing and ripped towels. Although they visited her at the hospital nearly every day, they enjoyed being close to her without the nurses watching them. The first night they sat on the floor next to her.

"She's so beautiful," Miranda said.

"Yeah, 'cause she looks just like her mom," Peter said, leaning in to give Miranda a hard, messy kiss. When they finally parted, he flashed his girlfriend a sly smile. "So I was thinking to celebrate Rainey being home, we could party a little."

Miranda's eyes opened wide. She had been hoping that they could stay clean. They had both committed to a sober life after finishing the initial withdrawal, but the craving for drugs was always there, sitting just beneath the surface.

"Oh, yeah? How little?"

Peter pulled a bag of heroin and two joints from his shirt pocket and waved them at her.

Miranda placed her palms on his cheeks. "I don't know. We've been sober for two months."

Peter took her hand. "You're right. We've been so good. But I miss that buzz, you know?" he admitted, leaning his face close to hers. "It's just a little taste to celebrate having Rainey home."

"It's never a little taste, Peter. You know it," she said looking from his face to the bag of white powder. "Do you have any works?"

Peter bounced his eyebrows, lifted his pant leg, and pulled a hypodermic needle from his sock. "Of course, I have works. Life wouldn't be the same without them," he laughed.

Miranda's right hand slid up and down, over the veins in her left arm. Her lips parted as she made firm eye contact with Peter. "We've waited so long to bring her home," she said, kissing the sleeping child's cheek. "Man, this is the happiest day of my life," she said, grinning.

It took only a moment's pause before she was following Peter, slinking away from Rainey's bedroom, down the steps, and to the kitchen table. With the briefest of thoughts of her baby in her rag pile upstairs, Miranda extended her arm and Peter tied it off with a shoelace.

Peter held the needle up for her to make a toast and she leaned in closer. "Here's to our daughter," Peter said and inserted the needle under her skin. As he pushed the potent fluid in, Miranda's eyes glossed over and she let out a ragged purr.

Peter watched the elation wash over his girlfriend. "Shit, babe. You look so sexy when you get off. I could do you right here on the kitchen table."

Miranda gave him a crooked smile and her eyelids fluttered shut.

A short time after Peter shot himself up, he lit a joint, took in a long drag, and pulled Miranda from the kitchen chair. With her back to him, he unzipped her jeans and bent her over the table. Miranda lazily complied, and when he slid his fingers inside her, she let out a sensuous moan. Dropping to his knees, he pressed his face between her legs. After a while he rose from the floor, letting his jeans drop to his ankles and plunging inside of her.

"This is the best celebration ever," Miranda slurred afterward, her eyelids drooping as she swayed slightly.

Rainey's first night home set off a long heroin binge for her parents. They had held onto the concept that their daughter belonged with them and, no matter how bad their addiction became, the baby was right where it belonged. Before Rainey was born, they'd gotten by on a small inheritance from Miranda's parents. But once they started taking drugs again, they blew through the remaining money. Desperate, Peter came up with the idea of letting other addicts pay to stay at their house overnight.

Within a month, and with the money they collected from squatters, Miranda and Peter were using several times a day. Given the crowds of people, the house became a breeding ground for drug dealers.

Rainey was often left for hours on the pile of clothing that was her bed while her mother and father got high downstairs in the living room. Though she'd been weaned off the drugs in the hospital, the infant was soon back on them through her mother's breast milk.

Chapter Four

S omehow Rainey survived the first several weeks at home. From the tainted breast milk, the child was undernourished, addicted, and manic. Then, when she was not quite three months old, a blessing entered the baby's life: Miranda's older sister Sophie.

Sophie hadn't dated much and never married, preferring to focus on her work as a professional photographer. She traveled most of the week throughout the region, and while she made a modest living, it was enough for her to buy a two-bedroom home in a middle-class neighborhood. Sophie and Miranda couldn't look more different, yet before addiction they were equally attractive.

Where Miranda once had an exotic look with her silky black hair and large light brown eyes, now she was gaunt, with dark greasy hair hanging like clumps of spaghetti around her face.

In contrast, Sophie had blond hair and blue eyes. She was just over five feet, six inches tall, and was slender, with long legs and a tiny waist. Sophie turned heads when she walked into a room. While many men had pursued her, she loved her freedom too much to get tied down. At only twenty-five—four years older than Miranda—she wasn't ready for a long-term relationship.

Sophie and Miranda had never gotten along, and their relationship had turned volatile in their teenage years. Sophie was a well-balanced child who had been pushed to the side by their parents, who were focused on Miranda's drug addiction, which began when she was only sixteen, after she met Peter. Sophie carried deep bitterness for her sister's selfish behavior, and Miranda hated that Sophie didn't understand she couldn't control her addiction and secretly thought Sophie acted the way she did out of jealousy.

Rainey was almost three months old when Miranda called Sophie to tell her about the baby.

"Hey, Sophie. It's me," Miranda moaned into the telephone.

"What's going on?" Sophie asked. "I haven't heard from you in almost three months. I've been calling you. Is everything okay?"

"Yeah, I had my kid. I named her Rainey. Anyway, she had some problems so they kept her in the hospital for a while. But she's home now."

Sophie closed her eyes and pressed her forehead to the wall. "Why didn't you call me sooner?"

"You know, me and Peter have been busy—going back and forth to see her at the hospital and all."

"Why did they keep her so long? What was wrong with her?" she asked, though part of her already knew.

"Ah, you know how it is. She had to get some of that methadone for a while and gain a little weight."

"That's just great, Miranda," Sophie spat. "You couldn't stop getting high while you were pregnant? Classic. Really, it is."

"Whatever," Miranda huffed. "Anyway, Peter and me have been sober for a while now. That's the only way those jerkoffs would let us take the kid home."

"Really?" her sister asked hopefully. "And you're doing okay?"

"Yeah, we're doing fine. Anyways, I'm calling 'cause I gotta buy my baby girl some stuff and I wanted to know if you'd loan me some cash."

"What kind of stuff?"

"You know . . . diapers, clothes, shit like that."

"How much do you need to borrow?"

"I need about three hundred," Miranda said, holding her breath while she waited.

"Are you sure you aren't using?"

"Yeah, of course, I just got done telling you that . . . can you help me out or what?"

"Yeah, sure. I can lend you some money. I'll drive it to your place on Saturday. I can't wait to see Rainey."

Two days later, Sophie got into her car and drove to Kensington. She dreaded going into the area and knew it wasn't safe. She drove through the depressed neighborhoods while hoping her niece was being cared for and thriving. Unable to have any children of her own, Sophie longed to be part of Rainey's life.

Standing on her sister's rotting, uneven porch, Sophie banged on the front door. Nothing. She tried to peer into the front windows, but they were covered with blankets or boarded up. After a few minutes, Sophie kicked the bottom of the door. Finally, Miranda pulled it open and eyed her sister up and down. Then she stepped out onto the porch.

Sophie watched her sister carefully. Her heart lay like clay in her chest. She had wanted to believe Miranda was sober. It pained her to see the familiar signs of her sister's addiction. She stepped closer to get a better look, Miranda's face was washed out, her eyes were bugged, and she had angry fever blisters clinging to her top lip. She looked into her glassy, red eyes, "You look like shit, Miranda. You're not sober—look at you—you're completely strung out. I thought you meant it this time. Come on, you're a mother now."

"I'm sorry I ain't as perfect as you, Sophie. But guess what? At least I can get a man and have a damn baby. That's more than you can do," she snapped.

Sophie felt like she'd been slapped. "You're such a bitch," she said, fighting back tears. "I can't have children because I was born without ovaries and you know that. What the fuck is wrong with you?" She paused and took a few deep breaths. "Look, I didn't come here to argue, I came to see my niece. For the record," she stated, making her voice more authoritative, "You should have called me when she was born; not wait three months."

Miranda rolled her eyes. "Hey, you know where I live. You could've checked on me just as easy."

"Really? The last time I was here you were six months pregnant and Peter, that asshole, threw me out of your house because I was annoyed that you were smoking. Remember that? Do you remember telling me not to call you again?"

Miranda shrugged, not wanting to talk about what happened in the past or fight with Sophie—she wanted her money and for her sister to leave.

"How is Rainey doing?" Sophie asked in a gentler tone.

The tight lines around Miranda's eyes softened, and for an instant she looked more like the girl Sophie remembered growing up. "She's okay. She cries a lot, like, a really high-pitched, never-fucking-stop-crying cry. Sometimes," she said, gritting her teeth, "I just want her to shut the hell up." She raked her fingers through her hair. "It's annoying as hell. I can't stand it. It gets so bad I wanna toss her skinny ass out with the trash."

Sophie, accustomed to Miranda's erratic behavior, focused on keeping her cool. She knew if she grabbed her sister by the neck of her shirt like she wanted to, she would stop talking. She wanted to know everything about her niece, so instead of reacting just said, "Yeah, I totally get it. One of the women I work with just had a baby and it's colicky. She said he cries all the time and she can't get any sleep."

Miranda snorted. "This ain't about sleep. This is about shut the fuck up, kid. I feed her . . . she cries. I change her dirty ass . . . she cries. I hold the thing . . . she cries. That's all she ever does. That kid doesn't know how to bring me an ounce of joy."

Sophie reached for her sister's hand and lowered her voice to a gentle hum. "Listen, we both know that you're using again." She paused, uncertain how to ask the next question without pissing Miranda off, so she just went for it. "Are you breastfeeding?"

Miranda looked away and Sophie's heart sunk. She pulled her sister in closer. "Really, Miranda?" she said into her sister's hair. "Your kid spent the first two months of her life in the hospital and now you're giving her more drugs. That's probably why she's crying all the time." Sophie rubbed her forehead and gathered her thoughts. "Look, how about if I pay for baby formula?"

"Yeah . . ." Miranda looked up at her sister and smiled. "Yeah, I definitely need money to buy formula."

Sophie shook her head. "What I meant to say is that I'll go to the store and bring some back for you."

"Right, because you don't trust me."

Sophie nodded. "That's true. I don't trust you with money. You're a junkie."

"So what? You think just because I like dope that I don't love my kid?"

Sophie wanted to say, yes, that's exactly what I think about you when you're high. Instead, she let out a loud sigh. "No, I think because you like dope you forget about your priorities. You and Peter are twenty-one. You've been doing drugs since you met in tenth grade. It's time to stop."

Miranda lit a cigarette and stared blankly into the garbage-littered street.

Sophie hiked her purse higher on her shoulder. "I want to see Rainey and we can talk more after. Are you going to let me in your house or what?"

Miranda shrugged, opened the rickety front door, and let her sister inside.

BUY NOW: A Little Pinprick (Rainey Paxton Series: Book One)

Book one and two of the RAINEY PAXTON SERIES must be read in order.

More books by Paige

Home Street Home Series (can be read in any order):
Believe Like A Child
When Smiles Fade
One Among Us
Mean Little People
Never Be Alone
My Final Breath

Rainey Paxton Series (must be read in order):
A Little Pinprick
A Little High

A Note From Paige

Dear Dearth Reader,

I want to take a moment to thank you for reading and supporting my work. I appreciate you spreading the word about my books to family, friends and co-workers. If you enjoyed this book please go to Amazon and leave a short review so that other readers can determine if this is the right book for them . . . great reviews mean so much to me and keep me writing. Thank you!

~Paige

www.ingramcontent.com/pod-product-compliance
Lightning Source LLC
Chambersburg PA
CBHW020646030726
47498CB00002B/393